THE DAY ZOMBIES RUINED MY PERFECTLY BORING LIFE

Boring Life Series #1

JEN NAUMANN

This is a work of fiction. The names, characters, places and incidents are products of writer's imagination or have been used in a fictitious manner. Any resemblance to persons, living or dead, actual events, locales or organizations is entirely coincidental. Any trademarks, service marks, product names or named features are assumed to be the property of their respective owners, and are used only for reference. Namely: Twinkies, *The X-Files*, Charlie Brown, *Sixteen Candles, Harry Potter,* Girl Scouts, Norman Bates, Bruce Banner, The Hulk

THE DAY ZOMBIES RUINED MY PERFECTLY BORING LIFE

Third Edition

ASIN: B008AK8KWM

Cover designed by Q Design Cover and Brand Premades

Model image © ValentinaPhotos

D o you ever wish you could go back in time to shake the living crap out of your past self and say, "Dude, you don't know how great you have it?" Maybe tell your naïve and less educated self to wake up and appreciate what you have? Take that second chance you've always dreamed about? Well I don't, because I know I wouldn't listen to myself anyway. I may as well bang my head against something repeatedly—it would have the same effect.

I can honestly say with 100% confidence that I had no clue how wonderfully pathetic my life was before now— before it flipped totally upside down. Not too long ago, I was a normal teenage girl. Not like necessarily average, but *normal* as in I tolerated the torture of high school, had decent parents, drove a crappy old car, liked to blow money on trivial things, blah, blah, blah.

My whole life I was stuck in an itty-bitty Minnesota town that's basically smack-dab in the middle of *nowhere*. And let me tell you, life there was *boring*. Not boring as in having the same mundane things to do with your friends every single weekend, but boring as in *there was nothing to do*. We had no mall, no bowling alley, no movie theater. *Nada*. We're talking the lamest of lame towns, right at my front door. But now I'd pretty much do *anything* to resume being bored.

Maybe a part of me *does* want to go back and have a little chat with my old self after all.

Chapter 1

Despite the energy drink I consumed as the sun was first rising, I'm less than alert when the homecoming queen drops me at the curb in front of my house. It's a relief to finally break free from her dad's old Lincoln that has a rancid stench of sunflower seeds and rotten cigars. I slam the rusty door and lean down to wave.

Mindy's blond hair sticks out wildly around her face from her loose ponytail and dark rings line underneath her bright green eyes—both results of our eventful night. I imagine my own reflection would give me tremors if I had some kind of mirror at my disposal.

"See you at the dance tonight!" Mindy beams wildly.

"Yay. I can hardly wait," I return, making no attempt to hide the sarcasm in my voice.

She honks the horn twice and pulls away. I hold my hand up until she's gone from sight. Although I get along with pretty much anyone and everyone, being in the company of royalty such as Mindy McKinney doesn't make me popular by default. There are only fifty girls in the entire senior class, and being in a school that small, your chances of being homecoming queen—regardless of your looks or social status—become much higher by default. Don't get me wrong; Mindy's certainly pretty and popular, but once you get to know her you eventually come to realize she has the personality of a tree stump, at best.

Having just returned from an all-nighter with some of my fellow senior girls, a nine-hour nap seems in order. For the record, it wasn't my idea to "decorate" the senior football players' homes for homecoming. I say "decorate" very loosely as transporting chickens from a classmate's farm to the players' garages was involved. We also placed large tire tractors in the middle of their driveways and wrapped their cars with endless rolls of Saran wrap. Most likely we'll get some kind of "disciplinary action" for our excursion—maybe even face suspension once Monday morning arrives. But what would senior year be without the threat of not getting to participate in the graduation ceremony?

I look up at our stellar stone-front house nestled just on the edge of the thick woods that separate us from town. We built the monstrosity ten years ago after my parents received a generous inheritance from my wealthy grandparents. I've never understood why my parents, who are hardly ever home, felt the need to have three extra bedrooms. I sometimes wonder if maybe they'd planned on having more children, but changed their minds once they realized we actually needed to be fed, clothed and given occasional attention.

Surprisingly, the front door to the house is wide open. We never use that door, not even on Halloween as my mom doesn't believe in giving sugar to other people's children—she thinks they're all too hyper even without it. Instead, my best friend and I like to hide in the bushes and see how many kids we can scare half to death until a parent comes by to chew us out. Last year there were hardly any kids who came out—I think the little buggers are finally on to us.

A gust of brutally cold wind blows through me and I look up to see clouds thickening. Holding my sweatshirt tightly against my body, I quickly cross the manicured yard to the open door and slam it shut behind me. My hollered greeting bounces off the peaks of the high ceilings, but it's met with silence. Figuring my dad's probably engaged in another bizarre project, I continue all the way through the house to our backyard.

The weeds out back have always been a major source of contention for my dad. Even though fall's here, he's known to be working on the weeds up until the first frost of the season. On more than one occasion, I remember him having to wear gloves and a stocking cap while doing it. According to him, they're on the *county's* property line— why should he spend his precious time weeding it when his taxes pay the county to do a perfectly good job of it?—or something like that. My dad is forever ranting about some political conspiracy theory or how the president's a horrible leader and will eventually cause the apocalypse in one way or another. I don't usually give that much weight to his ramblings—if I did, I certainly would've turned insane years ago.

But I find the backyard to be empty, too.

Despite the wicked wind pulling my hair up around my face, the trees in the forest seem to be unnaturally still, causing a cold trickle of fear to run down my back. I never used to be such a scaredy-cat, but Finn and I recently watched a marathon of horror movies and my overactive imagination can sometimes get the best of me. A few days ago I could've sworn on my own life that a lifelike doll from my childhood was staring at me—I spent an entire morning paralyzed in bed until I was completely sure she wasn't going to attack.

Deciding I just need a shower and a whole lot of sleep to reset my paranoid mind, I turn on my heels just as a faint moan drifts towards me. I stop at once.

Filled with a sickening dread, I shuffle over to where the now gold and red trees meet our backyard. The only thing I see moving is a small gathering of bright leaves. They circle in the sky just above me in a mini-tornado pattern before they flutter down and land at my feet. I stand and watch, fascinated.

The moan returns, more guttural this time. My attention's drawn back to the woods. Another sound like a heavy log being dragged through dried leaves comes from my right. Just a few yards away from where my dad thinks to be our property line, the outline of a person comes into view behind a line of nearly bare maple trees.

By her ill choice in fashion, it's obviously a younger woman coming toward me although the features of her face are not totally clear in the distance. Her long brown hair hangs down in straight clumps, swinging back and forth with each off-balanced step she takes. A bright pink t-shirt with the word "Boss" displayed across the chest in rhinestones clings tightly to her petite body and her long legs jet out from what I perceive to be a totally out of style pair of all too short gym shorts. Why she would be dressed in such skimpy attire on a cool fall day is beyond me, but I guess she could be one of those insane people who enjoys putting their bodies through the torture of daily exercise.

What this chick is doing in the back of our crappy old woods is a serious mystery in itself. From her ill style of clothing and neglected personal hygiene she'd be better off heading to the mall for an emergency makeover.

"Can I help you?" I finally ask her loudly. Then I

correct myself silently—probably nothing I can do would save her from the traumatic lack of fashion sense. "Do you need...something?"

Her speed quickens at the sound of my voice and the odd moaning amplifies—I suddenly realize *she's* making the horrible noise. *Great.* Lack of fashion *and* inability to communicate are apparently both problems. The wind slams a rotten odor into my nostrils, forcing me to hold my breath.

With each step she takes, it's clear there's plenty more wrong with the woman. Her head hangs down and off to the side as if the muscles in her neck have worn out. I still can't see her face clearly as that nappy hair covers most of it, but there's something really off in the coloring of her skin that seems to be more of a pale gray. And the deficiencies don't stop there. Not only is her skin discolored, but it's muddled and torn. It's far worse than having just forgotten to wash her face at bedtime.

I begin to fear that she's a leper.

My heart beat speeds up to a disconcerting rate. "Ah... are you okay? Do you need a doctor or something?"

As the distance closes between me and the tragically fashion-challenged woman, I freeze with fear. Hair still covers a portion of her face but her pupils come into view. They're completely white. And her jaw hangs down to reveal a majority of missing teeth. Wounds like boils on her face ooze blood. Together, the neglected appearance and nasty smell are simply nauseating—it's far worse than my original conclusion of a lack of fashion.

It occurs to me now:

1. This woman is definitely *not* okay,

2. If she gets any closer, she'll get her leprosy or whatever all over me, and

3. Being near her could result in great bodily harm or

possibly some kind of dismemberment if she is in fact violent, as I'm beginning to suspect.

Although my bowels have pretty much turned to liquid, a pulsating adrenaline shoots through my core. Conveniently enough, my dad likes to randomly chop down trees that he thinks are encroaching on our property line, so there's usually an ax to be found in the backyard. I scramble for it, holding it out between myself and the woman. But the ax is so heavy and my hands shake so badly that it probably makes no kind of threatening gesture whatsoever.

The woman raises an arm in my direction with impossibly slow movement. I shriek when her hand reveals five bloody stubs where her fingers should be.

I've certainly never been anywhere near strong and the very thought of confrontation freaks me out—just last spring when Darcy Sanderson threatened to punch me for kissing her ex-boyfriend I'd cowered behind my locker door and nearly cried. But I somehow manage to push this mutant of a woman away with the handle of the ax. She stumbles backwards and tumbles onto her back.

Having never purposely tried to hurt someone like that before, I instantly feel remorseful. "Sorry! Are you okay?" I ask, stepping forward with the intention to help.

But any trace of pity for what I've done disappears the second she scampers back onto her feet. One of her arms had landed underneath her and now bends unnaturally in the other direction. She opens her mouth with a slow exaggeration and makes an even more horrific sound. My pathetic attempt to defend myself has only pissed her off. I'm beginning to suspect there's something really, *seriously* wrong with her.

"Ohmigod!" I yell when she continues coming at me. At this point, not only do I think she's unable to comprehend whatever I say, I *know* she's physically incapable of *hearing* me—at least partially. Once she'd returned to her feet, her head flopped to the other side to reveal a giant gaping hole filled with blood where her ear should be.

I realize the smart thing would probably be to drive the ax into her skull and at the least hope to sever her spinal cord. But my experience with zombies is limited to what I've seen in movies and not coming at me *in real life*. You may like to think if a zombie ever attacked you that you'd be all badass and fight for your life like some kind of hero, but unless you've ever had a rotting human being approach you in your backyard and catch you off guard, you don't *really know* how you would actually react.

My screams sound very much like those of a four-year-old when I drop the perfectly good weapon to the side and hightail it back to the house. I run with such a burst of energy that I know I'd *finally* be capable of beating that do-gooder Christy Barts in the mile run—if only we were doing the yearly test in phy ed rather than me running for the preservation of my life. Funny how fear motivates a girl more than the mere threat of a lower grade.

I breeze past my empty house and run down the street like a totally insane person, screaming and throwing my hands around wildly in the cold air. A surge of adrenaline rages through my veins like hot lava as my feet pound the pavement in staccato bursts. A full three minutes pass before any other houses come into view, but I continue running down through the cul-de-sac with this new speed I didn't know I was capable of until today.

The few neighbors I spot outside are going about their business as if it's any other fall day. The old widow I only know as "Mrs. Gervais" is dressed in a super ancient barn-jacket that's ten sizes too large for her. She raises her wrinkled hand to wave casually in the midst of raking a pile of leaves as I dash by in a blur. Out of habit, I wave back.

The one and only Darcy Sanderson stands on the porch of her parents' house, looking as if she just rolled right out of bed. She hadn't been invited on our senior girl outing, although as a disclaimer, I wasn't in charge of the guest list. She gives me a predictable one-fingered salute while watching her stupid, yippy little dog take a dump in the neighbor's yard. Other times, when passing by, I've been tempted to launch that little hairball across the yard with a simple flick of my ankle, but I'm not into animal brutality. Besides, the poor thing suffers enough by mere default of its ownership.

In seeing how normal the rest of the neighborhood appears, I start to wonder if maybe I'd imagined the rotting woman dressed in her tribute to the 80's outfit. I *had* skipped dinner last night—everyone knows your brain's capable of crazy things when lacking in natural sugars. At least that's what my friend Brenda said when she was caught making out with someone other than her boyfriend last summer.

Once I've reached the front yard of my lifelong best friend's house, I finally allow myself to look back down the road in the direction of my own home. To my relief, the disfigured woman is nowhere to be seen. Aside from a handful of dead leaves dancing over it, the road's still.

I stop to clutch my sides when the runner's death cramps kick into high gear. My chest tightens to the point where I wonder if it's possible to have a heart attack when I haven't even been asked to the senior prom yet. Back in junior high, I went out for cross country to get a certain guy's attention. The coach nearly called an ambulance when I declared that I was dying after the first practice, but it turned out I was only having charley horse cramps. That was the first time I realized that I have a natural aversion to anything fitness related.

"Emma?"

I look up to find Finn leaning out a second story window of his house, giving me one of me his WTF expressions. "What're you doing?"

"Crazy…woman…at…my…house!" I yell between bouts of pain shooting through my lungs. My voice is high and squeaky, like a dog's chew toy. I clear my throat and try again. "There's a freaking *zombie* at my house!"

Finn shakes his head and sighs. "What? Hold on a sec —I'm coming down."

Before I can protest, he disappears from the window. In the few seconds it takes before he joins me, I debate whether or not to continue running until I reach the Mexican border. But who am I kidding? I probably can't make it another block as much as my sides are killing me. Quite possibly I'll die from the pain alone at this point.

In general, I'm not exactly what you would call an *athletic* person. My idea of exercise is going down to the mailbox by our short driveway. Frankly, I don't see the point in it—every time you eat something you take another step backward anyway.

When Finn appears in the doorway, I dart into his mediocre-sized arms for an embrace. While holding him, I decide his arms maybe aren't so much *mediocre*, but they're definitely *un-muscular*. Regardless, I squeeze him with all my strength and savor the smell I know to be Finn mixed with trendy cologne. I let my face rest against his super soft Darth Vader t-shirt for a minute before pulling back.

I take the opportunity to really assess my old friend up close. His nose and cheekbones are both smooth and his silky skin is always the most gorgeous shade of tanned brown no matter the time of year, making his dark brown eyes suck you in even more than they already do on their own. The way his shaggy brown hair tousles around his face makes him appear disheveled, but I know for a fact it takes a ton of hair products to achieve this look. He spends more money on that stuff than I do on my own mop of curls. My hair has a mind of its own. More often than not I just throw it into some kind of sloppy bun. Other girls spend all morning straightening their hair, curling it, or *whatever*, but that just seems like too much work.

As I study Finns' face, I can't believe I haven't spent all this time actively pursuing him. He's actually pretty hot, aside from his occasional dorky demeanor.

"I'm so glad you're home, Finn. You don't even know." When a dramatic sigh shoots out of me, my friend appears baffled.

"What's going on? What were you saying before about a *zombie*?" All it takes is his adorably crooked smile for me to instantly question myself. When we were younger I never really cared what he thought of me, but in the past couple of months I've started to develop a pathetic crush on my old buddy. Now pretty much everything I say is focused on whether or not he'll think I sound like an idiot. About eighty-six percent of the time, I'm sure he does.

I let out a nervous bubble of laughter. "Not exactly a *zombie*, zombie. I'm not really sure. You *know* I totally flunked biology last semester." It's not one of my prouder moments as I fumble in front of him. Maybe the woman's lack of communication skills rubbed off on me a little.

My friend grips me by my arms in more of a mocking gesture than anything. "Why's your face so red? Wait—have you been *running*?"

I purposely scrunch my face, knowing he hates it when I do that. He recently told me to knock it off because the senior guys rated me second most attractive female in our class even though they can never take me seriously. I'm guessing it has something to do with the fact that I would rather spend my nights hanging out with the guys playing video games than going to slumber parties to make out with pillows—or whatever they do at those things. I haven't been invited to an overnight girl party since the seventh grade when I drew a Hitler mustache on the hostess. Apparently some markers are a bit more permanent than others and people can get pretty uptight about their dance recitals.

"You say it like I'm not capable of running." Okay, so maybe I'm not totally capable. Not *really*, anyway. Athleticism doesn't run in my family—my parents are also more the type that tire just by listening to others talk about their exercise regimen.

"The only time I've ever seen you run is for gym class. You wouldn't be running unless something was actually chasing you." It irritates me when he chuckles at his own joke.

I glance back in the direction of my house to find the road still remains clear of disfigured corpses. "That's what I'm *trying* to tell you. I don't know what it was, exactly, but there was this *thing* wearing women's clothes…albeit really tacky women's clothes…but that's not the point. Its skin was all funky and it didn't have very many teeth—or *fingers*. And it had this ginormous hole in its head. But it was still walking—not necessarily talking though. But it came after me so I hit it with the ax handle. When it came back again I just ran."

He rolls his eyes to the top of his head while thrusting his head back and forth like he's trying to shake out what I've just told him. "Em, you get crazy like this every time we have a movie marathon. I'm beginning to think they're a bad idea."

"I'm *not kidding*, Finn. This is totally serious. We have to call like the police or the Red Cross or *something*. Whatever it was, it wasn't right."

My friend looks closely at me for a moment to decide if I'm totally pulling his leg or not. When his insidious little smile drops, I know he's finally coming to his senses. "You're being totally serious right now?"

We've been inseparable since like the *third grade* and he's supposed to believe everything I tell him. Well maybe not *everything*. I *had* told him Harry Potter turned evil in the last movie and killed all his friends but only because he bailed on our plans to see the premiere together. If he had read the books like I told him to, he wouldn't have fallen for it. I considered it a schooling in good literature.

I swear I try to resist the urge to smack him on the forehead, but sometimes I just can't help myself—my hands can have a mind of their own.

"*Ouch!*" he yells, grabbing my arm and holding it away from him. "Okay! *I get it.* You don't have to get all violent on me. We'll call the police."

"Thank you."

I've almost completely stopped quivering from my encounter with the backwoods woman. Finn always has this way of calming me, probably because he knows me better than anyone else on the planet. With heavy relief, I follow him down the path back to his house. But we stop short when a low shriek comes from not too far off in the distance. The sound makes the fuzzy hairs on the back of my neck stand erect.

We both freeze in place, barely daring to move our eyes to look at each other. We each have the same "deer caught in the headlights" look—and I literally know what that looks like. Finn was riding with me last spring when I ran smack into a giant buck. The windshield cracked into a hundred pieces and the front end of my mom's BMW was totaled. I couldn't get behind the wheel of a car for another month because I kept having flashbacks. Besides, a lot of those frisky buggers are always running around here like they own the place.

"What was *that*?" Finn finally asks.

I throw my hands into the air. "Probably more freaking *zombies*. How the hell should I know?"

I'm only being facetious but Finn's dark brown eyes grow larger. "Stay here," he says, pointing a finger at me as he edges over in the direction of his neighbor's house.

But I'm quick to run after him. "So I can get attacked again by another one of those freaky things while I'm standing here all by myself? Forget *that*. I'm coming with."

My friend ignores me and continues into the neighbor's yard. A second shriek resonates from across the street, this time in a higher woman's pitch. I jet into Finn, clutching him from behind in a serious death grip. I'm not a big fan of the sound people make when screaming in general, but after my earlier run-in, I'm guessing something terrifying is about to go down and we already covered the part about what a coward I become in the face of danger.

"Emma, let go." Finn's voice is steady and calm.

I shake my head in refusal. "No way!"

"Emma. Someone's coming this way and I think we should *run*."

Although I probably respect Finn the most of all the people in my life, I think my props to him grow even more in this moment. He sounds totally normal, yet when I peer around his body I discover that by god, he's right.

A short and slender decaying man wearing bloodied work attire limps across the yard toward us. His suit looks oddly out of place for the situation. His bright green tie is jerked off to the side like maybe he had tried removing it at some point, but his now messed up mind didn't know how to make his fingers work properly. He looks very much like my friend from the woods, with all-white eyes and a nasty skin complexion. Only this guy's missing an entire arm, and dark blood spews from the corner of his mouth. The slow and smooth movements he makes are like he's swimming under water.

I let out another eardrum-shattering shriek. Finn scoops me into his arms—albeit with more grunting than finesse—and pulls me off of my feet. At least I finally know what it's like to have Finn holding me, even if it *is* the last lame thing I do before I become a human chew toy.

All at once my head makes contact with a metal lamppost behind us, making a terrible ringing that circles through my skull. Finn's wide eyes stare back down on me as I either laugh or say something to him.

Everything turns black.

Chapter 2

I think I might be dead. Sharp pain radiates through my back. I'm lying on something lumpy and the temperature of the room is so cool that goose bumps have erupted all over my arms and legs. A dank smell of rotten water fills the air, making me want to hurl. Voices mumble nearby, low and unrecognizable. When I attempt to lift my head to look around in the faint light, pain explodes in my head.

"Em, are you okay?" Finn's voice asks.

I briefly close my eyes, realizing I'm at least alive for the time being. But when I open my eyes and figures begin to stand out against the near darkness, death doesn't seem like such a bad option.

Finn's older and totally moronic brother Cash smirks at me from a few yards away, crooked teeth flashing under his lip. His dark hair and dark eyes blend in with the darkness of the room, kind of the way the features of a vampire lurking in a direful cave would. My hatred for him seizes hold of me, boiling in my veins. The only time I remember wanting to full-on slug another human being in the face, Cash was involved. Not only is the guy a total jerk to Finn *and* me, but I'm pretty sure he's a bane to the existence of the entire human race. How unfortunate he wasn't eaten by one of these zombie creatures.

He clicks his tongue. "What a pansy ass, having to be *carried off* like that. I give her four hours tops to survive this nightmare."

I sit up, regretting the action when my head pounds furiously. "I'll have you know I hit one of those things earlier with an ax, Cash. *Your* pansy ass probably would've run away screaming like a little girl." Technically, running away screaming like a little girl is exactly what *I* did, but he doesn't need to know that.

Cash snickers and mumbles, "As if."

Finn lightly rubs my head when he catches me favoring it. "Are you okay?" His touch on my head spreads a million tingles through me. I slap his hand away, pretending to be annoyed by his doting. Lately, my body reacts strangely whenever I'm too close to him, so I usually try to avoid it at all costs.

My mouth is dry and there's a nasty taste of metal on my tongue. I sit all the way up and place a hand on my pounding head. "Where are we? What is going on? I should be heading to work soon."

Cash snickers again. "You've never worked a day in your life, you idiot."

Even though he's right, I choose not to acknowledge his statement. Instead, I turn to my friend. "Finn, seriously —what's happening?"

"We're in our basement shelter," he says. "These walls have thick enough concrete that we'll be totally safe in here from whatever's going on out there."

My eyes find a huge door with something pushed up against it. "You guys have a shelter?" I've spent over half my life in this house and never remember seeing anything like this in the basement.

Finn shrugs. "We never had a reason to come down here before."

"That's because you guys were too busy trying to figure out how to *get it on* in your bedroom," says Cash, chuckling at his own moronic humor.

"Shut up!" Finn yells over his shoulder. His expression turns apologetic when he looks back at me. "I'm sorry I didn't believe you right away. I never would've thought before today that *zombies* could really exist. It's like some George Romero movie has come to life out there."

"Did Jackhole over there see any?" I ask, motioning to Cash. The fact that the two of us saw one together doesn't make it any more real. I keep hoping we'll wake up any moment and discover this was a dream that had quickly deteriorated into a nightmare.

Cash answers on his own behalf, his voice snippy. "When I was on my way to Marley's they said something on the radio about a viral outbreak in southern Minnesota. They didn't say exactly what it is, but they're telling people to stay inside their houses. I figured it was nothing big until I saw a couple of them wandering in the field behind the high school."

Now it's my turn to snicker. "So instead of going to warn your girlfriend you ran back home to hide? How *noble of you*, Cash."

"Not that it's any of *your* business, but I tried calling her. She didn't answer so I left a message for her to meet me here." I can't be sure, but I think I can feel his eyes shooting daggers across the room into me.

I laugh carefully, so as not to hurt my already pounding head. "Just so long as *you're* safe, that's all that matters, right?"

"Why don't you go out there and look for her if you're so worried?" Cash returns. "Oh, that's right—you can't because you freaked out and had to be carried away."

Not willing to waste a perfectly good eye roll on the dark room, I sigh instead. "Whatev." When I stop and allow myself to think about everything he just said, the level of fear I experienced with my first zombie encounter returns, rising to an even higher level.

There's no way this is really happening.

Demons, werewolves, zombies—they're all supposed to be for *entertainment purposes only*. But if we're really facing some kind of supernatural being, why can't I get some ridiculously hot guy like Jensen Ackles to protect me? Instead, I'm stuck in a grave of concrete with my some-what attractive, but goofy best friend and his asshole brother.

This is so the way my life always goes.

I shudder. It's too much to process. "How could they call this a *virus*? It looked to me these people had more than just a cold." Then again, maybe I hadn't been so far off in thinking the woman in the woods had leprosy. "This has to be some really elaborate joke someone's playing on us for homecoming. Maybe it's those snotty junior girls— they were pretty ticked last year at the talent show when we switched out their music for squealing pigs."

Finn's teeth still manage to gleam bright in the dark-ness when he smiles. "Sorry, Em, but I think this is really happening. I barely got us into the house before we were ripped apart by that guy in the yard. Guess all of those zombie movies we watched were good for something, right?"

"That's not funny," I scold. "We're totally *screwed*. Not a single one of us knows how to handle a gun and you wouldn't believe how hard it is to actually *physically* drive an ax into another human being's body. Unless it was *someone who really got on my nerves*, I doubt I could really do it." Cash laughs quite maniacally, knowing full well that he's the one who I could probably chop up with little to no remorse.

I suddenly remember my parents hadn't been home and wonder if they're okay. My dad doesn't own a gun and my mom is an even bigger wuss than I am—plus she has this overly nice but sometimes ditsy way about her. If she were to be greeted by a creature in the woods as I'd been, she would be dead mere seconds after naïvely wanting to help them.

My parents are both really good people, but growing up they were more like my buddies than anything else. Quality family time wasn't a thing. I was raised like an adult and never babied or pampered in any way. Most of my life I was left to fend for myself, at times also having to take care of my parents' well-being when they were being irresponsible. They were always off to parties and events up in the metro area, asking Finn's mom if I could "hang out" with him whenever they left. Thus Finn and I developed a close relationship.

"I don't know where my parents are," I say grimly. "What if that chick from the woods ate them?"

Finn's voice is hard as he grabs onto my arms. "I'm sure they're okay. And we're going to be okay, too. We're safe down here."

Cash clears his throat. "Don't you forget—the guy who broke the school's all-time hitting record in baseball is sitting right here with you fools." He taps what sounds like a titanium bat against the concrete. It makes a wimpy, tinny noise that falls flat against the thick walls.

"Yes, but that was *before* the malted barley and hops invaded your brain cells," I answer dryly. "Your glory days were over the minute you became captain of the campus drinking team."

He taps the bat again. "You want to come over here and see about that?"

Finn holds his hands out to each of us. "Knock it off. You guys acting like a bunch of toddlers isn't going to help anything." Our pleasant conversation is interrupted by the faint, musical chime of the doorbell. Finn and I strain to look at each other in the darkness.

"Maybe these zombies are actually polite," I say, shrugging. The chime repeats a number of times with more urgency. "But still really, *really* hungry."

For one of the very first times I can remember in the past ten years, Finn doesn't laugh or return my quip with his own banter. He says to me, "Stay here. I'll be right back."

Glancing at Cash, I scramble to my feet despite my pounding head. "No thanks. I'm totally coming with you." If something happens to him, it may as well happen to me as well. I'm not going to spend the rest of forever trapped in the basement with the world's biggest douche bag, even if I'm incredibly nauseated now that I'm on my feet. I'd rather deal with a little spewing versus total damnation.

Finn sighs with an exasperated sound. "*Fine.* Cash, give me that bat."

"No way. The only way I'm putting this bat down is if I'm dead."

I step forward. "I can help you with that little problem."

Finn holds his arm out to stop my attack. "Then you're coming with us," he tells his brother.

Cash tags along willingly, without any protest. He's most likely too afraid to sit alone in the dark. Finn hoists me up by my waist to the slim opening in the concrete.

With the shadowy light from the basement's hallway I can see we're not in just any old room—it's actually finished off and specifically made to be some kind of shelter. I shimmy my way through the opening, falling awkwardly on a landing of stairs that can apparently be raised and lowered.

"You guys did a good job of making it convenient for the zombies to join us in there," I call out to them. I look back to the opening, deciding it's pretty tight even for me and add, "The skinny ones, anyway."

Finn slithers out behind me and leans through the opening to offer his hand to his brother, who has a little more difficulty getting his more muscular body through. By the time the three of us have all made it out, the doorbell stops.

"Maybe it's Aunt Linda," Finn says to Cash. They both sprint up the basement steps with obvious urgency.

Recently Finn and Cash's mom was locked up—as in *committed for being mentally ill.* I don't know all of the specifics, but according to town gossip she was convinced she was pregnant with Michael Jackson's baby. But who knows—with the recent discovery of zombies maybe something like that *is* possible. Finn hasn't said much about it, and I never push the subject. As much as I adore their mom and am grateful to her for welcoming me into her home over the years, she's always been a bit off-balance. Her commitment didn't come as any mind-blowing revelation.

Because Finn was only seventeen when it happened, their mom's sister Linda came to live with them. Their aunt is pretty cool most of the time, but she's sometimes a bit kooky, reminding me of her sister. If she's attacked by a zombie, she stands even less of a chance of survival than the rest of us.

We reach the landing of the stairway nearly in unison. I crash into Finn, who's stopped dead in his tracks. I follow his gaze across their elaborate home. The entire upstairs flows from one room to the next without any walls to separate them. Massive windows in the living room stretch across the length of the house, giving a phenomenal view of the same woods that continue past my house.

Well, normally it gives a phenomenal view. Today, not so much.

An obese, middle-aged man is pressed up against the glass, beating his fists in slow motion. Gaping holes in his cheeks reveal a lack of remaining muscles in his face, and his mouth hangs open. The old-school pair of striped overalls he wears aren't *totally* uncommon in our farming community, but the blood splatters across his midsection are certainly a new twist to the whole look.

His glazed-over eyes seem to be trained on something in the next room—either that or he's lost all control of his eye muscles. The poor guy looks weak, like he's maybe starving to death, but I remind myself he's probably most hungry for a man-wich.

I peer over at the front door, unsurprised to find whoever had been ringing the doorbell has split, probably scared off by Chris Farley incarnate.

Finn's hand reaches for mine with serious urgency. It's sweating and shaking as badly as my own. The three of us move together the twenty feet or so toward the kitchen, taking great care to not make any noise or sudden movements.

The modern kitchen with sleek black cabinets and stainless steel appliances holds a massive marble island in the center that can sit up to ten people. The island proves to be a great cover from impending zombie attacks. When we're safely huddled behind it, I exhale deeply.

"Who do you think was ringing the doorbell, and since when does glass keep a zombie from getting in?" I whisper as quietly as I can into Finn's ear.

"Since my sister had bulletproof glass installed," a different voice answers loudly in my ear.

I squeal with surprise, but a collective sigh of relief passes through the other two with the sight of their Aunt Linda squatting behind us, a big smile spread across her feminine face. "You never know what assholes would want to assassinate us with all the secrets we know." She winks rather dramatically, making me believe the woman must be seriously *nuts*, just like her sister.

Linda's tall and lean, also like her sister, and shares Finn's dark hair, brown eyes and good looks. When younger, I used to wonder why Finn's mom didn't have a boyfriend since their dad had died long ago, but the older I got I began to understand why she remained single. Their whole family has proven to be quite off-balance, and their mom's recent commitment was just more evidence of her instability.

"God, Linda, you scared the shit out of us!" I gasp.

Cash chuckles, his grade-school humor kicking in. "In that case, you better check your pants."

I roll my eyes, but don't justify his idiocy with a response.

"Where were you?" Finn asks his aunt.

"I was coming back from Mankato when the emergency broadcast started," she tells him, her lips tight.

I frown. "Why were you ringing the doorbell?"

She shakes her head. "That wasn't me. I came in from the garage. When I saw you guys come up from the basement I figured you had invited some friends over."

"Um…have you noticed what is going on outside?" I ask, motioning to the windows. "We don't know *who* was ringing the doorbell, but something tells me it wasn't Girl Scouts. Does anyone know what seems to be taking them so long to make their rounds this year?"

Finn and his aunt pass some silent knowledge between them when their eyes meet. "It's happening, isn't it?" he asks. The serious look he gives her is so foreign to his face that a shiver races up my spine.

Linda nods slowly. "I think so."

I moan. "Okay, what are you two *talking* about? What's *happening*?"

Suddenly, something large crashes upstairs. We all look up, expecting the ceiling to come falling down on us. A series of more loud noises follows. I hold tight to Finn's arm while fearing the worst is about to happen—I'm going to die in the same room as the world's biggest idiot. That's so not how I want to be remembered.

"Cash?" a female voice drifts down the stairway in the front hall. "Where are you?"

I snicker. "Look at that, Cash. Your girlfriend has come to save your sorry ass."

He shoves me roughly from behind, causing me to fall against Finn, but my friend holds me up before my head makes contact with the floor. Cash sneaks away, making an embarrassingly pathetic attempt at an army crawl.

"What if we catch this virus thing?" I ask Finn. "I haven't had any shots since I was like twelve."

Finn peers around the corner of the island to watch the decaying man still banging almost robotically against the windows. Linda rummages through some of the cupboards behind me. I don't really want to know what she's searching for. I can't even begin to imagine the garbled thoughts going through her head.

"Finn, did you hear me?" I ask.

"We'll be fine," he answers in a distracted and unconvincing tone.

"Phones have been down for the last hour," Linda tells us over her shoulder. "Internet's out too."

At this moment I realize my cell phone was in my pocket the entire time. Maybe before running to Finn's house I could have called 9-1-1 or tried my parents. But my mind doesn't seem to work properly when faced with imminent danger. Then it occurs to me—how am I ever going to find my parents without cell phones? What about the rest of the world? What if we're the only humans left and we have to fight all the zombies off on our own, and like start our own little community of non-zombies? I'm way too young to squeeze out any babies, but I'll do it willingly with Finn if mankind is counting on us—it's the least I could do for my country.

"Found it!" Linda exclaims with heightened enthusiasm.

Filled with trepidation, I look over to her and discover my fears to be warranted. She wields a small, black handgun, and her eyes are wild. I can't decide if I'm relieved or freaked out by the sight. Seeing Finn's aunt with a gun is like giving your elderly grandparent access to the Internet —it's a nice gesture, but probably will prove to be dangerous in the end.

"You know how to *use* that?" I ask nervously.

"She knows more than you think," Finn answers plainly. Linda loads little golden bullets into the gun and cocks it back before standing straight up.

Gasping, I frantically pull on her arm. "Linda! What are you *doing*? We don't want that big guy to have any more reason to want to come in here and eat us! If he sees you, we're toast—like literally!"

"I'm going to take care of that nasty son of a bitch

before he breaks my sister's window. She hasn't exactly had a chance to test it out before now and I don't know if the warranty will stick if she claims a walking corpse broke it."

She sprints away from the island and toward the front door. I'm shocked when Finn simply lets her pass by. My eyes dart to his. "What are you doing? Your aunt is already in danger of hurting herself, even without a gun. You have to stop her!" I reach out to slap him on the arm but he swiftly diverts the attack and a playful smile creeps onto his face.

"Emma, don't worry. She's got this."

I try answering him, but the words can't find their way out. He stands, so I follow suit. We watch through the glass windows as his aunt marches around the front of the house to where the starving zombie stands. Linda pulls the gun up, holds it to his rotting forehead with her arms taut, and fires off a couple of shots that hit him squarely in the brain before he collapses to the ground.

I gasp. Where did she learn how to shoot a gun?

She calmly pushes the unmoving corpse with her foot until she's convinced he's truly dead. After glancing around in search of more walking dead guys, she breezes back in through the front door. Throwing the gun on the countertop, she washes her hands in the sink like she's preparing to make breakfast. My stomach rumbles demandingly at the thought.

"Done that before, have ya?" I finally ask, my voice high. She had done everything so calmly, like it was no big deal, when in fact she just shot the reanimated remains of another human being.

She smiles smugly as she grabs a towel from the stove handle. "Emma, are you one of those people who believes that my sister and I are completely crazy?"

"Uh…" I shift my weight uncomfortably. How the hell am I supposed to answer without sounding like a jerk?

"Don't do that to Em," Finn scolds her, his eyebrows all scrunched together. "It's time to tell her the truth." I have no idea what truth he could be referencing, but it's kind of hot the way he stands up for me, even if it *is* to a family member.

"You mean like these aren't really zombies and this is all an convoluted play you guys are putting on for my benefit?" I ask with budding hope. "I mean, you probably owe me for putting that red hair dye in your shampoo bottle this summer."

Linda smiles at her nephew. "You're right Finn, I'm sorry. It probably *is* time to tell her." She takes my hands in her newly cleansed ones. "Emma, I'm sorry this family had to lie to you all these years but I assure you, I'm not crazy and neither is my sister. Elizabeth is actually a federal agent. She works for the government."

Chapter 3

Looking at Finn, I silently beg for his help. His aunt's quite *obviously* full-out, batshit crazy. But surprisingly, my friend's gaze turns sympathetic, just like it had the time I found out my boyfriend Ned was cheating on me with some random college girl. In hindsight, I probably shouldn't have been too surprised at the time. Someone with a name like that was bound to be unbalanced.

Linda's stare on me feels creepy. "I was an agent, too. I retired when I had a bit of a breakdown after the events of nine-eleven. Emma, we knew an attack of some kind was coming. Elizabeth had warned us. I just hoped something to this extreme wouldn't happen."

I blink my eyes dozens of times while trying to absorb this bit of information. Maybe I hit my head harder than I thought and I'm hallucinating. I've never tried drugs but once I overdosed on cold medicine and saw fairies over my bed. This situation feels oddly similar.

Between the discovery of zombies and learning Finn's mom works for the government, I'm convinced, at the very least, that I'm experiencing residual side effects from the energy drinks I was downing last night. Either that or Cash slipped me a hallucinatory drug while I was out.

Lip held between my teeth, I glance over at my silent friend. "What about your mom claiming to have Michael Jackson's baby? Does the *government* know about that?"

Finn only smirks.

Linda's light laughter fills the house, sounding totally out of place. "That story was just a fabrication to keep this small town from knowing the truth. I wish it were true though—at least we would know where to find Elizabeth." Although her lips are pulled into a smile, her eyes all at once appear sad.

My heart sinks with this information. "You don't where she is? Why haven't you told me any of this before?" I ask, my eyes wide.

Linda shakes her head slowly. "She went missing while on assignment quite a few months back. The bureau says they're looking for her, but I think there's more involved than they're willing to share."

"No one else knows all of this," Finn adds. Again, I look to him for help but he now looks just plain *sad* with the mere mention of his mom. Eyes blank, he gazes past the kitchen to where the zombie was recently massacred.

Just how long have they known of her disappearance? At least it would explain why Finn took his mom's alleged commitment so hard for the first few weeks. Even though I'm better at being "one of the guys" than acting all girly and being a sympathetic ear, we've always been pretty open with each other about everything. Or at least *I* have been with *him*. He asked me to quit sharing when I started giving him really detailed descriptions of my dates.

"You said she knew all of this was going to happen," I say to Linda. "How? And why didn't she warn people?"

"She put this family in danger just by telling us," she

answers. "We don't know the specifics or even what it's all about. She just warned us that when something unimaginable happened, we aren't to trust anyone we don't already know and that we need to use our own supply of food and water. She told me this the very last time any of us spoke to her."

I take all of this in with a heavy heart for both my best friend and the rest of civilization. I also can't believe all of Linda and Elizabeth's crazy notions over the years had just been for show. Once upon a time I actually felt guilty for laughing when my girlfriends and I coined the nickname *Looney Linda* for her. But I got over it the next day when I caught her doing nude yoga in Finn's backyard.

"They were talking about this on the news, but everyone was too afraid to really say what is really happening," says Linda. "They were calling it *reanimation of humans*. No one had the balls to say that the dead are actually walking. Last I heard they thought it was some kind of virus, possibly from ingesting some spoiled meat. They said the National Guard has already been deployed and is forming a barrier around the infected area."

"I told you being vegan was a good thing," I say to Finn with a snort.

Marley and Cash breeze into the room as if nothing out of the ordinary is happening. Marley grabs an apple and hops up to sit on the island. Cash rests his elbow on her knees and takes a bite of her apple. The two of them watch us as if we're getting ready for a picnic.

"What's up?" Marley asks when I won't quit staring.

"Not much," I say. "Just the usual…you know…hiding from dead corpses and such."

I have nothing against Cash's girlfriend Marley, per se, although she *is* dumb enough to keep dating him. They've been together for almost two years straight since first meeting in college, and they seem to be pretty serious—as serious as Cash is capable of being, anyway. Marley is actually pretty cool, and I have fun hanging out with her most days if I ignore her crazy tendencies that include the study of witchcraft. But once again, if zombies are real, who am I to say witchcraft is bogus? At this point, reality is becoming just a word and not looking like anything I'll be seeing again anytime soon.

"Yeah, I had to climb up the back of the house when a big one tried attacking me," Marley says casually.

"We told Emma about Mom and Aunt Linda," Finn tells his brother.

"Cool," Marley says, throwing me a condescending smile from behind her stupid, perfect red curls that frame her annoyingly adorable green eyes and pear-shaped face. Okay, now I have something against her.

I glower at my best friend. "*Wait a minute*. You mean to tell me Marley knew about this? I thought you said no one else knew! How is that fair?" Finn only folds his arms and looks calmly back at me. His self-control can be so overly irritating—sometimes I'm sure he only does it to agitate me.

"Finn didn't want to tell you because deep down he really hates your guts and wishes you would just go away," Cash says with a mouthful of apple. "But you just can't seem to take a hint."

I continue my attack on Finn, again ignoring his mentally defective brother. "*Dude.* I'm your *best* friend. Why didn't I get to know before now? Your mom is officially the coolest person I know, only all these years I didn't even *know* it!"

Linda places her hand on my arm. "It was my call, Emma. Finn wanted to tell you a long time ago but I didn't think it was safe. Marley isn't from around here so there was less of a chance of the word getting out."

I chortle, my eyes switching from my friend to his aunt. "*What* are you saying? Like I have a big mouth or something?"

Cash snorts loudly. "You only announced to the *entire school* that you made out with Eric in the backseat of his dad's Mustang. What do *you* think?"

I whirl around to glare at him. "I was telling *Carolyn* about it, you nimrod. I didn't know she was in the middle of a live student council webcast!"

Cash shakes his head, scrunching his nose and lips up. "Why else do you think she would she be talking to the computer?"

"Carolyn can be a bit eccentric at times!" I yell back at him. Truth is I was so excited over my steamy make-out session that I hadn't even bothered to pay any attention to what my friend had been doing at the time. In the weeks to follow I received quite a bit of guff from the entire student body for that one.

I finally snap my mouth shut. I guess I have to accept the situation for what it is and can't get mad at my friend for something ~~Looney~~ Linda had decided. I huff in annoyance and turn away from Finn.

"So now what?" Cash asks. "What's our plan?"

Linda turns to assess her more annoying nephew. "I came to get you guys the hell out of here, that's what."

"Before we become someone's main course?" I add sarcastically. Linda doesn't answer. She only glances my way, her troubled eyes telling me everything I need to know —she's just as afraid and clueless as we are.

* * *

TURNS out the Benson family had been keeping even more secrets from me. Like the safe room we were in earlier—it was a far cry from being "just a shelter." Finn purposely hadn't turned the lights on so I wouldn't see just how prepared his mom and aunt are for this very type of crisis. They also failed to mention there's a heavily bolted door we could've used earlier that leads directly outside past a set of stairs.

A mountainous wall of metal storage shelves holds an impressive supply of bottled water, both cans and packets of some kind of food, plus a whole bunch of other stuff one may need if the world happens to be ending. A handful of big mattresses line the walls in camp-style bunks, and a large metal door with a keypad lock sits in the rear end of the room.

"The room is chemical-proof, lined in a high-grade metal," Linda explains by way of giving me an official tour. "We designed it for up to ten people to survive up to three months in any type of attack. Elizabeth had always feared we would be using it for when terrorists struck again one day. But between us girls, I'd rather deal with zombies than *those* assholes."

I only look back at her in awe, unsure to how respond to all of this. I still wonder by the excessive measures they've taken if there isn't still just a sliver of crazy somewhere inside the sisters, dying to find its way out.

Linda crosses the room to the large metal door and types in a code on the keypad. The door swings open to reveal what must be the biggest collection of guns known to man—or southern Minnesota, anyway. I won't even pretend I know anything about guns, because I seriously don't. I come from a more tree-hugging, loving type of family that doesn't think weapons of mass-destruction are necessary. The collection includes short guns, long guns, very large guns, black guns, silver guns…you get the picture—whatever the technical names are for them, they're packing a serious variety in their arsenal.

"Each of you needs to carry more than one gun," Linda says as she passes them out to her nephews. "We'll stop by Emma's to see if her parents have returned. Marley and Emma can practice shooting a few rounds there."

Marley stares blankly down on the big gun that Cash hands her.

I hold my hand out. "Wait a minute. Are you saying we're actually going to *go out there*? Why don't we just sit it out for a while? It looks like we're good to go with all this stuff. If we got rid of Cash it would be like a little vacation down here, only without any beaches—or any kind of sun. Okay, maybe it would be more like a prison stay. But it's still got to be better than going out there and being gnawed on, right?"

Linda shakes her head. "I'm just going by Elizabeth's directions, Emma. She told us to evacuate the area as soon as possible."

When Cash starts rambling on to his aunt with *his* take on the zombie infection, I zone out and assess my own mental status. I've become numb to everything that's happening. My mind begins to wander all over the place—from the night before (would the zombies have found the chickens in the garages by now and eaten them as appetizers?) to the president (maybe my dad *was* right all along and the president has caused this Armageddon) and finally to school (will they be able to reschedule the homecoming game or will there be too many dead players?).

Finn slings the strap of a large gun over my shoulder and stuffs what must be bullets into my pocket. His expression remains impossibly solemn as he dresses me for what is beginning to feel like a war. I watch my friend with a new appreciation.

He certainly has a great sense of style, which is rare in this town. He has changed into the new faded jeans and cobalt blue hooded sweatshirt we picked up just last weekend. I love what the vibrant blue color does to his already handsome face. He has never openly enjoyed it when we shop together, but neither do I. We usually hit our favorite stores in the nearest mall—an excruciating hour away—and bring our selections to the register without taking the time to try anything on. We're more concerned about the entertainment that will follow, which has involved seeing who can ride on the mall's giant carousel the most times backwards without throwing up.

I've always seen my best friend as the goofy, *amusing* person that I know him to be, but never really paid attention to how seriously *good looking* he is until just recently. Then again, maybe I'm just trying to make the best of the situation. If the five of us are the last ones on earth it would be comforting to think my only option in men is a really good one.

I never would've dreamed Finn would be so calm and collected when it felt like the world may be ending. When watching scary movies together he would sometimes hide behind the blanket with me like some kind of pansy. Looking back, maybe that had been him trying to make a lame ass move on me. In this moment of clarity I realize my crush on him has evolved to something much deeper. I frown up at him while he's still pushing the bullets into my jean pocket.

"Finn, do you actually expect me to *use* all of this stuff? And why do I get the feeling you already know how to shoot a gun? You're too chicken to even kill a little *spider*."

A sluggish, coy smile comes to his lips. "Yeah, well spiders haven't ever tried to attack me in my yard, either."

I beam back at him like some kind of perverse crack addict. "You could have just taken me for a date on the shooting range somewhere if your family was so concerned about an impending attack of this kind. You know me—I would've been cool with that. Just think—we could have played Cowboys and Indians with Cash, only with *real* guns."

He shrugs and continues placing supplies on my person. "It wasn't necessary. I knew I'd be around to protect you if anything monumental were to happen." His eyes meet mine behind his mess of thick eyelashes and I suddenly *know*. He's into me, too. How long had this been going on and why was I too much of a moron to have noticed it before?

Linda interrupts our sappy moment. "Finn and Emma, you two start loading the car with as many supplies as you can carry. Food and water, soap, deodorant, whatever you think we will need. We may be stuck in a vehicle together for a good while."

I groan at the thought of being stuck in a vehicle with Cash for more than ten *seconds*.

When I take a step forward, I nearly collapse from the additional weight of the weapons Finn has strapped on to me. My slender 5'7" frame is a bit wimpy for any kind of Rambo-type getup, but I don't want Cash to rip into me again so I continue following Finn to the supply cabinets with as much pep as the weight allows me to muster.

Linda continues to give orders to Marley and Cash. I only half listen to what she tells them. My mind is still reeling from the fact that she had once worked for the government.

I've been hanging out at Finn's house forever and never

suspected they were actually lying to me about their lives. Sure, their less-than-modestly furnished home—which includes the biggest flat screen television I've ever seen and an Olympic-sized pool inside a separate guest house in the backyard—is a bit elegant for someone living solely off her dead husband's estate, but the official story they fed me was that Finn's dad was a wealthy lawyer who was killed in a car accident.

Elizabeth was often gone for what I was told were art gallery shows—she was supposedly this starving artist traveling all over the world. Before now I had no reason to even suspect that they would be lying to me about such a thing—I've even seen some of her paintings.

I frown at Finn. "So you're saying all those stories about your mom being an artist and traveling the world were just a cover. What about those paintings she showed me? Were they really just some color by number thing?"

Finn smirks. "She really does that stuff, but only as a side hobby. Whenever I told you she was going on some gallery tour, she was actually on assignment for the government. Mom really got a kick out of the places she pretended to be visiting."

I observe him for a moment. He's putting on a brave face, but it's one I know too well. Deep down, he's freaking out. "The government has to eventually find her though, right?"

Finn blows a breath of air from his cheeks. "I sure hope so. They don't claim to have any leads, but Aunt Linda is convinced there's more to the story."

I hold open a large black duffel bag Finn hands me. He begins filling it with bottles of water and granola bars. I want to ask where the good stuff is—like candy bars and cupcakes—but the mood in the room is quite serene, so I keep my thoughts about our crappy food choice to myself.

Instead, I decide to pursue this whole "mysterious dad" scenario.

"What about your dad? He wasn't really a lawyer, was he?"

"You're catching on quickly," Finn answers, not looking up.

I'm careful to use a gentle tone, something I've rarely used in conversations with him. "Do you remember him?"

He shrugs one shoulder up. "No. He really did die when I was a baby. It just wasn't a car accident that killed him."

I gasp. "You mean…your *mom* did it?" I whisper. The off-kilter Elizabeth I thought I knew would be easily capable of flipping out and losing her shit, but I guess it's also possible this new person I have just learned of would probably kill her husband if he became some kind of threat in her line of work.

Finn gives me this incredulous look. "Don't be an *idiot*, Em. He worked for the government, too. Only he died shortly after he got too close to the truth."

My mind immediately goes to my days of being obsessed with *The X-Files* series and I gasp again. "You mean…as in the whole *we're not alone* thing?"

He laughs and I'm caught off guard by how much I seriously adore the sound of it. "*Emma!* No, not *that*. Mom wouldn't tell me what exactly happened but I think it had something to do with terrorists. My parents were both involved in the Gulf War. We had to go into hiding with my mom for a time after nine-eleven, too."

My eyes light up with my newest thought. "Do you think *terrorists* could somehow be responsible for those disturbingly gross people walking around out there?" I've been throwing the word *zombie* around like a Frisbee, but truth is, I don't know what the technical definition of a *zombie* is. I haven't seen any of them eating actual human *brains*, per se, and that's what zombies always seem to be doing in the movies. Maybe these people just have mad cow disease or something.

Finn's eyes drift over to where his aunt is still filling bags with weapons. "I don't know, but Aunt Linda sure seems to be gearing up for something big."

* * *

WITH EVERYTHING LOADED into the back half of Linda's shiny new black Suburban—which seems ironically fitting for her ex-government status—we head out in the direction of my house. We're completely silent as we assess the damage to the neighborhood. Our once peaceful community looks more and more like a war zone the farther away from the Bensons' house we travel. The walking corpses appear to have moved on, but they left a trail of carnage in their wake.

Quite a few of our neighbors have turned into some-thing resembling road kill. I can hardly identify their twisted remains. Random arms, legs and unknown body parts lie in the road and in a few of the yards.

My stomach lurches, deciding it can't take anymore. The sick feeling is worse than the time Finn and I got stuck on the tilt-a-whirl for twenty minutes at the state fair after trying deep-fat fried Twinkies and pickles.

"I think I need to vomit now," I say, holding my hand to my stomach as it twists and grumbles in protest.

Cash looks back at me and rolls his eyes. "There's a shocker—Emma's gonna lose it."

"Shut up, asshole!" Finn snaps at his brother, putting his hand on my neck. "Linda, pull over—*quickly*."

My hand is already pulling on the door handle before the vehicle has totally stopped and I leap out. Unfortunately, my feet land just inches from where Darcy Sanderson's bloody remains lay, her body ripped to nearly unrecognizable shreds. Her legs are twisted unnaturally with one bent in one direction and the second stretched out straight in the other. One of her arms is severed and rests just inches from her head, looking like a turkey leg after Christmas dinner. Blood is everywhere—I don't think it's possible for all of it to be from her. Her once blond hair is now a cheap strawberry red, and her remaining lifeless eye stares straight up at me from its socket.

I inhale deeply to unleash a scream that will surely break records on the Richter Scale when I'm startled into silence by a pair of arms slipping around my waist.

"Don't look," Finn's voice beckons smoothly, turning me away from her.

My legs give out underneath me, but his arms hold on tightly to keep me upright. Finn again lifts me up into his arms and carries me back to the vehicle. My chest is tight with the horror consuming me. Sure, Darcy became a total witch and tortured me numerous times over the past couple of years after our friendship took a downfall, but I'm not some pervert that gets off on seeing people disfigured unless it's in some brutal horror movie.

Before I crawl into the back of the Suburban again, I catch Cash gaping out the window at Darcy's mangled body. For once, he has nothing smart to say to me, which is good—I have no snappy comeback, either. There are no words for this.

Chapter 4

A side from my incoherent ramblings, the car is once
again silent as we drive the last few yards to my
home. I pull myself together long enough to debate
whether or not I want to go inside with Finn. In the end, I
know I do want to go. If my parents have either been
zombified or chewed up I need to see it for closure
purposes, no matter how grizzly the proof.

"Stay close," Linda says to us. Finn grips my hand
tightly as we follow her in through the front door. Linda
holds a smallish gun out in front of her as we walk through
each room of the unusually still house. After we've made a
quick sweep of the general living area, I huff out a blast of
air in relief. The house seems undisturbed, without a single
drop of blood to be found.

"Dad's car is gone," I tell them, discovering the hook to
be empty where he always keeps his keys. The whole house
is as neat as a pin, mostly because none of us are ever
home. The bright, recently remodeled kitchen is still
immaculate from our cleaning lady's last visit on Thursday.
The kitchen is rarely used for anything more than making

sandwiches, however, as my mom has never been into the whole cooking thing. More often than not we eat frozen meals or something greasy from one of the town's wide variety of three crappy restaurants.

Linda lowers her gun. "What were they doing today?"

"I think Mom had an appointment to get her hair done downtown," I answer her. "I'm not sure what Dad was doing, though. He may have gone with to make sure she wasn't 'taking a second mortgage on the house to get beautified,' as he always says."

Linda and Finn exchange a look, attempting to be secretive, but I catch it. I drop Finn's hand to fold my arms in front of me and glower at them. "What?"

Finn reaches out again, pulling my hand back into his and speaks gently. "Linda drove through town earlier…" He lets his voice trail off and searches my eyes with his, not knowing the best way to continue.

"Most of the people in town have…vacated," Linda finishes for him. But I know what she's really trying to say is anyone left behind was dead.

"But she heard on the radio that the Guards were being disbursed in the area. Maybe they already went through town and got everyone out," Finn adds.

"How did we miss the Guards coming into town? Just how long were we your creepy basement, anyway? Why didn't your mom plan for a radio in her master dungeon design?" I'm grumbling in frustration more than anything. My visions of being rescued from this nightmare are fading.

"By the time we got into the basement, the phones were down and there was nothing but a high pitched squeal on the radio," Finn explains.

Linda frowns at him. "It sounds like someone was messing with the local frequencies."

A new hope fills me. "Do you think the Guards will come back to get us?" No offense to Linda, but being in a military vehicle with a bunch of burly men toting weapons sounds like the safest place to be at a time like this. Plus, maybe there's some kind of portable brig they could throw Cash into, for good measure.

Linda shakes her head. "I don't think so, honey."

Finn turns to his aunt. "Did they say on the radio how contagious this virus thing is?"

My stomach lurches at his implication. "As in is it possible we're infected? You mean I could turn into one of those freaky things? You guys remember I don't eat meat, right?"

I look to Linda, demanding an acceptable answer. No way am I going to become a zombie—not when I've just realized my deeper thing for Finn. I'm far too interested in the possibility of the upcoming steamy nights we may have together to allow myself to become a rotting freak of nature.

Linda squirms with the pressure of my questions. "I don't know much more about the whole situation than you do. Only what I heard on the radio, which wasn't much."

I frown at her answer. "You mean aside from the fact that you used to work for the government? Surely there's something you learned in basic training. Or maybe you have some old connections that can get us out of this mess, right? Don't lie to me anymore, Linda. You need to be straight about this."

"Em—" Finn begins, but his aunt holds her hand up.

"She's right. You two are adults and deserve to know the truth."

"What if we can't handle the truth?" I ask without bothering to sensor my mouth. Finn nudges me sharply in the rib cage. Although it probably isn't the best time to mockingly quote famous movies, I can't seem to help myself. Whenever I feel like I'm under attack or facing the possibility of becoming a flesh-eating ghoul, it's my nature to respond with humor.

"They were saying it's possible we've been exposed to some kind of infection…I mean I don't think they know for sure," Linda says. "My ex-FBI status may get us places, but I don't know just how far. I think our best chances are to just hightail it out of the Midwest—it was what Elizabeth told us to do."

Cash and Marley suddenly come barreling into the house, frightening Linda enough to raise her gun and take aim at them. The two automatically raise their hands in surrender. Linda curses under her breath when she realizes what she has done before lowering the gun. Cash and Marley drop their hands and sigh.

"There's another one coming from the woods," Cash tells us. Marley's eyes are wider than normal and she looks spooked by whatever they saw. I wonder if maybe it was her first contact with one of the walking corpses.

I blow out air in exasperation. "Here we go again," I sigh, dreading the thought of another zombie encounter. I'd reached my tolerance level immediately upon meeting the first ill-dressed one.

Linda holds her hand up to us. "You kids stay here. I'll go check it out."

"I'm going with you," Finn insists, standing at her side.

I pat his back. "Good luck."

I'm certainly not going back out there with them.

His eyes settle on mine. "It will be okay."

I nod, even though I know he has absolutely no control over the situation and can't promise me anything at this point. He disappears behind his aunt and through our back door. I stand with my arms tight against my body, wanting to ignore the uneasy feeling creeping into me, and curl my lips at Cash and Marley in what probably appears to be a rather terse smile.

Marley drops Cash's hand and steps toward me. "Maybe you should grab some of your things while we're here."

I nod mechanically. "Good idea. I'll be right back."

My childhood home feels oddly surreal. I wonder if this will be the last time I set foot inside. I've spent a big chunk of my life here and have so many inept memories connected to it. Will I ever experience the perverse joys of adulthood?

Wandering back through the long hallway to where my impressive bedroom is located, I decide being an only child had been a good run—dozens of picture frames holding memories line the walls to prove it. I run my fingers over the glass frame holding a picture of my shirtless dad, tall and lean, holding a younger version of a pigtailed me in front of a large waterfall in Jamaica. We're both soaking wet but have these giant, identical grins plastered on our faces.

My parents took me on this trip with a group of their friends who were first opposed to toting a bratty little ten-year-old with, but their opinions changed when I became skilled at refilling their glasses of rum. I even saved a few of them from drunkenly breaking their necks on the mossy rocks when journeying up the multi-tiered waterfalls. For as long as I can remember, my parents have always treated me as an intelligent person and not some little kid, which was their reasoning for bringing me on that trip, and many others that followed.

Walking into my elaborate room, I know my favorite of all perks had been the decorator my mother hired every couple of years to give me the coolest and most sophisticated looking room of anyone I know. I'm usually not very girly, but the room is just plain sick. The massive iron and glass chandelier looming over the bed and tan suede chaise lounge sofa are just the start of it. My dad insisted on buying me the colossal walnut desk that takes up the entire corner on which my laptop and other electronic toys sit. A large flat screen television is mounted on the wall across from my bed, connected to killer surround sound and video gaming systems that tend to make all my guy friends sickly green with envy.

I stand staring at my ginormous four-poster bed shroud in layers of luxurious soft materials, remembering the numerous times Finn and I had lay together watching movies or even just hung out talking about stupid stuff like his brother. He had even slept over here more than a dozen times in the past year. Our parents never cared since we weren't ever anything more than friends. Even if we were, I'm not sure any of them would've noticed.

Sadly, the beautiful bed would've made for a perfectly romantic setting, had we realized our feelings for each other before the threat of impending doom.

"What a waste," I say angrily to the empty room.

Seconds later, the sound of something bumping into the wall comes from the hallway, tearing me away from my trivial thoughts.

"Give me a minute, you guys," I call out. "I'm just saying goodbye to my listless love life in here."

I'm answered with a high pitched moan.

Each hair on the back of my neck pricks up to life. That gut-wrenching fear that can make a person totally paralyzed or completely insane seizes hold of me once again.

I'm about to be attacked by another one of those ghouls in my own bedroom.

My eyes frantically search the room for some kind of weapon. Teddy bear…pillows…a boring paperback book that I couldn't finish…an unread tabloid magazine.

"Hey—I totally forgot about that!" I say. Then a flash of something silver near the magazine catches my eye. I dash forward to find my silver baton from junior high marching band buried in the carpet. I grab the baton, spewing a line of swear words as I run to my walk-in closet with the ridiculous weapon clutched to my chest.

The closet door is barely closed behind me when the newest zombie stumbles into my bedroom, tripping over the doorway. Through the wooden slots it's difficult to fully assess the straggler. Bits of generic women's clothing and shocks of white hair appear to me. When her stench drifts into the closet with me, I hold my breath.

The she-zombie moans again, her head dancing around like a bobblehead while searching the room. I will my heart to quit pounding furiously, as surely the zombie has some keen sense of hearing or other super powers. She limps past the bed, closing in on the space between us. I try to put myself in the shoes of someone strong and brave, like Arnold Schwarzenegger, but scratch the idea when I remember that I suck at accents.

Whether it's actually my erratic heart-beat or my labored breaths that betray me, isn't clear, but quite suddenly the zombie jerks her blood-soaked head in the direction of my hideout.

In this moment, her identity becomes too clear.

"Betty?" I gasp out loud. I'm so baffled that I momentarily forget I'm supposed to be hiding from this flesh-seeking monster. But our housekeeper of fifteen years is hardly the flesh-eating type. She's a good foot shorter than me and is on the heels of eighty. Poor Betty has always been quiet and kind, even tolerant of my deplorable hygiene habits that include leaving a trail of dirty underwear anywhere from my closet to the bathroom. My mom always says it's fitting my best friend is a guy because with my terrible hygienic habits, I'm more like the son she never had and never wanted.

I find it just depressing that somewhere in Betty's garbled mind she still thinks of work as a priority and has found her way back here. As her decomposing arm reaches for the door and she lets out an excited cry, however, something tells me it's not dirty underwear she's searching for this time.

I suddenly remember the gun Finn had holstered to me and want to kick myself. By now a pattern of forgetting about available life-saving tools (like my cell phone) has clearly been established. My hand shakes so badly when it curls around the cool metal barrel, however, that I probably have a better chance at accidentally shooting myself than taking out our slight housekeeper who is barely capable of lifting a full laundry basket. The gun jumps around in my trembling fingers like a fish fresh off the hook.

Just when I've myself convinced that I merely have to pull back on the metal trigger thingy, something flashes from the other side of the closet. I look up in time to see Betty's head drop off to the side, her neck separated from her shoulders. Her corpse slumps to the ground. Blood splatters across my bedroom, covering the walls and carpet. A few drops even sprinkle through the slats of the closet door I'm hiding behind.

I scream for reasons other than seeing my perfectly gorgeous room ruined.

Linda stands where Betty's corpse had been, clasping my father's ax firmly in her hands. She appears to be perfectly calm, despite having just taken the head off another human being. Although I'm in shock, it's kind of cool to witness my best friend's aunt being badass.

I fling open the door to the closet. "You just killed my housekeeper."

Don't get me wrong—I'm not complaining that she saved my life. I'm just really, really freaked out seeing Betty's head severed like that, just inches from my face. This is the same woman who had meticulously ironed my jeans every day for years without protest.

Linda's face turns to a deep scowl. "Did I get any blood on you?"

I look down and my hands flutter wildly about, assessing my body—it's surprising they can even function as shook up as I am. Thankfully, I seem to be blood free. My carpet and walls have taken the brunt of the attack. Between the sight of the dark blood and Betty's eyes staring blankly up to the ceiling from her decapitated head, my stomach's ready to purge whatever's left of the energy drinks. I whirl away from Linda and begin to ralph.

She reaches out to hold my hair away from my face. "There are more of them coming from the woods, Emma. We need to leave."

Finn comes flying into the room but stops short when he sees Betty's corpse. His expression changes from one of concern to deep sympathy when he spots the pile of puke at my feet.

He rests his hand on my shoulder. "Shit, Em. Are you okay?"

"Peachy," I say, giving him an artificial thumbs up.

Finn turns to his aunt but runs his hand across my head, petting me like a dog. "They're getting closer."

"We have to get out of here," Linda says, pulling on my arm with urgency.

As we run from my childhood home, I don't have the

common sense to grab a picture, family keepsake or any memento, but I'm still holding that stupid baton under my armpit.

* * *

WHEN OUR LITTLE legion of misfits rides into town at law-breaking speeds, the comments on the obvious slaughter that took place are minimal. I'm not a contributing member to any intelligent conversation that goes on anyway. Occasionally I'll ramble off some random memory having to do with Betty and how I should've been nicer to her.

Finn has been holding me against his chest since we left my house. He strokes my head with each comment I make, which only adds to the raging emotions that are piling up. I know Finn's afraid more than anything that I'm going insane. Truth is, I may be in agreement on that one.

"I spit my toothpaste right on the sink and didn't wash it off. Not one single time," I tell my mostly disinterested audience. "Who does that?"

Cash groans, turning from the front seat to scowl at me. "We get it, Emma. You were a total bitch to the cleaning lady and you're a disgusting pig. None of this is news to anyone."

Finn reaches over the seat to slug Cash on the arm hard enough to make an actual punching sound and mumbles, "Shut up."

"We'll just make a sweep through town to check for any stragglers," Linda tells us. "I have enough gas loaded up to get us a few hours from the Canada border."

Finn turns his attention from me to his aunt. "Wait, we're going to Canada?"

"I think it's our best chance," Linda answers. "It was what your mom told us to do, anyway."

I can deal with moving to Canada, only I don't know anything about hockey and I'm pretty sure I won't be able to speak their language.

"Don't we want to, like, stay in the States with Elizabeth working for the government and everything?" Marley asks. "You guys must have some kind of pull being family of someone so high up."

From somewhere deep in my hazy mind, I agree it's a good question. I'm one of those people who is crazy proud to be an American and don't like the idea of being locked up in some other third world country for not being one of their citizens.

Linda seems to mull over this thought, then says, "No. If the virus has spread as far through the Midwest as they think, it will take us longer to go in any of the other directions and our chances of getting out of here in time may be diminished."

The loud click of a tab opening a can comes from the front seat. We all watch as Cash takes a casual sip from a can of cheap beer. He lowers it and sighs in satisfaction before realizing he's being watched. He frowns before raising his shoulders. "What? If the world is coming to an end, I'm pretty sure the rules about drinking before noon went out the door."

Linda grumbles at his side and snatches the can away, pitching it out her window. "I need everyone to have a clear head through all of this. We can't afford any distractions. That means no alcohol, no social networking, and no hanky-panky."

Surely the last regulation is reserved for Cash and

Marley, but I'm stabbed with disappointment from it all the same. I'd been hoping that under no condition will I die a virgin and from the way Finn's vibes toward me have changed I'm pretty sure he's up to the challenge.

Marley turns her mouth down at Linda. "How are we going to social network when our phones don't work?" Another valid point for Team Marley—Linda had told us all phones and Internet are totally down.

"Who would want to Facebook right now, anyway?" Cash chimes in. "Shane Frommie—about to be bit by a zombie because I'm standing here, updating my status like a total moron instead of running." But truth is, Cash is addicted to the website and would probably be among those doomed when taking time to creep on other people's statuses. I blocked him a year ago when he wouldn't quit writing imbecile things on my wall.

Linda ignores them, already engaged in another train of thought. "The food and water we brought with us are safe to ingest, but you kids cannot, under any circumstances, eat or drink anything else until we're sure it's clean. Elizabeth said not to, and we don't even know how this virus was spread. Most likely it did have something to do with our water or food, as that's the easiest way to mass distribute a chemical agent like this one we seem to be dealing with. You need to be extremely careful not to get any blood or bodily fluids of an infected person on you."

The urgency in her voice causes the panic in me to multiply. She's making it sound more and more like this is some kind of terrorist attack. I'm infuriated to think that terrorists are using our friends and neighbors to wipe each other out. They could have at least been a bit more selective about who is worthy of becoming a soulless weapon in their quest. Maybe they could have used an intelligence test or something of the sort—at the very least I would've been happy to provide them with a list.

"Do you think there's a cure for this?" I ask. My exceptional candor surprises me—it's clearly a sign I'm beginning to crack.

Linda's eyes meet mine in the rearview mirror. "I sure hope so."

No one speaks again until we've reached the heart of downtown. The handful of mom and pop stores that have remained open in the sluggish economy are now deserted just like the failed businesses surrounding them. A few cars are parallel parked to the curb like any other day, but a minivan is upside down in the middle of the road and a few smaller cars are crookedly lined up on the sidewalk with their doors wide open.

I try not to imagine the scenario that made them desert their vehicles in such a fashion. I'm grateful I hadn't been here when the proverbial shit hit the fan—especially after spotting the maimed body of my favorite lunch lady. She had always given me seconds on tater tots, even though the First Lady's harebrained plan to keep us all waif thin strictly forbids it.

Linda slows down to peer into the hair salon where my mom would've been. "It looks empty, but I'm sure your parents got out of there in time." She turns to give me a reassuring smile, although it comes to me a little too late. I'm already freaked out, even though my dad's car is nowhere to be seen.

The salon does not appear to have made it through the outbreak unscathed. A pile of female bodies can be seen through the broken windows, as well as a collection of mannequin heads whose once perfect hairstyles would never again be the same.

Linda parks the vehicle around the corner from the

salon and grabs her gun from the dashboard. It's still hard to adjust to seeing the Looney Linda I once knew morphing into a total Sarah Connor—minus the physical difference in muscle mass and overall movie-star quality and charm—right in front of my eyes.

"I'm going to survey the area for anyone who remained behind." She turns to Cash. "You're coming along."

Cash's eyes dart to his brother. "Why do I have to go? Why can't Finn?" He sounds just like the whiny little brat he was ten years ago. Come to think of it, his body size is probably the only thing that has changed. I want to laugh at how ridiculous he's being, but all joy seems to have temporarily left me.

Linda opens her door and gives her oldest nephew a warning glare. "Someone who is good with a gun needs to stay behind and watch after the girls. Don't take it personally, kiddo, but you're not the quickest on your feet, either."

Now the laughter comes back to me in a choking burst. I have to say, it feels really good. Tears run down my cheeks and my stomach clenches from all the jiggling. Finn's chest shakes for a minute under me as he laughs along, but then his grip on my arms tightens, attempting to settle me when I can't seem to do it on my own.

I'm holding my stomach and wiping my eyes when Cash throws me a murderous glare before hopping out of the vehicle. In my defense, I think the laughter had just been a release from the horror of seeing my longtime family employee butchered in front of me only minutes before. Crying has never really been my thing—it ranks right up there with sappy chick flicks and smutty romance novels with pansy men airbrushed on their covers.

"Do you think they'll find anyone still alive in there?" Marley asks Finn once my delirium has ceased. "What if everyone else in town was killed today?" Her questions are doing nothing to calm the terrified part of me that thinks Linda will find my slaughtered parents.

Finn watches his aunt walk toward the salon. "Linda thinks everyone left. I'm sure most of them made it out in time."

I love the vibrations his chest makes into my ear canal as he speaks and the warmth his body projects on to mine. Being this physically close to him is something I could easily get used to on a regular basis, assuming we live through the Rapture and everything.

I'm able to lose myself in the fantasy of being alone with Finn until I see something scurry in the street from the corner of my eye. The figure was larger than an animal but moving with too much speed and agility to be another walking corpse. When I turn, it disappears behind the brick corner of a store.

"Anyone else see that?" I ask, pointing. "Something just moved over there. I don't know what it was, but I'm about sixty-four point eight percent sure it wasn't some kind of walking dead person."

Finn uses exaggerated care as he pushes me away to grab the large gun resting by his feet. He's definitely into me, for sure—in the days of our friendship he would've simply knocked me onto the floor.

"We're coming with," Marley tells him.

I nod. She's right—I'm not going to sit in this vehicle and wait for something to pull me out like those other cars parked on the sidewalk. If any zombie redneck tries attacking me in the street, I could easily outrun it with my record-breaking running skills I discovered earlier in the day.

Grumbling to himself, Finn holds the door for Marley and me to jump out. I gratefully accept his hand when he offers it. If nothing else, his touch reminds me I'm not stuck in some horrific nightmare and, better yet, that I'm not facing this zombie debacle totally alone. Plus my raging hormones are all for it.

We carefully creep in the direction of the figure, the three of us moving in total unison that would've made my preschool dance teacher totally ecstatic. Finn lets go of me to lower the gun with both hands so I take hold of his waist and cower behind him.

"Is someone there?" Marley calls out in a soft voice.

I turn to give her an incredulous look. "Um, hello? Were you expecting one of those dead people to answer that? Did you maybe think they'd be all, 'yep—step closer so I can eat you?' Why don't you just start yelling fresh meat here?" But as quiet as her voice had been, mine is amplified to the same degree, mostly from the nerves rushing through me.

"Emma?" a young voice asks from behind the wall.

Finn turns to look at me questioningly.

"Um…yeah. Who is it?" I ask flippantly, as if someone had been ringing a doorbell.

"It's me, Jake." My twelve-year-old neighbor steps onto the sidewalk.

Chapter 5

My cutie patootie neighbor is obviously traumatized from the events of the day. His large brown eyes that are normally lit with mischief dart around nervously. His shirt and pants are ripped from what I'm hoping to be a narrow escape from some kind of close quarters and not an attempted attack of some kind. His hair is not styled in his favorite teeny-pop sensation 'do but sticks out wildly from his head, looking just as stressed as he is.

Although I don't really have any sympathetic tendencies in me, the sight of my poor little friend all frazzled like this is heartbreaking. I don't want to imagine what horrors he has seen during the day. I run over to embrace him.

He squeezes me back for the slightest of moments but then pushes me back. "What are you doing?"

I frown, knowing for a fact the little shit has a crush on me. His sister is a junior and told me last month she found a notebook with my name scribbled on it a hundred times. But I guess if he wants to play Mr. Tough Guy around me, I'm cool with that. The little man has a reputation to uphold.

"Oh, sorry. I just wanted to see what it felt like to have your..." I look down at his arms that have less meat than Finn's "...long arms around me."

In his defense, he's only in sixth grade and I totally remember what a brutal time that was. I'm not tall by anyone's definition, but he comes up to my armpits and you can about see his bones protruding from underneath his skin. The infected had likely passed him over, deciding there wasn't enough meat to bother.

He gives me this little freaked-out gaze. "Okay, psycho."

"Are you alone?" Finn asks him.

Jake's face floods with relief when he realizes our male neighbor is with me, and in possession of a firearm. It's such a typical guy reaction. "Yeah. I was throwing a football around with some of the guys in the schoolyard when a bunch of those crazy assholes came running at us. We couldn't figure out what the hell was wrong with them, so we all just started running and ended up in different directions."

I narrow my eyes at him. "Are you supposed to be swearing like that?" My intentions are all for good. I don't want him to lose all innocence just because the world seems to be coming to an end. Some things in life are worth preserving.

He snorts. "You really think anyone is going to give a shit right now?"

Marley steps forward to cut into our conversation. "Have you seen anyone else? Any normal people, I mean?"

Jake surveys her, unsure what to think of the company we're keeping. Her unusual piercings on her face and ears along with the tattoos across her neck are something the rest of us are used to by now, but I guess they come off as a little extreme to people meeting her for the first time. I figure if someone wants to stretch their earlobes out excessively and create the need for more plastic surgeons in America, good on them.

"Who are you?" Jake asks. At least they're still teaching stranger-danger to kids these days.

"It's okay," I tell him. "She's Cash's girlfriend."

He raises a single eyebrow at her. "On purpose?" Finn and I both chuckle. I'm suddenly reminded why I've always been a big fan of this kid's.

"What about your parents?" Finn asks.

Jake looks back to me, the lost-boy look resurfacing. "They're at my grandparents' place out in Wisconsin. I was staying at a friend's house."

"What about your little friend?" I ask.

He makes a failing attempt to swallow and his eyes water. "One of those assholes got him. It freaked me out so I hid behind the school. I didn't come back out until I heard trucks going down the highway. By the time I made it down there, I saw the last National Guard truck leaving town. I tried jumping and yelling for them to stop, but they were too far away."

"You're coming with us," Finn decides.

Marley examines Jake more closely with a critical eye. "Are you sure you weren't bit or anything? Have you been drinking water or eating anything recently?"

I step between them, holding him behind me. "Give the kid a break. He probably just witnessed half the town turning into a smorgasbord."

Jake doesn't need to thank me—his giant brown eyes peering up at me say it all. I only hope his lack of answer doesn't mean he had been bit or eaten something poisoned. As hard as it had been to even think about harming our cleaning lady, it would be even more difficult to shoot my little buddy—especially when I'm probably infallible in his mind.

We return to the vehicle where I give Jake a bottle of water and some fruit snacks. He pretends to take it all in stride, but it's obvious he's hungry and thirsty as fast as the snacks and water disappear. Finn paces nervously around outside of the vehicle, waiting for his aunt and worthless brother to rejoin us.

I lean over the front seat to look back at Jake. I claim shotgun as no one else seems to be paying any attention at the moment. "We're heading to Canada," I tell him.

Panic fills his eyes. "But what about my parents? What if they come back here looking for me? I can't just leave the country!"

I don't know much about kidnapping laws when it comes to little kids, and can only hope this isn't breaking one of them. I so don't have the stomach for prison food. "I'm not…quite…sure," I answer truthfully. "Finn's aunt knows a lot about this stuff, and she seems to think we should head north. I'm sure your parents would be okay with us taking you somewhere safe. We'll be able to find them later, when all of this is over."

With this information, his panic becomes full-fledged and he starts flailing his arms around like a Muppet. "Finn's aunt? You mean you're going by what Looney Linda thinks is best?"

I guess my friends and I aren't the only ones to use the cruel moniker, although I probably deserve credit for being among those to come up with it. I look to Finn for help but he's too busy walking in circles like some brainless cat, thankfully oblivious to our conversation.

"She's not really crazy," I say, fidgeting with my fingernails.

Jake rolls his eyes with disbelief. "You mean just like her

sister, who really did have a kid with Michael Jackson's ghost?"

I stare at him, wondering how I'm going to get around telling him the truth that isn't mine to tell. Linda didn't exactly say I needed to keep their secret, but they had taken great care not to share it with me all these years, so I'm not about to let anyone else into our little circle this easy.

"Yeah, but MJ's attorneys took the kid away before she even had a chance to name it," I finally answer.

Jake blinks his eyes rapidly. "Really?"

I shake my head once. "No, not really. But you will just have to trust us. We know what we're doing." Maybe I'm being a bit overly cocky in pretending to be part of the group in the know, but I have a duty to sound intelligent to this kid who probably hangs on my every word in adoration.

His oval-shaped little face turns ashen white as he points his finger to something behind me. "Are you sure about that?"

Marley leans over the seat with her eyes wide. "Oh, shit!"

My inner voice begs me not to turn to look out the back of the vehicle, but I don't always have control of my bodily functions—another reason my mom says I act more like a guy than anything. My aversion for the whole situation takes a major upswing when I see the object of Jake's concern.

A jagged line of zombies is coming directly at us.

I try to make some sort of noise to get Finn's attention, but I'm only able to repeat Marley's sentiment on a much softer level. My outside voice seems to have fallen into my stomach.

The infected shuffle and sway down the middle of the

street from the opposite direction of where Linda and Cash had gone. There are dozens of them, appearing to be in the form of all shapes and sizes, but comprised entirely of grown men and women. My eyes sweep back and forth with the alleged ADD I've had since I was a small child, trying to decide if I can recognize any of their distorted faces. But their skin is so mottled and mangled with decay, I hardly recognize them as fellow human beings in general.

Although the four of us are completely outnumbered by the herd, they're moving so slowly that we could probably run around the block a few times before they would get to us. Still, it's pretty damn horrifying to see them headed in our direction.

Marley and Jake are screaming with urgency when Finn jumps into the driver's seat. "Hold on!" he shouts, slamming the vehicle into reverse.

Of course, the commotion we make interests the town's unwanted visitors. Their pace quickens and their elevated moans can be heard even through the glass of the car's windows. Either Marley or Jake winces loudly from the seat behind us.

"Hurry, hurry!" I urge Finn, waving my arms wildly around in the air when he pauses rather than springing into action. He looks in both directions before laying on the horn.

I squirm when the feral anxiety reaches its peak inside of me. "What are you waiting for, traffic? All you're accomplishing right now is making sure these things are really good and pissed off!"

"They'll be back any minute," he tells me calmly. The admiration I felt for his same display of calmness earlier has completely disappeared by now. I'm tempted to punch him—hard.

"Go!" Marley screams from the backseat, her neck

craned to the side where the zombies are becoming even closer. "What are you waiting for?"

Finn reaches behind him for the seatbelt and I follow suit without having to be told.

"Seatbelts, guys!" I yell at the others.

Jake is jumping up and down while beating on the back of Finn's seat, also screaming for him to drive away. Marley jumps over the kid to strap him down before putting her own on. My eyes fly to Finn's face, finding him stoic as he simply lays on the horn again. He taps his thumb against the steering wheel in slow beats, looking like he's waiting for a meal in the drive-through.

"Are you insane?" Marley cries from the back seat.

I want to answer, "Yes he is," but I'm still Team Finn— at least for the time being. I envision myself jumping from the car and letting loose a round of ammunition into the wall of walking dead that are close enough to throw a snowball at. But that's yet another unrealistic fantasy of mine brought up from watching too many action and horror movies.

Instead, I scream like the crazy person I'm becoming. "Go! Go!" I yell.

All at once, Finn pushes his foot down against the accelerator. But instead of turning the steering wheel away from the zombies like a logical person would, he turns directly into them. This is the first time I consider my best friend may possibly be really, truly batshit crazy, just like the rest of his family at least pretends to be.

"We're all going to die!" Jake squeals from the backseat, his voice suddenly two octaves higher than usual— which I'm sure could be blamed on impending puberty.

I continue screaming until I'm certain everyone in the car is deaf. Marley joins in, her voice lower than mine, making a fingers-on-chalkboard-type harmony to mine.

The vehicle is traveling at such a high speed that a good handful of zombies merely ping off the hood like bowling pins when we make impact. The vehicle hardly stutters from the force. When I realize we passed by the monsters unscathed, I somehow find a will to quit screaming.

Finn lets out a joyful cheer when we've fully broken through their line. "Guys, calm down. This isn't just any old vehicle."

I turn to the buddy I used to bake cookies with in grade school, my face most likely blank to mirror my total flabbergasted state. How he can remain calm through this crazy nightmare is way beyond me.

Marley's hand flies over the backseat, connecting with Finn's arm with a loud slapping noise. "You asshole! You could have killed us!"

Finn continues driving down the road at a much slower pace. Predictably, the remaining zombies turn on their heels to follow us. "I knew we would be fine. This thing is government issued. Not only is it bulletproof—"

"It's zombie proof?" I interrupt. Finn laughs and hits my knee gleefully. I move a little closer to the door, adding to the distance between us, and give him a confounded look. "I'm seriously beginning to worry about you."

Finn grins at me with a whole lot of mischief behind his warm eyes. "They're moving away from Aunt Linda and Cash, right? We'll just get them a little further down the road and hightail it back to downtown. They will have heard the honking and be waiting for us."

"What do you think is taking them so long, anyway?" Marley asks. "Why didn't they come as soon as they heard you honking back there?"

"I'm sure they're fine." Finn says, his voice hollow.

We keep the slow pace for a few more blocks. I grow angry when Finn allows the distance between us and the ravenous monsters to shrink. I try to avoid looking in the side mirror that's quick to remind me OBJECTS IN MIRROR ARE CLOSER THAN THEY APPEAR. I'm already uncomfortable at how close they've become.

"Can you maybe hurry this little zombie parade along? I know we're not on any kind of time schedule or anything, but the sooner we can distance ourselves from the possibility of slaughter, the better I'll personally feel about this, anyway."

Marley is quick to second my opinion. "Yeah. Seriously, Finn."

We pass by one more block before Finn tells us, "Hold on." We're all a bit more prepared this time and cling to the vehicle for our lives when he whips around the corner at death-defying speeds. He takes no care in missing curbs or avoiding anything else. We bounce around wildly in our seats as much as the seatbelts will allow. By the time we reach downtown, I'm pretty sure I would throw up again if there was anything left in my stomach.

Jake giggles when the car screeches to a halt in front of the salon. "That was awesome."

Finn turns to grin at him like a total and complete goon. Miraculously, Cash and Linda appear beside the vehicle within mere seconds. But they aren't alone.

"Way to burn up the gas, nimrod," Cash tells his brother while hopping into the backseat of the car. Marley and Cash proceed to break one of Linda's rules—big time —but Linda is too busy helping the newest member of our survival club into the vehicle to catch them.

A tall and totally scrawny eighth grade boy with freckles and strawberry blond hair flashes me a smile full of old-school, silver braces with the colored rubber bands and everything. All I know about the kid is that he's known by the nickname Cheese.

"What up?" he says to me.

I can't be sure that I even want to know how he had earned his nickname. I sigh heavily while watching him crawl into the backseat and settle in beside Jake before both of them are smiling at me sideways.

"Aren't there any big, burly men that survived this day?" I ask. "I mean, seriously. It's beginning to feel like we're running some kind of day care here."

"Hey—I'm only a couple years younger than you," Cheese says, all matter-of-fact like.

Linda scoots her youngest nephew over so she can drive, causing him to push up against me. I hug the door as closely as humanly possible, not really gaining any leeway. Although I've decided Finn is really cute and all that, I've also seen a psychotic side of him that makes me think it's time to reassess my standards.

Linda is all smiles when she praises her nephew. "That was a smart move back there, Finn. We were watching you from above the salon."

I snort beside him. Smart isn't even close to the word I would use to describe his actions.

Jake is quick to add his ten cents, only the terrified boy in him does not pay up. "Oh my god, that was wicked insane!"

"Insane is right," Marley says. "Do not ever do anything like that again, Finn."

The idiot in Cash can never stay quiet. "Yeah, bone-head," he adds a delayed second later.

While Linda pulls the vehicle away from the war zone that had once been our small-town community, Finn speaks with his voice low. "This virus must have been going on longer than we thought. Did you see how decayed they looked?"

I can't see Linda from my door-hugging position, but I

imagine her frowning as she does when deep in thought. She has a way of making her thick eyebrows appear to be one solid caterpillar whenever she does that. Her dark eyebrows stand out against her pale face and much lighter, brown hair. I don't think she has ever dyed her hair, either. But it goes with the whole look that has helped to make her appear insane.

"I only hope your mother knew what she was talking about when she told us to head north," Linda says back to him, her voice also low enough so only those of us in the front seat can hear.

* * *

WE TRAVEL many miles through the countryside where there's nothing much other than rows of corn and soybeans ready to go that will probably never be harvested. We see an occasional walking corpse or abandoned car with dead mangled bodies nearby, but the highway is pretty much clear of any other vehicles. The lack of cars is seriously unsettling. Where are all the other people?

"Guess meeting up with the Guard in Mankato is for sure out," Cash grumbles as we pass the last exit for the city. Seeing other people would be a major day-brightener, but I remember what Linda had said about being quarantined by the Guards and know I wouldn't want to be stuck in this area where it's possible to catch this virus. I still can't help but wish we would run into some other normal human beings at some point.

We're probably a good ten miles beyond the exit when a couple of jets flash overhead, making a very earth-shattering whooshing noise that rumbles deep inside my chest.

JEN NAUMANN

The feeling is not too much unlike the time when I was little and my dad made me go to a NASCAR race with him down in Kansas. The only thing that had kept me from slipping into a boredom-induced coma had been the vibrations I felt every time the cars passed.

"Whoa!" Jake exclaims excitedly from the backseat.

Everyone in the car cranes their necks to watch the jets continue on. They shoot through the sky at such a fast speed that even I find it a bit exciting to see something so out of the ordinary flying our skies.

"What would a Marine Corp jet be doing here?" Cheese asks.

All eyes move on to him except Linda's, although she keeps glancing at him in the rearview mirror. I lean forward enough to see her look of concern. Her eyebrows do the caterpillar thing again as she asks him, "How do you know that's a Marine jet?"

"I...ah...used to build model airplanes," Cheese stutters. He's quite obviously still into making planes but doesn't want to expose his geekery to a car full of virtual strangers. I make a mental note to school him on how we're all capable of serious geekery and should learn to embrace it. It's just another one of life's little lessons I learned from Dave Grohl.

"Do you know what kind it was?" Linda asks, the panic in her voice becoming evident.

Cheese meets her eyes in the mirror. "I think they were AV-8Bs."

Linda pushes down on the accelerator with urgency. "Everyone have their seatbelts on?"

I hold on to the door and Finn's legs when the vehicle shoots forward at death-defying speeds. "What's the deal with these AV ate babies?" I ask her. "Why are you freaking out?"

Cheese is quick to correct me in a huff. "AV-eight Bs."

"Whatever." I wave him off. "Just let it go."

Linda cuts in with her answer. "They're primarily used to destroy land targets."

Marley sits forward to lean on the back of our seat, her eyes filled with dread. "What? You mean they're going to like bomb someone?"

Linda purses her lips tightly. "I can't say that for sure, but I really hope not."

Dread fills me, wondering if my parents have gone to Mankato. What if I never see them again? What if we do make it to Canada but they decide to close the borders?

The idea sinks in that this group of oddballs I'm stuck with may be the only "family" I'll know from now on. What if I'm forced to spend the next fifty Christmas mornings with them? I shudder at the thought of seeing Cash and Cheese in pajamas.

We all turn to somberly watch out the back window in the direction the jets had headed, waiting to see if our beloved shopping city is about to be destroyed.

A heavy realization seems to be hanging over all of us.

This is it.

Our lives will never be the same.

Chapter 6

After passing through the more agricultural area of the state and nearing the metropolis, we finally see other vehicles. Marley, who is taking on the role of most paranoid throughout all of this, keeps an oral tally of the people in each vehicle. Every time we stare into the car beside us, we're met with the same vacant stares right back. People wonder just as much as we do who the survivors are and if they're worth teaming up with.

"Hey!" Cheese shouts after Marley has counted the forty-fifth person. "It's Zander Anderson!" We all gape out the window on his side of the vehicle, wanting to see if he's telling the truth. I let out a happy squeal when I realize he's right. Our senior quarterback is driving his dad's obnoxious Hummer with his fourteen-year-old brother in the seat beside him.

I reach over Finn to lay on the horn and wave wildly at my friend. "Linda! Pull this rig over! C'mon!"

Linda peers over her nephew to see who I'm so excited about before her eyes return to the road. "We're not stopping."

Zander strains his eyes to look at me and nearly goes off the road when he waves back with matching enthusiasm. He honks back over a dozen times and has this giant smile planted on his face. I motion for him to pull off to the side.

"Seriously, Linda," I snap. "You have to pull over now. All you have to do is move the steering wheel a little bit to the right. It's easy enough to do."

Linda grumbles and slows the car down, pulling off onto the highway's shoulder. Zander parks the Hummer behind us.

"We can't stop for every person you know, Emma," Finn scolds.

"Are you kidding me?" I narrow my eyes at him. "You're jealous right now? He's a friend, Finn, a classmate. We can't just drive past without stopping. What if they don't have any weapons or supplies? Would you rather we give him the finger and keep on driving?"

Finn looks away from me. I know I've called him on the carpet for that one. What a typical guy reaction. I'm all excited over seeing my hot ex-boyfriend and he's all defensive. Of course it was while dating me that Zander realized he was more into guys, but I'm not about to tell Finn that. I'm having way too much fun watching him squirm.

"We're not giving any of our supplies away," Linda tells me.

I try to make my eyebrows look as fierce as hers when she's upset. "Not even a gun?" Before she has a chance to answer, Zander is standing next to my window. I push the door open and thrust myself into his arms, being sure to direct a sultry look in Finn's direction that he can chew on.

"It's so good to see you, Emma!" Zander hugs me back tightly before letting me loose. His little brother and I exchange an awkward embrace as if it's some kind of duty just because we're from the same town. I catch Zander glancing at the gun holstered to my body.

I smile happily. "I'm just so thrilled to see a familiar face—you know, one that doesn't want to tear mine off."

Zander's smile fades and he glances nervously at his brother. "That isn't funny, Em."

I sigh impatiently. "You know me, Zander. The world may be coming to an end and this is apparently how I'm able to cope. Deal with it." When we first started dating he claimed to be drawn to my sense of humor. Certainly he doesn't expect any less of me now. Not everyone can have their cake and eat it, too.

The back door to Linda's vehicle opens and the band of gypsies all pile out to stand beside us. Zander's little brother and Cheese give each other some kind of special little junior high greeting. It's entertaining to watch Finn size Zander up. They've been in the same small class since preschool, but Finn clearly wonders just how much of a threat Zander still may be. I swear he even puffs his chest out a little when he takes his place beside me.

"Where are you heading?" Linda asks Zander.

Zander's trepidation to talk to Looney Linda is a little too obvious. He turns to me as if I'm the one who asked. "We're going to my grandparents' place up north. Before my parents were killed, that was their plan. Dad figured there'd be less exposure in the north woods."

The way Zander's winces loudly as he looks away, I wonder why so many girls still insist on wasting their time chasing after him. It's so blatantly obvious he's not your typical Midwestern high school quarterback.

I lean in to wrap my arms around him again. "I'm really sorry about your parents." He cries a little harder and sniffles in my ear. I pull away when I'm scared he's getting snot in my hair.

"Do you know if anyone else got out of town?" Marley asks him with hopeful eyes.

Zander wipes the tears from his eyes with his index finger. "Stupid cell phones are down. I haven't heard from anyone, although we saw a van full of juniors and seniors from our school turning into Mankato awhile back."

Finn and I exchange worried glances. "We need to be moving along," Finn tells him in a gruff voice that I don't believe I've heard until just now. I turn to give my best friend a stern what-the-hell-is-wrong-with-you look. He's taking this whole chivalry thing a little too far.

I rest my hand on Zander's arm. "Do you guys have any guns? Knives? Batons? Nunchucks? Any weapon of any kind?"

Zander's eyes are unblinking and scared—a look that I'm all too familiar with by now. It's the same one I see every time I've glanced into a mirror today, although admittedly my reflection is not nearly as charming as his.

"No," he answers. "But we did grab some canned food and bottled water from the pantry."

"I don't know that I would ingest anything just yet," Finn tells him. "We don't know what is safe at this point."

I take a step closer to Zander. "I'll ride with you." If Linda isn't going to let me share our weapons, I'll take the ones she has given me. Zander has never been into the "brutality of hunting poor little innocent animals"—his words, not mine—but has to be more skilled at handling a weapon than I've proven to be, by default of being a guy.

Not a whole lot of thought has gone into my plans before this moment, so I'm not sure why I pull that idea out of my butt. All I know is that I don't want to see my friend walking around defenseless. Granted, Zander is a hulking 250 pounds and has the muscle mass of an alleged steroid user, but still—these decaying corpses walking around aren't necessarily easy to take out with one's bare hands.

Besides, it doesn't hurt that I won't have to ride with Cash anymore, either.

"You will not." Finn grabs my arm and brings me closer to him.

"That's okay," Zander says, his face direful. "You guys have your little group and I don't expect Em to want to come with me and Darrin."

I glower at Finn and pull my arm from his grip. "But I do want to, Zander."

Finn folds his arms in front of him. I'm growing tired of the always sullen and serious Finn and hope my almost-never-serious goofball of a best friend will be making another appearance sometime soon. "Then I'm coming with you," he says forcefully, leaving zero room for any more protest from me.

Truthfully, I like the thought of there being another person in the vehicle with us. As annoyed as I am with Finn right now, it will be comforting to have him at my side —even if he continues to act like a macho jerk.

Linda growls angrily at all of us. "Everyone just calm down. We are not splitting up."

"Well we won't all fit in your vehicle," I say, hoping she'll see the obvious. "Finn and I can ride with Zander and Darrin. We'll stay close to you and everything will be fine."

Everything will be fine is a total load of crap and we all know it, but sometimes sayings like that just leak out of your mouth, much like a bad case of diarrhea. Or like the lady at the gas station who always says, "Have a nice day." You know she's miserable standing behind that counter all day and hates you for getting to have a life while she's stuck at work, but she forces herself to say it anyway. We're all guilty of saying insincere things at one point or another, if only just to make the moment not totally suck as much as it truly does.

"I want to come, too," Jake says, stepping beside me. I look down and pat his head with gratitude, which apparently irritates him. He jerks away from my hand, but otherwise makes no attempt to move from my side.

"Fine," Linda mutters angrily under her breath. "But for now just take a few supplies with you. We can redistribute everything once we've settled somewhere."

We scurry around like a Chinese fire drill until we're formed in our new groups. Finn steals the seat in the front next to Zander right away, forcing me to sit in the second row with Darrin. Linda steers back onto the highway and Zander follows a little too closely behind for my comfort.

"What about your parents?" Zander asks, meeting my eyes in the rearview mirror. "What happened to them?"

I shrug, hoping not to let on just how worried I've become for their safety. "Don't know. At this point I'm hoping nothing happened to them."

Darrin sits forward, his eyes dancing. "I heard the virus came from a fast-food chain."

I nod, thinking the idea probably isn't too far off. "Maybe they just put it in the super-sized stuff to punish those who shamelessly stuff their faces."

"Do you guys think this is going on everywhere?" Zander asks. "You know, like all across the entire country?"

I went to New York City once in middle school with my mom and favorite aunt to skate in Central Park and watch the Rockettes' holiday show. The thing I remember most about our trip is passing by a billion people every time we went anywhere. If this virus has hit there, all those people will be totally screwed—they will have a better chance of being eaten than catching a taxi, anyway.

"We heard it was just the Midwest so far," Finn answers, the annoying gruff tone returning to his voice. I'm disturbed to see my friend turn into a jealous zealot. "But before we left town there was a different group of them coming in from somewhere else. Who knows how far they had actually traveled by foot but they were already starting to decay."

"Do you think it's just like in the horror movies?" Jake asks, his eyes growing wide. "You know, like if you get bit or blood on an open sore, then you change into one of them?"

I turn to him. "Don't know. Are you volunteering to try it out?"

When Jake doesn't answer, Zander changes the focus of conversation to the pranks my friends and I had performed just hours before for homecoming. He's also concerned for the demise of the chickens left in all the garages, but more so than I had been—he actually wishes he could go back to set them all free. I know either way, they will be eaten by zombies or a bunch of mindless people at some fast-food chain, so either way their fate is pretty much already sealed in a lose-lose situation.

The mischievous night before seems like it had happened a whole lifetime ago. I wonder how many of the girls have survived or if I'll ever see them again. Certainly the homecoming queen is dead by now—she's so tragically naïve and manages to function on a third of the brain cells the rest of us possess. Come to think of it, that's a good explanation that applies to a majority of our school's cheerleaders. If school ever does resume one day, maybe there won't be any more annoying cheers of "V-I-C-T-O-R-Y."

Maybe this whole apocalypse thing isn't all bad.

We're south of the Twin Cities somewhere when the

small herd of traffic begins slowing down. I have no clue where we are exactly and really hope there won't be a time where I have to know my way around the state in order to survive. I'm just lucky to find my way around our 15-avenue little town at times without getting lost. That actually happened to me once, but I blame the crappy navigation system in my dad's car.

The cars surrounding us begin to completely stop. The most disturbing thing I find when looking in each one we pass is that there are very few people in each one, closely followed by the fact that no one seems to be over the age of twenty. Normally I'm all for an adult-free environment, but to see so few actually making it past the outbreak makes me fear our chances of survival are seriously diminished. If all the adults are gone, where will we get the money to buy stuff?

"What's going on?" Jake asks from behind me.

I laugh nervously. "Maybe Cash has to tinkle."

"Stay here," Finn says over his shoulder. He shoots me a warning glare to let me know he isn't kidding around—I'm not to leave. I salute him smartly before he opens the door and is gone.

Jake is bouncing around behind me, getting all riled up. "What do you think is up there? Maybe it's the National Guard again or maybe there's a bunch of zombies blocking the road. What if it's the Army and they're not letting anyone past?"

Never would I dream of striking a kid under normal circumstances, but I consider the possibility of throwing him out to the next zombie we pass. His adorableness will only take him so far with me. I wish he would stop yipping like an excited puppy so I can hear myself think.

The car beside us rolls their window down on the passenger's side. A husky college-aged guy in serious need of a shower and comb pokes his head out and cringes when the sun hits his bloodshot eyes. He starts yelling something muffled from our side of the glass, but loudly enough that the veins in his neck pop out.

Dozens of others around us have gotten out of their cars and walk farther up in the direction Finn had gone. Between the activity outside and the anxiety festering in my gut I have a sudden need to get the heck out.

"Screw this. I can't wait around here like some kind of zombie bait." I open my door and shut it again before anyone inside can protest. I peer into Linda's vehicle on the way past and instantly regret doing so. Cheese is riding shotgun, oblivious to the hot and heavy action going on the back between Cash and Marley. I make a mental note to add brain bleach to the list of supplies we're going to need. Wanting to separate myself from the debacle, I speed walk past the line of cars when I hear my name yelled behind me.

"Wait up!" Jake yells, running toward me. He looks so young and innocent weaving through the line of cars and I suddenly hope I won't be his only hope of a maternal figure through his teen years. Everything I know about life's mysteries came from an American Girl book my mom once gave me, and I'm sure as hell not about to go back to my blood-stained room to retrieve it.

I use the authoritative stance Finn's mother sometimes used when scolding me as a girl. "You were told to wait in the car, young man."

"So were you!" He squeaks in his pubescent voice. He glowers at me quite seriously, daring me to prove him wrong.

I snort and relax my body language. "Okay, you got me there. Come on."

Quite a few cars are spread out around us. I still look

closely into each one we pass by, hoping to find my parents or any other familiar face. An alarming lack of adult figures is still unaccounted for, which alarms me. Everyone knows our generation won't last more than a few days without being able to afford Internet or cellular phones.

We aren't anywhere near the end of the line when we catch up to Finn. He stiffens as soon as he realizes we're standing beside him. "It would literally kill you to listen to me for once, wouldn't it?"

"Literally," I answer in agreement. He's not just mad at me—he was actually frightened by our sudden intrusion. I loop my arm through his and teeter on my tiptoes to try to see past the heads of the people standing in front of us. "Does this line ever end? It looks like one of those horribly long ones at Disneyland. Maybe there's actually some really cool ride up ahead that we don't know about."

Finn turns to look at me. "Something's wrong."

"What do you mean?" I ask. I finally spot his Aunt Linda quite a few feet ahead of us. Her back is to us, her brown wavy hair falling over the collar of her bright purple windbreaker. She's also poised on her tiptoes, straining to see or hear something being said to the crowd ahead of her. A large group of other confused and scared citizens are clustered around her, reminding me of the mosh pit at hard rock concerts—it's like she'll get sucked in and disappear at any moment.

"We were both standing up there and we heard something—Linda told me to wait back here until she got some more answers."

Suddenly there are Army soldiers swarming from seemingly everywhere around Linda. They direct people to follow the others ahead, their voices loud and abrupt. Linda turns our direction and attempts to escape, but she can't break past the mass of limbs blocking her way.

The people are now in full panic mode, not knowing where the Army is taking them or why they're taking them, so they push up against each other frantically the way a herd of sheep do when spooked by a loud noise. A few people fall down to the ground in all of the madness and their loved ones or just random people who don't want to squish them struggle to help them back on their feet.

"Run back to the vehicle!" Linda yells in our direction, trying to move her head past a man's arm that's blocking her view.

"Why? Where are you going?" Finn yells back. He holds one hand under my elbow and one at the small of my back. I'm excited from his touch all over again when I realize he's being protective.

"Take as many back roads as you can and don't stop for anyone!" Linda yells. "Don't worry about me! I'll find you—" Her last words are muffled from the flutter of movement surrounding her. All at once, the crowd opens up and finally swallows her, like some kind of creepy wave —if waves were made out of people and not water. We watch in horror until we're sure she's gone. The mob of people is very slowly but very certainly floating in our direction.

"C'mon!" Finn yells to me. "Run!"

I blindly reach out for Jake and drag him along when Finn pulls me by my hand in the direction of our vehicles. My feet continue moving along, but everything else has become numb. I glance behind my shoulder to see the sea of people getting closer by the second.

"We're really leaving her?" I ask Finn. "Can't we just leave Cash instead?"

Finn doesn't answer. He continues pulling my hand, his speed picking up. Once we're next to Linda's vehicle, he yells at Zander and the others to hightail it into the

Suburban with us. The tone of his voice is urgent enough that not only does it bring a shiver to me, but it gets the attention of those in the Hummer. Within seconds, they're piling into the back of the Suburban with wild eyes.

With the growing number of passengers in back, it's becoming an uncomfortable fit, but Finn is behind the steering wheel and driving away before anyone has time to settle in. We're still packed in like sardines with the other cars and there's little room to drive away without hitting them. We've gained very little leeway on the mob that continues creeping toward us.

I turn to my certifiable friend while bracing the dashboard. "Uh, Finn…"

"Hold on!" he yells over his shoulder at everyone in the back.

I whip the seatbelt over my chest, knowing full well what crazy driving skills he's capable of in this pimped out vehicle. Cheese fumbles with his own seatbelt beside me and I briefly wonder if he's even supposed to be in the front or if he should be strapped into some kind of booster seat in the back. I reach out to help him until we hear it click into place.

Finn pushes on the newer black Camaro parked directly in front of us with a minimal bump, then accelerates. The driver is not inside, but a pack of spoiled and large college boys are. One of them sticks his head out the window and starts yelling with veins pulsating at his neck.

I shoot my hand out to lock all of the doors, hoping like hell they're made with some kind of reinforced material. The large boys in the car we're attempting to relocate without their permission don't look like they're in the mood to play right now.

"Finn…" I say nervously.

"What's going on?" Cash asks. "Where's Aunt Linda?"

Finn continues focusing on the task of moving the angry boys out of our path. The tires squeal on the pavement and other people get out of their cars to see what the commotion is all about.

Cash leans over the seat until he's hovering above Finn's shoulder. "What are you trying to do? Where is Linda?"

The man-child who has been yelling out the Camaro's window jumps out and starts walking towards us. His arms are easily larger than my entire torso and his neck could fit an entire basketball down into it. I wonder if he had possibly grown up near a power plant.

My fingers nervously push the door locks repeatedly. "I'm thinking this guy doesn't appear to be exceptionally happy with you right now, Finn."

"I've got this," he assures me. He slams down harder on the accelerator, pushing the Camaro into another vehicle ahead of it. The steroid junkie tries to open Finn's door and begins beating on the window. If I were catholic, I would be crossing myself, but I'm not, so instead I cross my fingers and hope Finn won't get killed.

A low humming noise comes to us from somewhere in the distance, gradually turning into a loud chopping that resonates throughout the sky. Everyone—even the massive crowd that looms only feet away and the young freak of nature standing beside Finn's window—stops what they are doing to search overhead.

Numerous helicopters invade the sky until it seems completely peppered with them. Rather than being comforted by the presence of other humans who are well enough to drive an aircraft and who are a part of our very country's own defenders, the humming they create seems to be more of a warning or invasion. The angry mob breaks apart as people scurry to their cars seeking shelter from the high winds the helicopters bring.

I turn to assess Finn's mental health just as he finally makes our path clear. The vehicle jerks forward then makes it safely off the road and down an incline into the ditch. No one makes a single noise as the SUV climbs over the rugged terrain—we even take a few signs out along the way. We're jostled back and forth in wild movements when Finn goes down the side of an overpass and across a shallow river.

"Are we in the ditch right now?" Jake asks at one point.

Our eyes are glued on the aircrafts hovering over the spot from which we've just escaped. Although it comes as great relief when we become more distanced from the car pileup, new concerns are growing.

"Those were also military helicopters," Zander reports from the backseat. No one says anything to this.

"What happened back there, Finn?" I ask in a quiet voice. "What did you and Linda hear?" Predictably, he won't answer me. I lean over Cheese to see my old friend actually has pools of tears in his eyes.

Chapter 7

The sun is barely gone from the sky when the chorus of whining begins. Our passengers are either hungry, tired, or have to pee. Although Cash and Marley are technically older, I know Finn and I'll become the leaders of this doleful little pack. We've been handing out small portions of snacks to everyone in the past couple of hours of driving, but there are only so many granola bars a person can ingest. I'm starting to fully understand why my parents decided to quit after one child.

Finn sticks to the back roads as his aunt had instructed, and we find ourselves in unknown territory somewhere northwest of Minneapolis. We see occasional drones of the infected everywhere we go, but easily breeze past them without incident. Some of the main roads we pass by are bottlenecked with cars from people forgetting how to drive in their attempts to flee. In general, it's beginning to feel like we're the stars of some really cheap end-of-the world flick made by a bunch of art students in which the director and actors have no clue what they're doing.

"When are we going to stop?" I ask Finn. "As much as

I've enjoyed cuddling with junior over here, it would be nice to find something to eat and a place to sleep for the night." Cheese has been leaning against my shoulder for the last hour or more, his mouth hanging open as loud snores erupt in regular intervals.

"How about we grab some infected food from the nearest drive-through and pull into a hotel where we unconsciously wait for another attack. Is that the kind of plan you were hoping for, Em?" Finn snaps. He's obviously very tired, but I wonder what he heard to make him so upset.

"Sounds good to me," Cash answers from behind us.

Whirling around, I face Cash's girlfriend. "Marley, I really hope you don't make the same mistakes Cash's parents made. Please tell me he uses a condom." Marley actually giggles but Cash reaches forward to punch me in the arm. I see the attack coming and bend over Cheese to avoid the contact.

"Are we really going to just drive straight through to Canada?" I ask Finn. "What if we get there and find out they have more infected there than we do? Worse yet, what if they still require a passport to get in? I don't have one and most of these guys probably aren't even old enough to get one. Or, what if we get lost in this country where we don't even know the language."

"Guess what, Em? I don't know. I have no idea where I'm going or what the future holds for us. I'm just as freaked out by all of this as you are, and I'm sorry."

Although Finn is clearly frustrated with me at this point, I'm able to look past that and become excited at the mention of "us" and "future" in the same sentence. I blame those stupid teenage girl hormones—they've never done me any good except for the time I used my period as an excuse to get out of a football quiz in gym class.

"I never said this was your fault," I mumble. "I just plan to blame you for it."

We've been traveling down a twisted gravel road inside a tall wooded forest of pine trees for the last twenty minutes. A dark cabin hidden among the trees appears every now and then, but after a few more minutes of silence have passed we come upon an older looking log building—too big to be a house or cabin—that's all lit up like my Uncle Steve at family gatherings. The windows in the front of the building are covered in boards. The well-manicured lawn around the building is still. A dozen or so cars are parked in the front, none of which show any signs of unwanted attacks.

Finn looks at me with question before turning back to the building, tapping his thumb against the steering wheel. I stifle a yawn, thinking nothing sounds better than a night of sleep on a real bed. All this running is making me feel so totally exhausted. Plus I would do anything to get away from Cash, if only for just a few minutes.

"I vote we stop in," Zander says. "What's the worst that could happen?"

"A pack of wild zombies waiting for us inside is top on my list," I say.

After a minute of deliberation, Finn groans and pulls the vehicle up next to a red compact car. I'm suddenly grateful for our crazy, souped up vehicle. With a miniature car like that, there's no chance of surviving anything that doesn't involve clowns.

"Em and I will go check it out," Finn announces.

"Look at you!" I say to him. "You're beginning to wise up through all of this!"

But the rest of our passengers moan and shout in protest. Finn throws his hands up in defeat. "Okay, fine. Everyone come in then. I don't care. Just make sure you lock this thing up. We don't want someone else absconding with our supplies."

The vehicle comes alive with everyone rustling to get out. It has been a long day locked in with mostly pubescent boys who apparently have yet to learn the necessities of deodorant and any other crucial personal hygiene tips.

Our crew scurries up the front steps of what now is appearing to be some kind of resort. A sign advertising fishing excursions and other special events has been violently ripped from two wooden stakes and lays on the nearly-dead grass. Someone was obviously not amused by the offer of their "all you can eat" buffet.

Finn tries to open the front door but it only moves a few inches.

"Maybe we should knock," says Jake.

I snort. "What would be the point of that?"

Finn pushes the door with his hand. "There's something pushed up against it."

Cash and Zander step up to throw their shoulders into the door alongside Finn and within seconds the door pushes back, the object behind it groaning in protest.

When we enter, our shoes click loudly against the stone floor and the sound resonates throughout the seemingly empty building. What the rustic cabin lacks in taste, it makes up for in size. We walk into a massive hall with a high ceiling and large exposed beams holding it all together. A cozy gathering spot filled with numerous outdated, mismatched couches is positioned around a multi-story fireplace covered in old bricks. A large brown moose head stares down on us from over the mantel. Many other animal heads scattered about also watch us from all over the dull white walls.

The lodge smells like musty carpet and smoke from a recent fire. The front check-in desk is crudely covered in brown paneling, looking like something a ten-year-old threw together. A notebook rests on the small countertop, but there's not a computer anywhere to be seen. I've never seen a building this outdated and guess it draws in a lot of men on fishing trips. The place practically screams "man cave."

"I think we found the end of civilization," I say with confidence.

We stand around taking the crappy place in until a friendly-enough looking, slender older woman with white-blond hair appears from behind the front desk toting some kind of large gun in her hands. Immediately upon seeing her gun we all instinctively hold up our hands like a bunch of idiots, despite the fact there are more of us and we collectively possess more firearms than she does. My mom always warned me not to underestimate the power of stupid people in large groups.

"How'd you get in here? What do ya want?" the old woman asks. Her voice is deeper than Finn's and her beady eyes glower with distrust. On a closer examination of the woman, "friendly" had been the wrong assessment and our surrender is probably warranted. She may be slender, but there's a demeanor to her that screams biker bitch—her leather studded jacket and Harley Forever tattoo on her hand being a dead giveaway, as well.

"We're just looking for a place to sleep for the night," Zander tells her.

The woman lowers her gun and looks over her crooked nose to assess each of us. A bead of sweat has formed over her lip and her watery eyes look like she may have some kind of nasty cold coming on. "How do I know you ain't one of them zombie creatures?" she asks with her sickly eyes narrowed.

I lean into Finn and whisper, "Oh boy."

Finn takes a step closer to the woman. "From what you've seen, they're not able to carry on a conversation like this, right?" His mouth twitches for an instant. I know he's having a difficult time not snickering as a look of understanding crosses the woman's face. The process is so slow and drawn out, it's as if we can actually see the thought passing through her mind.

A younger woman appears out of the door behind her and our group sighs in relief at the sight of her. She's cute as a button with an innocent face. Her plaid, country-style shirt in red and white checks shows off her slender figure. Her long blond ponytail—which looks to be the victim of a bottle job gone very wrong—hits against the side of her head when she looks from us to the biker woman.

"For God's sake, Wanda, put that gun down. They're obviously just a bunch of kids looking for a place to stay." She's probably closer to Cash's age and I notice she's wearing the same earrings I bought myself a few weeks ago. I immediately know anyone with that good of taste can be trusted. It doesn't hurt that she's another female to interact with that doesn't appear to want to suck face with the most annoying person on the planet, either.

The old woman brings her gun down, but continues looking at us with her jaw set and her arms firmly planted on her hips. It would seem her trust in strangers only goes so far. She finally grumbles in protest before walking away.

"Do you have a bathroom?" Jake asks the younger woman.

I turn to discover him dancing around, but trying to be subtle about it. "No, Jake," I tell him, rolling my eyes. "Places like this don't have a bathroom. You have to go out back and use the woods."

"There's one down the hall back over there," the young

woman answers, throwing me a confused glance while she points into the distance.

Jake looks from the woman to me, apparently waiting for my permission. I motion for him to scurry along and he bolts for it. Zander and Darrin follow closely behind him.

"Is this your place?" Finn asks the younger woman.

She shakes her head, that horse-like ponytail slapping her again as she does it. "It's my Pa's. I came home to visit my grandmother when this whole dead-walking thing started up. We've all been holed up in here for a few days, hoping it will just pass by."

"A few days?" Finn repeats.

I snort incredulously at her. "I don't know who stopped payment on your reality checks, but I don't think this dead-walking thing is going to just 'pass by,' as you say."

Her eyes flicker to me for a second before answering Finn. "My grandmother tried attacking us on Tuesday when we got here."

Finn and I exchange worried looks. Maybe heading north to Canada isn't the smartest plan. The outbreak started north of us long before our pleasurable interactions with it began.

"I'm sorry about your Nanna turning all cannibal and everything," I say to her. "But have you heard anything more about the virus? Like if it's hereditary or anything?"

My last question may be unnecessary, but we're possibly going to be staying in the same building for the night and I don't want to worry about her deciding to follow in her grandmother's footsteps while we're all unconscious.

Her doe-like blue eyes blink rapidly with confusion. "How would a virus be hereditary?"

I shrug. "Death is hereditary, isn't it?"

"We have no idea what this virus is," she says, her

words slow. "We haven't been able to use any phones since it all went down and there aren't any working radio stations, other than an emergency broadcast that says to stay indoors until the National Guard arrives to help."

My stomach twists into knots at the thought of the military coming. They hadn't done the city of Mankato any good from what we could tell.

"Have you seen any of these walking-dead around here lately?" Finn asks, searching the large room for any signs of battles fought, but there aren't any to be found. The room, although tragically outdated, appears otherwise untouched from zombie attacks.

The ponytail swishes again. I suddenly wish I had a pair of shears. "We seen a few during the daytime, but they don't seem to come around at night."

I shudder, her improper grammar like nails on a chalk-board. "You mean you saw them?"

She looks back at me with confused eyes.

Cheese steps forward to share his wisdom. "Maybe they're just like the rest of us and they can't see anything at night. They did start out as humans, after all." With his interest in comic books and other unusual things, he may very well be the most knowledgeable among us on this kind of thing. Either he has a really good point, or I'm simply in agreement because I'm dying for a night of good, un-inter-rupted sleep. Had I known all this drama was coming, I maybe would've skipped the senior girls' night out and rested up.

"Are there enough rooms open for us to stay the night?" Finn asks, giving her what I think to be his best smile. I try not to be annoyed by the overt way in which he seems to be flirting with her. But sadly, he must think he has something resembling charm that she won't be able to resist.

The younger woman smiles brightly in response to my Finn and a stupid little dimple forms on her right cheek. "Sure."

Seconds later, my hand shoots out and clamps over Finn's. He raises his eyebrows in question, but his fingers wrap through mine an instant later, making my insides turn to goo. If zombies aren't going to make me cherish my deeper feelings for my lifelong friend, then this bleached blonde bimbo apparently will with good old-fashioned jealousy.

We wait in awkward silence for the bathroom buddies to return before she leads us down an equally outdated hallway to show us to the empty rooms. I can't decide if I'm amused or horrified by the brown shag carpet lining the walls. A few yards down in the middle of the long wall there's a mounted fish randomly hanging by itself, taking up maybe a foot of space.

The kids in our party chatter excitedly as they trail behind us. The girl introduces herself to me and Finn as Casey, but when I say, "Hey Casey" she's quick to correct me. "It's K-C. They're initials."

I bob my head in recognition. "Initials—got it. I'll write that down for future reference."

The carpeted hallways seem to never end, but K.C. finally stops outside of a large room with a number of bunk beds. "There's a few smaller rooms available if any of y'all want more privacy," she says, her eyes flickering to me and Finn.

The younger boys and Zander run to the bunk beds while the rest of us follow K.C. to the next door where Cash pulls Marley inside and slams the door behind them.

Our hostess stops at the next door and motions to Finn and me with her head. "You two can have this room. If you need anything, you can find us in the apartment behind the front desk."

I should probably be ashamed at how happy I am to see her look at the two of us with jealousy, but I'm not. It does make sense for the two of us to take a room together, as we've shared a bed many times before. Although in the past, I hadn't felt this totally crazed ardor for him that has been growing throughout the day. But my hands are sweaty at the thought of us finally being alone. What if both of us are too nervous to make the first move?

I can't say a zombie attack would be completely unwelcomed at this point.

Finn mutters his thanks to K.C. without any other comments and pulls me into the room with him.

The room is an echo of the rest of the lodge—large and outdated. A small double bed sits under a high window and a little white dresser faces it on the opposite wall. The two items of furniture are dwarfed in the spacious room. More tacky brown car siding plasters the walls and the olive green bedding looks like it was picked out sometime well before electricity was invented. The room is certainly nothing fancy or even close to resembling anything pleasing to the eyes, but probably enough to get by if your only goal is to hold a rod while sitting in a boat all day and passing out from too many beers late at night.

I throw myself onto the rock-hard bed, surprised by the exhaustion that floods me the minute my head touches the pillow. "I know we have old Wanda watching our backs and everything, but aside from that, do you really think we're safe here? Didn't your mom tell you guys not to trust any strangers?"

Finn makes a noise that's most likely supposed to be a laugh, but he has thrown himself in the narrow spot beside me and his face is pressed against the mattress, muffling any noise that comes out.

"Finn, are you planning to tell me what you guys heard back there before we just abandoned your aunt, or what?" I rest my hands under my head and continue rambling when he doesn't answer, hoping to strike a nerve. "I mean I'm not judging you or anything, but the woman has been like a mother to you, and we just left her there with nothing more than a couple of guns. You could have at least thrown her a bag of fruit snacks or a couple of—"

Finn's hand clamps over my mouth and his face hovers just inches above mine. "Shut up for a second," he whispers urgently.

I suck in my breath. The tension in the air between us makes me wonder if he's choosing this very moment to finally kiss me. I've kissed a fair amount of guys in my day, but I wonder how it will feel to finally do it with my best friend. Will it be like kissing the brother I never had? Will his lips feel thin and cold or voluptuous and heavenly warm? I've kissed some pretty inexperienced guys and hope the few girls Finn has been with taught him a thing or two about how to kiss properly.

But his eyes turn to the door. I sigh deeply, unable to tolerate his lips being that close to my face when he clearly has no intention to take advantage of the moment. A series of shuffling noises coming from the hallway must be what grabbed Finn's attention. We sit frozen in place together on the bed, his hand still clamped over my mouth. But a few seconds of quiet are followed by a knock on our door.

I pull his hands away. "I really hope that's room service. I'm starving."

Finn yanks out the gun that he had stuffed down the back of his pants at one point during the day. My pulse quickens not in fear of who is behind the door—I know by now zombies in general don't tend to knock—but with the excitement of watching my would-be paramour in action. Finn slides over to the door quietly and looks out the peep hole. He reaches out to unlock the door, letting Cash in the room. I utter a line of curse words at the sight of him.

A cruel grin plays on Cash's lips when he looks between the two of us. "Wait. I'm not interrupting anything, am I?"

I jeer at him. "If you're looking for pointers with Marley, I'm guessing anything you try will be inadequate, so you may as well just give it up."

"What's going on?" Finn asks his brother. I'm annoyed he's getting so good at completely ignoring me. My old BFF would've either laughed or joined in on the verbal attack. Cash is also annoyingly getting better at letting my jabs slide.

Maybe the world is coming to an end.

Cash turns to face Finn. "Do you think it's a good idea to be in separate rooms tonight?"

A bursting laugh leaves my lips. "Would you feel better if we got you a nightlight?"

Finn steps between the two of us. He must mistakenly think we won't bicker as much if unable to see each other. "You heard K.C. say they haven't seen any zombies at night. The windows in this place are either high enough up that no one is going to sneak in through them, or they were boarded shut like the ones out front."

I mumble angrily when he pronounces our hostess's name correctly. I decide I'll start calling her Casey again, only to perturb her.

"Yes, because they did such a good job of boarding up the front door, right?" Cash asks with a snort. "We don't know who else is in this place. There were a lot of cars parked in front. I say we go find out who else is around before we decide to camp here. Maybe there's a whole gang of bikers planning to steal from us in the middle of the night."

I bring my nails up to my teeth and chatter my jaw for his benefit. "Maybe you're just afraid they're planning to steal your virtue."

"You need a muzzle for your girlfriend," Cash tells his brother, giving me a look that would make an innocent baby run screaming from the room.

Finn glances at me briefly. "It's how she deals with stress. Get over it."

My heart soars happily. Not only does Finn know me so well, but he does not correct the part where Cash had called me his "girlfriend." If only we were in Vegas—I would be insisting we get married right here and now at some tacky little Elvis-themed chapel.

Cash waves me off with his hand. "Whatever. Are we going to see who else is here or what?"

Finn leans into the hallway and takes a moment to mull it over. "Yeah, you're probably right. Tell everyone we'll meet in the hallway in ten minutes."

Cash is momentarily pleased when he starts to leave the room, but his mouth turns down when he looks at me again. "Maybe you should leave Miss Sunshine in here. She could use a good month's worth of beauty sleep."

I smile sweetly at him. "You should talk. Maybe you should go take a sleeping pill…and a laxative, while you're at it."

Finn chuckles and shuts the door before his brother can respond. "Why are you still at his throat when we're all just trying to survive this as a group? You really should consider lightening up a little, Em."

I give him my best eye roll. "We're talking about the same guy who purposely puked all over my pillow on prom night. And the list of pleasantries doesn't even begin to end there, if you will remember. I could go on all night."

Finn and I had gone to our junior prom as friends and afterwards went to a massive coed lock-in at Billie Colbert's house. Cash and some other degenerate graduates crashed the party, totally bombed out of their minds. Even while highly intoxicated, Cash has the presence of mind to harass me, although he still has the intelligence of a total imbecile.

Finn comes over to sit next to me on the bed. "Yeah, I guess you're right. I'll continue to be mad at you for riding him, but you can delight in the fact that I secretly love it when you do."

My eyes lock on his. "Do you know what else I delight in?"

He leans in closer to me, making my breathing labored. "What?"

It would be so easy to lean in and finally see what it would be like to kiss him, but instead I push on his chest with enough force to knock him down on the mattress. "When you give me some kind of freaking clue as to what wigged you out back there!"

He runs both hands through his hair and I fall back to lie next to him. We turn to face each other, our noses nearly touching. I've looked into those eyes a million times before, but this time there's a mischievous glimmer of what I think to be hope for things to come. I'm guessing he can see the same emotion in my own eyes so I squint, hoping to look annoyed instead.

"I don't know if you can handle it, Em. I would hate to see you turn totally insane right now and lose your shit."

I smile innocently. "You know I'm not the type to suffer from insanity. I would totally love every minute of it." I try to act coy, but the way he holds out is making me uneasy. Just how mind-shattering is this bit of information?

"Are you sure?" he asks. I nod. "Okay, but if I do decide to tell you, you have to promise you won't tell the others. We don't need everyone losing it."

"Cross my heart, but make no promises whatsoever of wanting to die. That would just seem a little too morbid right now."

He inhales and exhales deeply before speaking, watching me carefully with his beautiful eyes. For a split second, I want to tell him I take it back and suggest we just make out instead, but he speaks before I can change my mind. "A couple guys told us they heard some of the Army guys talking. Em, they're planning to bomb this entire area, from Kansas all the way up to the Canadian border and may go out as far as Chicago and Denver. The Army is planning to keep everyone locked in the area until it happens sometime in the next week. Whatever this virus is, they're planning to wipe it out before it spreads any further."

I open my mouth to say something, but my voice has quit working. I guess Finn was justified in worrying that I would "lose my shit."

The room suddenly turns black.

Chapter 8

My face stings from being lightly slapped, although everything around me is still consumed by complete darkness. I faintly recall some kind of dream in which zombies had invaded earth and we were all going to die. I giggle at the idea of it.

"Em!" Finn's voice calls out.

My eyes finally find the control to open. Finn's face hovers above me, plastered with wild concern. I giggle again and reach for him, wondering for a minute if I'm still stuck in a dream. Deciding I probably am, I let my eyes shut again. "I totally love you, Finn. You know that, right?"

He mumbles something like "not a good idea" and strokes my hair while repeating my name. I pat his face a few times in reply with my eyes still closed.

"Em, look at me." He rarely uses a forceful tone of voice with me, so I peer through my heavy eyelids at him. "I promise we'll be okay. We have a few days before it will even happen. We'll get out of here in plenty of time."

I let my eyes shut again. "Okay, sounds great." I have

no idea what he's rambling about, but taking a little snooze sounds like a good idea at the moment.

Finn moans, sounding frustrated. "Em, just stay here for a second. I'll be right back."

"Okay, terminator," I return with a chuckle.

The minute he leaves my side, my mind drifts to thoughts of homework and violin lessons. I hope Finn wrote down the chapters we had to read in our English Lit class, as Mrs. V is a real stickler for details and doesn't take many excuses—I would know as I've tried them all.

A few seconds later I hear the low muttering of voices outside the door. They grow louder until there's a timid knock at my door. "Come in!" I call out with my eyes still closed.

"Shit. What did you do to her?" Marley's voice asks. Great—if she's here then the village idiot is most certainly with her.

"Just stay with her," Finn's voice says. "We're going to check out who else is staying in this place. We'll come back before long with some of the food from our supply." I love the sound of Finn's voice, low and smooth. I can envision the slight hint of his Adam's apple dipping up and down as he speaks. One day I plan to push my lips up against that apple and make him recite poetry to me. I make a mental note to add that activity to my bucket list.

His voice drifts back out into the hallway and the mattress buckles underneath me with the weight of someone sitting on it. I open one eye to see the back of Marley's flaming red hair.

"What up, Mar?" I ask.

"What is wrong with you, Emma?" When I don't answer, she says something quietly to herself, then, "I think I know what is going on."

I open my second eye. "You do?"

"Some heavy duty dark magic is at work here, that's what." She says the words in a dreamy tone and they don't sound directed at me.

I snort loudly through my nose. Marley is back on one of her mumbo jumbo kicks. Finn and I used to steal her phone and text bogus messages, pretending to be from her dead ancestors, knowing it would set her off. Predictably, it always did. At times, I'm amazed she'll even still talk to me after some of the pranks we've pulled.

She continues on with her theory of whatever she's mumbling about. The conversation seems to be held mostly for her benefit, anyhow. "Did you know in Haiti they will dismember the bodies of their dead because they're afraid they will come back to life? Other cultures warn of such a thing being possible, too. I remember seeing pictures of metal bars surrounding graves in case the people rose from the dead. If only I could get my hands on a book of shadows right now. Maybe I could find something on how to stop all of this."

I lightly slap the side of her cheek. "You're pretty."

Her eyes narrow at me. "Have you been drinking?"

I stop and try to think back to what I'd been doing a few minutes earlier. My brain has apparently blocked events of recent memories from my conscious mindset. I sit up with due care and blink rapidly. "I don't think I have. I don't know. Have I?"

She sighs dramatically. "Nevermind. Let's go see how the guys are doing."

I follow her out, surprised by the tacky room we're in. Nothing registers as being familiar. I blindly follow Marley out into a dark hallway lined in carpet, of all things. We continue on to a giant gathering room with stuffed animal heads on the walls. As I take everything in, a sudden twinge of familiarity starts sneaking up on me.

"This place is kind of creepy," I say, looking around. "Was this some kind of deal Finn found online?" It wouldn't be the first time he made us stay at a Norman Bates-style motel. Last summer we went to his cousin's wedding in Wisconsin and stayed in a motel with paper-thin walls and door handles that didn't totally lock. I fell asleep sitting against the door with my cell phone in hand.

I'm almost amused that I can't remember where we are, or how we even got here. Maybe I was drinking. Finn's good for taking me to wild parties that involve stupid jack-holes who like to spike our drinks.

Marley continues to ignore me and leads me over to a closed door behind the front desk. We enter a little apartment filled with strangers. There's an odd pairing of young women and men, with a few really young children. Most of the young adults appear to be recently graduated and closer to my age. Only a couple really old adults—like my parents' age—are present. There are obvious motorcycle enthusiasts present with some Star Wars type nerds, a few possible band geeks and a dash of other somewhat normal teens. Many of them seem freaked out when Marley and I suddenly enter the room. I blame their reaction on Marley's unusual looks and bright, shocking hair.

It's a relief to find Finn mixed in the crowd. Then I see the neighbor kid beside him, followed by my old boyfriend Zander and his little brother. Even the goofy kid from middle school whose name is something silly is comforting to see. It's almost like the ending of that stupid old Wizard of Oz movie my mom makes us watch every Thanksgiving. The only thing missing is an annoying little yippy dog.

But all happy thoughts go out the door with the sight of Cash. I guess he's as good as an annoying little yippy dog. For some reason I think of my nemesis Darcy Sanderson and her little mutt.

Finn's eyes meet mine, and I'm shocked when there's a pleasurable spark passing between us. His eyes flash to Marley's before turning his gaze back to meet mine.

"How are you doing, Em?" His words are slow and deliberate in the same way I answer my parents whenever they ask me stupid questions.

"I'm good, Finn. How are you?" I answer, using the same exaggerated slowness on him.

Having a room nearly full of strangers staring at us while we're having this awkward little conversation is unnerving. I wonder how they would react if I busted out into a dance routine—at least they would have good reason to stare. I begin to move my hands and feet for the beginning of a jazz number.

"You weren't kidding about her," Zander says to Finn, not taking his eyes off me. Finn leans over to whisper something into his year.

Finn steps forward and pulls me away from my dance. "Come with me for a minute." All at once, the strangers in the room break into hushed conversations. At least the attention's off me. Finn takes my hand and leads me back into the front lobby. The current running through me from the touch of his skin against mine is impossible to ignore, so I snatch my hand away.

"What is with the room full of yahoos back there?" I ask. "Better yet, where are we? Were we drinking again last night? Why was I in some random bedroom? Did I take advantage of you?"

Finn's eyes search mine. "What's the last thing you remember?"

"Um…something having to do with saran wrap and Zander Anderson's toilet? Oh, wait—is that why he's here? Is he mad at me? I won't take credit for the three pigs in his backyard. It was totally Carolyn's idea to write the numbers one, two, and four on their backs."

My old friend brings his hands to his temples and rubs them in slow, deliberate circles. "That's it? No reanimated dead people come to mind?"

I cock my head to the side. "Reanimated dead people?" Some kind of recognition tries to break through my memory. "Oh, wait. Did we watch another horror movie last night?"

Finn roughly drapes his arm around my neck and pulls me close to him for a pitiful hug. "What are we going to do with you, Em?"

"First of all...ow." I pull away when his arm yanks my hair. "And B, are you going to tell me where we are or what? I thought we were going to make our mandatory appearance at the dance tonight." Dances are not our thing, but we agreed we have a duty as seniors to show our faces before hitting what could potentially be the second biggest party of the year. Our town is painfully boring the other three hundred and whatever days of the year so we have a tendency to get creative at parties. My favorite had involved sneaking into the school to cover the senior hallways in hay and fill the air-conditioning ducts with glitter.

Finn attempts to keep a straight face, but I can detect a mischievous sparkle in his eyes. "You decided you didn't want to go to the dance anymore. You signed us up for a hiking excursion in Canada for the weekend. Remember?"

"I what?" That totally does not sound like me. I despise any kind of exercise. I get enough of it by just pushing my luck. "Finn, what exactly did I drink?"

Grinning, he rests his hands on my arms. "Trust me you were pretty out of it. But you pre-paid for this trip and now we have to go."

"Why is Jake here—and your a-hole brother, for that matter? Did I sign us up for babysitting services, too?"

"You wanted them to come with. You said something about trying new things and making new friends. You went on about being a responsible senior and setting an example. Don't you remember?" Finn seems very amused for some reason, and is hardly able to hold back a smile that plays at the corners of his mouth.

"Obviously not, but this really sounds like loads of fun. Can't we just sneak away and leave them all here or something?" I scrunch my nose at the thought of wandering through the woods with Cash. Then again, maybe we would get lucky and run into a pack of wild bears or wolves that are sweet on jerk meat.

"And leave them all stranded here?" he scolds me with open mockery. "This trip was your idea, Em. I'm not letting you back out. Let's go back to our room and eat something before getting some sleep. You're going to need a ton of energy for our big hike tomorrow."

I continue to protest, but he leads me back into the funky little room where we eat a totally bizarre meal of unheated, canned beef stew—Finn tells me I insisted we rough it out on our trip. It takes all the will I can muster to choke the mushy stuff down.

Finn checks in with the others in the hallway before we crawl into bed together. The room's very dark and Finn's body pushed up against mine has a totally different vibe from usual. He even falls asleep with his arm draped over my side. We've been best friends forever, but never really had a lot of physical interaction between us aside from the usual punching and slapping.

Lying perfectly still, I'm unable to sleep with the barrage of questions that have begun swirling through my head. How is it I don't remember coming to this strange place? Better yet, why would I suggest we go hiking of all things? I'm not big on high school functions, but can't imagine a situation that would call for me to blow off one the biggest parties of the year, unless there was alone time with Finn involved. Because I'd been boneheaded enough to invite all these other geniuses, it doesn't seem like a possibility.

After what feels like an entire hour has passed by, Finn's loud snores become so obnoxious I can't lie still anymore. Normally I would plug his nose until he chokes on his breath, but I'm obviously not going to get any sleep anyway. I slip on my boots and grab my sweatshirt before heading back down the tacky hallway in my ripped jeans and royal blue Foo Fighters T-shirt from the concert Finn and I went to last spring.

My master plan is to hang with the stuffed animal heads in the ugly couches I'd spotted earlier and play some Angry Birds on my cell phone. But when I pull it out of my pocket, I nearly yell out when I discover the battery is dead.

"Great," I mutter. I look up to find a seemingly normal-looking older woman with long white-blond hair already sitting by the fireplace. She's clad in a black Harley Davidson T-shirt and has numerous visible tattoos. Although it seems kind of late in the year for a motorcycle ride, I guess there are some people who actually like to gawk at the yellow leaves or something.

The woman's gaze is fixed on the colorful flames of the fire someone had started.

"Hey," I greet her somewhat cheerfully. "What's up?" My phone may be dead but at least I'll have someone to talk with for a while.

The woman's head rotates slowly in my direction. Her eyes are unfocused and vacant while her face either has a horrible case of bad acne or some kind of measles. I shiver. She looks super macabre but I try not to show my aversion to her and flash a horribly forced smile. I decide the part about her appearing to be normal had been a bad assumption on my part. She gradually turns back to face the fire.

I shiver again. This lady is obviously not your average, everyday biker type just out for a joy ride. Something is definitely wrong with her. I just hope her condition is not contagious.

"Sorry," I say, taking slow steps backward. "You look like you're pretty into the whole 'being alone' thing right now. I'll just give you some space." When I take another step my body suddenly slams up against something solid.

I find a hulking guy behind me and jump to the side, squeaking in surprise (even though he's madly good looking). On first glance, his face is broad and square and his features are sharply defined. He's a big guy. Not like eats-too-many-cheeseburgers big but works-out-for-hours-every-day-by-lifting-cars-over-his-head big. Though he's wearing an Army uniform—dark green camouflage shirt and pants with thick black combat boots—his sandy colored hair is a bit longer than the usual crew cut. I know for a fact that kind of hair wouldn't fly with any military regulations, so maybe he either stole the uniform from a soldier or he's on the run.

He holds a mammoth-sized finger up to his full lips, motioning for me to be quiet. I look down to find his other hand occupied with a very large and very menacing looking gun. My eyes pop wide in fear. I've only seen that kind of weapon in movies.

This is so typical of my life. The night before my very first hiking trip (and really any kind of strenuous outdoor activity) with my friend—whom I'd been hoping to get lost with down some dirt trail—and I'm about to be murdered in a totally outdated lodge by some crazy AWOL freak.

I spin around to run for what I think to be my only chance at survival, but his large arm cradles me and pulls me backward. He holds me tight with my back pressed up against his rock-hard chest. I'm surely about to die of a heart attack at this point from either fear or the thrill of his sculpted body pushing up against mine. My lungs fill up with a quick intake of air in preparation for a scream when his arm suddenly moves away from my waist and his massively thick hand clamps over my mouth.

His breath is hot on my ear as he whispers, "Don't move."

A whimper is lost underneath his hand when I wait for my life to suddenly end. But from the corner of my eye, I discover he's not pointing the gun at me. Instead, he's aiming for the batty old biker lady with the kooky eyes.

"Hey!" he calls out rudely. "Say something to let me know you're human."

Realization that GI Joe is not right in the head spreads through me like a bad case of the stomach flu. I pull his hand down with both of mine for fear that I'm about to blow chunks. His hand moves back down to my waist in more of a protective gesture than anything, which is enough to calm my stomach momentarily. But I'm not a complete idiot—there are still parts of me missing, like, quite obviously, my mind—and the fear is still stirring inside me.

I quietly watch along with him when the old woman moves her head in our direction. The way in which her head continues to turn without her body moving is highly unnatural and sends more chills up my spine. Her face has begun to change in the minute or so since she last looked at me. Her skin is now a pale gray and her eyes are glazing over, turning completely white. The sores on her face have broken open and fresh blood seeps out of them.

"Oh dear god," I whisper, pushing up against GI Joe. Every nerve in my body screams in fear. "Maybe we should call for an ambulance, or takeout." We live in a society where there's a better chance of pizza being delivered well before any authorities will arrive.

The woman opens her mouth to let out a low, inhuman sound, like some kind of busted coffee bean grinder.

Nothing could prepare me for the shot that GI Joe fires into the woman's skull. I watch in horror as a mass of dark blood and spongy brain tissue explodes around her with the impact of the bullet. Her body first jerks violently, then slumps lifelessly into the chair like a ragdoll. The room becomes silent aside from a small ringing that may possibly just be in my own ears.

GI Joe lowers his gun to his side. "That's what I thought."

Finally, I'm able to scream. And I don't hold back.

"Hey!" GI Joe yells, grabbing on to my arms. "You're okay! She was in the process of changing!"

As much as I struggle to break free, the guy will not let go. I gulp in small breaths of air, hyperventilation setting in. "Changing into what?" I croak. "What in the hell was wrong with her? What in the hell is wrong with you? Let go of me, you murdering asshole!"

The room quickly begins to fill. The same mixed up-crew I'd seen earlier in the apartment huddles together with wide eyes. A few of them are in some type of pajamas, but most are fully dressed and carrying some kind of weapon—guns, bats, holy shit is that a freaking machete?—held at attention. GI Joe finally drops his hold on me, but I push myself back into his arms, hoping for protection.

Has everyone in this place lost their freaking minds? Why are they holding weapons? What is with all the violence? Why isn't anyone else freaking out from the sight of the murdered biker lady's guts splattered all over?

Finn joins the mix, appearing confused and groggy from his interrupted snore fest, but at the sight of me in another guy's arms, he darts forward to pull me away. "Are you okay?" He glares up at the soldier, but we all know he's of no threat to the much bigger guy.

My insides are shaking just as much as my voice. "He just shot someone!" I point to the chair where the bloody corpse still lays. "I mean something was definitely not right with her and she gave me the serious willies, but still!"

"She was starting to change," the soldier says to Finn. When they look at each other, I can actually see an understanding pass between them before Finn nods. My jaw drops. Apparently my friend is among those losing their mind.

A young woman sporting a bleached blond ponytail steps over to assess the dead woman. "That can't be! She was just fine just a little bit ago! Last I seen her she was goin' outside for a cigarette! You guys all saw her, right?"

The gangly teen I know from school whose name still escapes me stands beside the blonde. The way everyone looks at the murdered woman with such casual interest is disturbing. "There's a bite on her hand," he says.

I shudder with his words. What in the hell could have bit her—a bear? If she really did have some kind of virus, is it possible I caught it? I wipe my arms with my hands, as if that will do any good.

"Where did you come from?" Finn asks the soldier. He leans in to look at the guy's name tag on his chest and adds, "Payton?"

The Payton-guy's eyes flicker from me to Finn, maybe

wondering if we're a couple from the way Finn holds on to me. "North Dakota. I was deployed when this all started up, but some of our orders became questionable when the feds got involved. A bunch of us went AWOL to find our families before things get out of control."

Once again, my love of movies has totally paid off—I so knew this guy was AWOL. But what does he mean by "things" starting up? What could be going on that involves the government? And why am I still the only one freaked by him having just shot a woman in cold blood?

"Okay, all of you need to take it down a notch and explain to me what the hell is going on here," I say, unable to hold back any longer.

"What's her deal?" Payton asks Finn, flicking his thumb at me. "Are you telling me she doesn't have any clue about what is going on out there? How long have you people been holed up in this place?"

Finn shrugs at this, much too casually for my comfort. "She's got some kind of amnesia thing going on. It just started up a few hours ago."

I realize with a start that he's talking about me. What does he mean by amnesia? Is that the real reason why I can't seem to remember anything? But why isn't anyone afraid of this guy who just shot a woman for having a little cold? I turn to Finn, but the plethora of questions building are too overwhelming for my lips to form.

Payton reaches down to pick up the gun, his eyes not leaving mine. "Has she been showing any other unusual behaviors?"

Before I can really process what is happening, he's pointing his gun directly at me.

Chapter 9

"Whoa!" Marley yells out, stepping in to position herself between me and the soldier. "Don't be getting all trigger happy! Nothing's wrong with her! It's some kind of trauma induced thing! I know this—we studied it in my psych class last semester!"

Payton does not lower his gun but frowns at Marley.

"We don't know that for sure," says Cash. "He should just shoot her to be on the safe side."

I'm completely floored when Marley turns to give him a look of death. The fact that Cash's girlfriend is trying to save my ass from anyone is quite monumental. Apparently everyone has lost their mind.

"What if she's infected?" the bleached blonde asks, her eyes silently accusing Finn. "You should've said something before about her condition."

Very slowly, every set of eyes in the room seems to be focusing on me.

A prickly, sickening sensation spreads in my gut. It seems quite possible I'm about to be stabbed or shot by someone in the immediate future. My handle on reality suddenly seems as if it has broken. I shrink backwards into Finn.

"Look, she's not showing any other symptoms. It just happened before we went to bed," Finn explains, his grip on me becoming tighter.

Cash snickers, the juvenile in him flaring. "In that case, you probably traumatized her when you took your pants off, you idiot. Just let the guy shoot her so we can move on."

I've put up with a lot of crap from Cash over the years, but his suggestion to shoot me two times in a row is just too much. "That's it!" I yell, using all my strength to break out of Finn's hold and lunge toward his brother.

A lot of shuffling takes place over the next minute as my friends position themselves to keep me and Cash apart. I twist to the side before I'm pushed down to the floor by Cash. Payton takes advantage of the confusion it has created and steps in to grab a hold of me, pulling me away from the group.

"Let go of her! She's not infected!" Marley yells when she sees what has happened. She steps forward to beat on Payton's arms with her fists, but as strong as he is, she may as well bang on a steel drum—it would have the same kind of impact, but be a bit more entertaining.

All at once, an ear-splitting gunshot thunders over our heads. Everyone except Payton and me automatically crouches down, screaming. I'm too busy debating whether I'm stuck in a really crappy nightmare or if I've completely lost my mind. With all the squabbling and shooting taking place, people are acting like it's the end of the world or something.

"What's goin' on out here?" a deep male voice demands. A frail old man with skin so tight it's nearly translucent stands on the opposite side of the room with a shotgun in hand. He wears a large white cowboy hat and a bright red dress shirt with one of those whacked-out string tie thingies around his neck. A stark white mustache the same color as his hair extends to the bottom of his chin. I laugh loudly at his outlandish getup even though it so isn't appropriate at the time, considering he just shot a gun inside a building.

"This is my lodge, and if ya ain't civil with each other then ya ain't welcome to stay here," he announces, his face scrunched up like he just ate a sour jawbreaker.

"Cash," I say, pointing to the door. If anyone can't be civil, it's him. The over-the-top eye roll Cash directs my way is expected and only solidifies my point.

A few people—including Finn, who yanks me away in a harsh movement from Payton's clutches once again—begin standing, but most of those in our group continue to crouch low, holding their hands up in surrender.

The bleached blonde points to where Finn and I stand. "It was these newcomers, Pa."

Pa? Between the old man's outlandish get up and their ill use of the English language I feel like I'm suddenly watching a twisted version of Little House on the Prairie where Pa is a creepy old pedophile and Laura has taken on the role of the neighborhood skank with cheaply colored hair.

"We're not here to cause any problems," Finn tells the old man. "There was just a misunderstanding."

I'm having a hard time keeping up with everything. I still don't know what we're doing here and whether or not we do, in fact, want to start any problems. But, as back-woods as these people are, they seem to have enough problems of their own without our help.

I point at Payton. "This guy is the one who came in and randomly started shooting people."

Colonel Sanders lowers his gun and squints over at the soldier. At this point, I can't be sure if his vision is bad or if that's how he makes his brain function. "You some kind of military soldier, son?"

"Wow," I say, unable to hold back. I so did not know there were active rednecks living in our state. All that's missing is a pair of dueling banjos and a rickety old porch.

"I was in the Army, sir, but I left to find my family," Payton tells him. He speaks each word with great pause to the old-timer, apparently also detecting a little slowness on his part.

The white-haired old man raises his gun again. "Abandoning the U.S. Military is a pretty serious offense, soldier."

My throat drops straight into my stomach when it dawns on me—the old man is intending on shooting this guy for leaving the Army. I love our country and have great pride toward anyone in the military, but it seems a bit harsh to execute him on such short notice just for being AWOL. The American in me wants to step between them and protect the soldier, but then I remember this is the same guy who was ready to shoot me just moments ago.

Finn leans in to whisper loudly at me and our cowering crew, "I think it's time for us to leave."

The old man cocks his gun back and actually takes direct aim at the soldier. "Be sure to take this AWOL piece of shit with you when you go."

"Oh hell no!" I yell in protest, taking a step forward. First this Payton guy shot a woman right in front of me, then he considered shooting me as well. I'm not going anywhere with someone who is apparently looking for extra target practice.

"He's not ours," Finn tells the old man in agreement.

Payton holds his hands up in surrender, not taking his

eyes off the crazy old man wielding the gun. "I don't think I have a choice in the matter," he mutters to us.

"You don't need to shoot anyone," Finn tells the old man. "We're leaving."

"What about our things?" I ask. Although I don't remember coming here, we must have packed a bag for the trip.

"We didn't bring anything," Finn whispers to me. In my apparent bout of amnesia, I must have really taken this hiking thing seriously.

All those who remain watch in silence as Finn tugs on my hand and motions for the rest of our friends to follow along. Laura and Pa seem to have the most satisfied looks of anyone as they watch our departure. I grumble angrily when Payton walks alongside us, but my protests are drowned out by our group's grumblings for being kicked out. The night is cold and dark when we step outside, causing me to shiver involuntarily.

"If Emma could keep her shit under control we wouldn't have gotten kicked out!" Cash yells to his brother with an angry line etched between his eyebrows. The only thing that keeps me calm in this moment is picturing my fist making contact with his annoying face.

Finn, however, turns on his heels, nearly spitting on his brother when he speaks. His breath meets the cold air in little white puffs. "Don't pretend like it's her fault when you're the one who started it, Cash! God! You can be such an asshole!"

Cash doesn't say any more—his little brother appears menacing enough for him to know not to argue anymore. Finn holds the door open for me on the driver's side of a black Suburban we're apparently traveling in. Payton has already claimed shotgun, forcing me to sit sandwiched between the two guys. The others have piled into the backseats behind us.

I'm ashamed to admit this new guy smells pretty dang appealing. His body is giving off some other attractive vibes as I sit close to him, even though he had seriously considered shooting me just minutes ago. I snuggle in as close as I can to Finn.

"If he shoots me, it's all on you," I say to my friend, using my best angry voice. "Literally. My brains will be splattered all over the place."

"He's not going to shoot anyone," Finn says, his eyes locking on the soldier's. "Are you?"

"So long as she stays human," Payton answers. As he regards me from a few inches away under the interior light of the car, I notice for the first time his eyes are a beautiful shade of piercing blue. Try as I might, it's hard to resist what is turning out to be my very own live-action hero up close and in person.

"Human?" I snort, turning to him. "You...hope... you're...staying human." I stutter on my words, his irritating good looks and charms flustering me to the point my speech is impaired.

He smirks at me, his eyes dancing. "How's that?" I glare angrily back at him when I can't form a response, which only makes him laugh. "That's what I thought."

"So what's the plan now?" Cash asks. "Do you expect us to sleep in the car?"

Finn puts the car into drive. "You pansies can sleep, I'll drive. It will be better the sooner we get to the Canadian border, anyway."

Our stowaway holds up a hand that looks more like the paw of a large animal. "Whoa—hold up a minute. You don't want to go to Canada."

"We're going hiking." I inform him. "If you don't want

to come with you can get out now, Sergeant Nobody-Asked-You-to-Tag-Along."

A few people listening in from the backseat chuckle spastically at my response. I'm beginning to suspect the hiking trip was something Finn made up.

"It's Payton to you, and I'm telling you guys, Canada is not a place anyone wants to go right now. The government is planning to wipe that country out in the next seventy-six hours. That's why I got the hell out of there. Our best bet at this point is to head south."

Finn shakes his head insistently. "I was told Canada is the only safe place."

I do some verbal thinking to myself. "Why would anyone want to wipe out Canada? I forget they're even there half the time."

No one bothers to answer me, but Payton looks over at Finn with his chest puffed out. The stereotypical male hormone-driven argument has begun to set in. "I don't know where you got your information, but I can tell you exactly what the U.S. Army is planning based on the direction of the federal agency, and forcing an attack on southern Minnesota wasn't a part of it."

Finn has stopped the vehicle to argue his side. The intensity bouncing off between the two guys is thick in the air. I wait for them to rip their shirts off and start pounding their chests, but apparently it's only a fantasy that I've cooked up in my own mind. Their shirts stay on for now.

Finn frowns. "How would you know what the federal agency is planning? I thought you went AWOL."

"Before I left, word got out that some big shot federal agent was orchestrating the attack on Canada. For all I know, they're going to wipe out the rest of the country, too. They were pretty hell-bent on containing this virus at any cost. Why do you think I left?" Payton is quite obviously thinking he's superior at this point with what he perceives to be super-secret military knowledge.

Finn sucks in a breath of air. "Any chance you heard the agent's name?"

Payton looks up, maybe in search of any brain cells that haven't been affected by steroid use. "I don't know— some lady who is pretty high up there, I guess. She took over by the order of the Army General. I think it was Benson or something like that."

Looking to Finn, I'm almost physically able to watch the color drain from his face. I reach for his hand that trembles against the steering wheel, but he snaps it from my reach. The vehicle is dead quiet, waiting for someone to dare speak up. As one would expect, the king of dipshits is the first to say something.

"How do you know any of this?" Cash demands. "You could just be making all of it up to get a rise out of us."

I turn to give him an incredulous stare. "Really? I may not know what is going on right now but I know you just met him. He doesn't know your last name, moron. Why would he randomly decide to use it when he doesn't even know who you guys are?" I turn back to look at Finn. "But while we're on the subject, could someone please fill me in here? Is this Benson woman a relative of yours or what?"

Finn sighs deeply beside me before resting his head on his arms. "Em, I'm sorry I broke you. Believe me. I really, truly am. But if you could please just shut up for now and let those of us in the know figure out what is going on, I would really appreciate it."

I should probably be offended by the abrupt way in which he speaks to me, but because he rarely uses that tone of voice, I know pushing it would not be a wise choice. I press my lips tightly together. Not speaking up will be a serious challenge.

"You know this Benson woman?" Payton asks.

"Pretty well, yeah." Finn nods while looking into space.

Cash clicks his tongue. "Why should we listen to this AWOL a-hole?"

Even I cower a little when Payton turns his thick neck to address Cash. I decide in this moment the last thing I would want to do is to hurt someone of Payton's size, although it's still on my list after he pointed his gun at me.

"Because with all that I know, I'm probably your best chance at surviving this," he tells Cash.

Finn studies our stowaway. "Do you know anything else about this Benson woman? Any mention of where the federal headquarters are?"

Payton turns back around and shrugs. "Not specifically, but I think a lot of the command is coming from somewhere out of central Iowa. That seems to be the safe zone, for the time being."

Finn thinks about this for a minute before turning back to exchange a look with Cash. He drums his thumb against the steering wheel. "I guess we're heading to Iowa."

The laughter bursts out of my mouth like a whale spout. "Everyone is talking like the world is coming to an end, and you want to go to a state whose anagram is I Owe the World an Apology? Are you serious?"

Finn puts the vehicle into motion. "Payton, man, I sure hope you're right about all of this."

* * *

WHEN I REGAIN consciousness from my impromptu nap, I find myself leaning against Payton's mass of a shoulder. Lifting my head, I discover a pool of drool left behind on his uniform. I give him a toothy smile before leaning away.

But he smiles down on me coyly. "Good morning, sunshine."

My eyes squint up at him, but not from the bright, early rays of daylight that assault the vehicle. It's common knowledge that I'm so not a morning person and don't like chipper people around when I'm trying to adjust. "It's Emma," I tell him sharply. Finn makes a low, satisfied "humph" sound.

"Are you having any particular memories involving flesh-hungry human corpses yet this morning?" Payton asks, his eyes steadily watching mine.

I frown up at him. "Seriously, dude. I just woke up." I shut my eyes and try to think back. Memories involving whatever he just said are not trying to break through, although I do recall some creepy nightmares having to do with Cash and a drone of rabid monkeys.

"Nothing comes to mind," I say. "Are you trying to say that's what all of this is about? You shooting that kooky old lady back there? All this talk of us being bombed by the Army? The reason you were considering shooting me, too? That's why you're concerned about people being human?"

This would seem to be a really insane explanation for everything, but one of the voices in my head tells me it's feasible—although the voice sounds suspiciously like the same one that told me at my cousin's wedding that apple puckers is only a mixer and does not contain any alcohol.

A mischievous grin creeps across Payton's face. "Basically, yeah."

I turn to look at everyone still conked out in the backseats. The way their mouths hang down in their deep slumber, they could easily be zombies themselves. "Do they all know about these corpses?"

Payton is nodding, the grin still tugging at his mouth. "Everyone knows."

I cock my head to the side and take in his rugged charm. "Are we talking actual zombies, or are you totally messing with me right now?"

He looks back at me with his face stone-cold sober. "Actual zombies."

"Pretty sure I warned you that we weren't going to drop it on her like that," Finn grumbles angrily. "You don't know her. It's not a good idea."

The first sign we pass is in the crooked rectangle shape that's known to be Iowa. We must have crossed the border sometime while I was busy leaving my DNA on the big guy. On the side of the road I see what would appear to be a deer carcass alongside the road on a normal day, but as we pass I realize it's a disfigured human. I only see a flash of it from the speed Finn is going, but there's enough time to see the man's organs are pulled out from his body the same as any other roadkill.

"That's just nasty," I say with fascination.

From behind the steering wheel Finn gives me the whole are-you-crazy look I probably deserved well before this moment. "That's it? You're not going to freak out or anything?"

I consider this for a moment, but then shrug. "Well, I would say it really sucks and everything, but if the world didn't suck we'd all fall off, right?"

I'm not sure what else he wants me to say. I just hope this means we will get some kind of free pass and won't have to finish the rest of our senior year.

"Maybe you should give your girlfriend more credit," Payton says to Finn in a very condescending tone.

Finn clenches his teeth for a moment. "She's not my girlfriend. We're just friends."

Although it's true that we haven't openly admitted to any such thing that I know of, a small part of me dies with his words. An end of the world romp is probably in order with the news they've just given me, but that could prove to be difficult if he still sees us as "buddies."

I sit up taller, hoping to cushion my bruised ego. "Yep, and that means I'm officially on the market, as they say." I throw a playful wink at Payton and his grin widens tenfold.

"How about we focus on surviving this apocalypse before worrying about who you're going to take to the prom," Finn says. The resentment in his voice is shouting, although he's speaking quietly. I have to push my lips together to keep from laughing at him.

Payton clears his throat uncomfortably. "How exactly did you snag this souped-up rig?"

Finn refuses to look at Payton when speaking. "Our aunt believes in being prepared for the inevitable." The need to win my affection displayed by these two is becoming rather embarrassing—they could at least make a more valiant effort.

The scenery doesn't change as we continue on. We continue down gravel back roads and only occasionally pass vehicles going at crazy fast speeds. The land is flat and un-harvested crops stretch as far as the eye can see. Abandoned vehicles and dead bodies are becoming a common sight, but at least we don't see any actual walking corpses.

"Whoa! Look at all those combines!" Jake's says from the backseat.

We turn to see that sure enough, there's a field just full of combine harvesters of all different shapes, sizes, and colors approaching on the right. The field they had been working in is nearly finished, but the doors of each and every one of the machines are wide open, like the owners had to flee with only a moment's notice.

"Looks like they were probably rallying together to help someone who got infected," Zander says. "They must have all ran off when word of the virus got out."

"Or when a bunch of zombies started chasing them around in the field," Marley mumbles.

My eyes are wide when I turn to Finn. I give him a lopsided grin. "No," he says firmly, turning back to face the road. "Not now."

"What?" Jake asks, popping his head up through the seat between us.

"I could sure use a potty break," I tell Finn, placing my face just inches from his. I poke him in the side repeatedly until he chuckles loudly.

"Forget it, Em! We don't have time to screw around." But he's failing miserably at trying to keep a straight face.

"C'mon, Finn! If this is really some kind of apocalypse as you said earlier, shouldn't we take time to have a little fun before we all die?" I ask. "Besides, you promised."

"What are you two morons talking about?" Cash asks.

Finn turns to me and I see a flash of my old friend that's every bit as mischievous as I am. "Fine, but only for a short break."

Chapter 10

I sit behind the wheel of the green monstrosity while Finn hovers over me to show which controls to use. Our friends stand in the field below, looking significantly smaller from our heightened viewpoint. They all had thought we were joking when Finn first pulled into the field, but now watch with amazement.

Finn spent last summer working for the local sweet corn packing plant and got to drive combines as part of his job. One night he snuck me in with him—it was the most amazing experience to drive through the fields in the dark and see the lights of the massive machines as they passed us by. I made him promise he would give me another ride, but he was "let go" the next week when he failed to show up for work one day. The firing was kind of my fault—on my urging, we had hopped into my car last-minute and driven to a Beastie Boys concert in Chicago. At least we both had a total blast that night. We even got kicked off the tour bus—although it was empty—so that kind of made it all worth the trip for both of us.

I hurry Finn's instructions along with my hand. "I thought you said these things have like this autopilot thing now. How hard can they be to drive?"

I reach down and turn the key over. The ginormous machine comes alive seconds later with a loud shudder. I throw a few fist pumps into the air and honk the horn, laughing hysterically at the wimpy beeping it makes.

"This thing is the size of a house but they give it the horn from a motor scooter! Wouldn't you think they need something a little more demanding so people know they're coming?"

Finn stands nervous next to me. "Just remember, Em— someone spent over a hundred grand on this thing. If they haven't turned into a monster yet, they'll probably want it back again someday. You have to be careful."

Using the lever he showed me, I make the machine pull forward. We both bump into the windshield with the force of the movement. Finn leans over me to push on a different lever and our speed slows. Our friends below scatter away like a bunch of little field mice as we jerk ahead.

"This is awesome!" I say loudly to Finn. He laughs and crouches in the small seat next to me, watching in amusement as I weave through the other parked combines. I push on the lever that I now know will increase our speed and beep the horn again.

"Emma, come in, over," a voice calls out from over my head.

My eyes widen. "Is that for moi?" I look up to the black square box with red dots flashing and tons of dials. I finally wave my hands in frustration. "I have no idea how to run that thing."

Finn pushes a button and grabs the black square thingy with the cord hanging from it. "What's up, Zander?"

"Take a look to your left, over," Zander answers. We both jerk our heads in the direction as told, laughing when we discover the Anderson brothers in a smaller yellow combine beside us. They wave with giant smiles and I wave back before honking the pathetic horn. Their rather wealthy uncle owns half the fields in our county, so it really doesn't come as a surprise that Zander knows how to drive a combine.

Just moments later, a third and even larger combine in bright red appears on the other side of them. Jake waves wildly from the driver's seat. Payton stands over him with a less than amused look and Marley perches in the extra seat, her eyes wide with a seemingly equal mix of fear and excitement.

Finn and I laugh at the unusual sight of our friends behind the large machines.

We all may be in the process of losing our minds, but at least we're stopping along the way to enjoy some of the little things this doom and gloom brings with it. If the end of the world is really here, at least we can say we had a little fun in the end.

* * *

WITH THE EXCITEMENT of driving my very first combine wearing off, I find my patience to continue riding in this smaller vehicle deteriorating with every mile of un-harvested crops that pass by. When I was in middle school, my parents once decided to try a vacation more suited for children and drove me to Orlando. We were not far from home when I had what the emergency room thought to be a bit of a nervous breakdown from being locked up. We ended up catching a plane in Milwaukee and my parents never tried taking me on a road trip again.

The vehicle is quiet as most of the passengers are sleeping out of boredom or just plain lack of sleep from the interrupted night before.

"The virus has obviously spread down this way," Finn says to me and Payton. "But why haven't we seen any actual people anywhere? We can't be the only survivors."

I shrug my shoulders beside him. "Maybe this is Iowa on a normal day."

"They have quarantine camps spread out all through the Midwest," Payton says. "Maybe they've collected all the survivors."

"You really don't know where to find any of these camps?" Finn asks him.

Payton shakes his head. "At one point they were talking about posting maps of everything but I got out of there before that happened."

"That was great timing on your part," I mumble. The feeling of being caged in sweeps over me when it appears we will never see another town again. I'm jonesing for an energy drink and some kind of chocolaty treat. If this is truly the end of life as we know it, there had at least better be some kind of candy bar at my disposal.

We come to the edge of what could potentially be a town, although painfully small, when the vehicle starts to slow. Finn curses like a sailor and steers us off to the shoulder. The Suburban shudders all at once and the engine kills.

He sighs and mumbles to himself. "Damn gas gauge must be broken." He jumps out of the vehicle and disappears behind it. I turn to Payton, but discover he has already gone out the passenger's door.

"Where are we?" a sleepy Marley asks behind me.

"Still stuck somewhere in America's armpit," I answer. Drumming my fingers on the dashboard for only a moment while debating on what to do, I decide to follow the guys out of the vehicle as sitting still is not a trait I possess. I find Finn standing on the bumper, stretched up to see what is on the top of the vehicle. From the irritated look on his face, it's obvious that he's not pleased.

"The freaking fuel is gone!" he yells, whipping some kind of rope off to the side. "Someone at the lodge must have stolen it!"

"I can't imagine any of those outstanding citizens doing such a thing." I say, thinking of the old man who wanted to shoot all of us. I bite my lip and look to the small town on the horizon. "Maybe that little village over that way has a gas station." The overwhelming need to get away from the vehicle and stretch my legs again is a priority, followed very closely by the need to gorge myself with something unhealthy.

"Can I come, too?" Jake asks. We look behind me to discover the car has been emptied. Everyone is gathered around and staring at Finn, waiting for some kind of verbal plan to take shape.

"We're all going," Payton says, taking action as the new leader of us misfits. "We need to stick together." The large gun he used to kill the zombie woman is resting on his jumbo shoulder and his square face is etched with serious intent. He stands with his legs slightly apart, fists firmly placed at his sides. I take a minute to appreciate the perfect movie poster the moment creates. The name "GI Joe" continues to suit him.

"Everyone, grab a weapon," Finn says, agreeing it's our only option, but also trying to take the lead again. He's quite obviously threatened by the new freeloader and doesn't want to lose control to him.

Finn opens the back of the vehicle and hands out guns to everyone as they step forward. I stare at the supply in awe wondering why Finn's family would have access to so many guns. Other than in unrealistic action hero movies, I've never seen such a huge collection of weapons. I'm guessing one person owning that many isn't even legal, unless you're a terrorist.

Payton stands next to me, also marveling at them. "Your aunt was seriously prepared for Armageddon." He enthusiastically takes another gun in addition to the one he has already acquired and looks it over like it's his precious.

Finn places a small gun in my unwilling hands last. I stare blankly back at him. "Seriously? Finn, what in the hell am I supposed to do with this?"

Payton quickly takes the gun and does something to it with a flash of his hands before placing it back in mine. "You clock them over the head with it and run like hell."

Finn gives Payton a look that would kill him, had it not been lost on his backside now turned to us. We obediently fall into line behind the soldier as he leads us to the mysterious town. The irony of our odd group walking on a deserted road with weapons over our shoulders isn't lost on me. I start humming the Darth Vader evil-sounding tune until enough dirty looks eventually silence me.

Although there aren't any actual tumbleweeds blowing across the street, there may as well be—it's completely abandoned. The town, if it's even big enough to be considered one, probably isn't too different now from what it was before this virus thing hit. We walk in through a residential area of no more than a dozen rundown homes that can't be any bigger than one bedroom in size. No cars are parked in the road or next to any of the houses, making me wonder if everyone left town before the virus even hit or if they simply couldn't afford any vehicles. Although I grew up in a small town, this one is so miniscule in size I wonder if they even have electricity.

Our shoes hitting the pavement are the only sounds to be heard. An unnatural vibe hangs in the air over our heads and you can almost taste that something is wrong— either that or I'm so hungry that I'm just envisioning food related things.

With nearly half of the people in our entourage under the age of sixteen, motherly instincts I didn't even know I possessed until this very instant begin to surface. I pull Jake into my side and hang my arm over his shoulders. "Stay close."

He looks up at me with a questioning gaze. If only I had a penny for every time someone looked at me like I was crazy today—I would probably have a whole nickel or even a dime.

But Jake's eyes change into something devilish. "You do remember that you agreed to go on a date with me after all of this blows over, right?" He's obviously trying to take advantage of my temporary memory loss so I give him my best sympathy-filled look. "I'll think about it the day you start needing to shave."

Jake frowns and rubs his hand along his baby-smooth jaw line.

We reach a small gas station that appears to have been the town's sole business at one time, although it looks old enough to have shut down a few decades ago. The last price advertised on the rusty sign hanging over the single pump is $1.30, but Finn lifts the handle to check anyway. No one is surprised when he finds it to be dry.

"Now what?" Marley asks, her eyes settling on Payton.

"We start walking south." Payton points in the direction that must be south, but I wouldn't know my directions in my own neighborhood without the use of a GPS.

"You really think we're going to walk?" the skinny redheaded kid from school asks. "What if we run into a pack of infected people?"

"What's that kid's name again?" I whisper to Finn.

"Cheese," he snaps back with irritation.

"We'll bring enough weapons to defend ourselves and whatever supplies we need," Payton says. "We'll be okay if everyone sticks together." Most of what he says is lost on me, sounding more like the teacher from Charlie Brown. I'm so completely mesmerized by the mass of muscles on his arms that brush across his solid chest as he moves that I nearly forget how to walk.

Cash shakes his head. "I'm with the kid. None of us knows where we are. The next town could be a hundred miles away."

Payton shrugs and shifts the larger gun he holds further out on his shoulder. The muscles under his shirt flex and make the material taut for a second. "Stay here then."

"I'll go." I'm quick to volunteer—anywhere that gorgeous goes is fine with me. Finn already announced that I'm not his girlfriend so I don't care what he does at the moment, despite his icy glare.

"We're all going," Finn grumbles. "Like Payton said. We're not going to split up, and staying here certainly isn't going to solve anything."

A faint, faraway collection of moans drifts over to us, causing those of us who heard to look beyond the gas station. The recognition of what is happening begins to appear on the face of everyone in attendance, one by one. I'm the last one to register that the noise is close to the same creepy noise the old lady in the lodge had made just before Payton shot her. My eyes dart back to the mass of muscles that have a way of making me feel more comforted.

Payton, having the heard the noise as well, positions himself between me and the direction of the impending threat. He even slips his hand into mine. Chivalry is far from dead with this guy, and I'm almost able to forget the fact he once pointed a gun at me and that we're about to be attacked by a bunch of mindless monsters.

"This way," he says in a commanding whisper, pulling furiously on my hand. We fall into a sort of crooked line as we sneak past the fuel pump and into the small building that once had been the actual station. The noises become louder just as Zander is the last to enter. He pulls down on the bars against the glass doors to lock them—they click loudly into place, sounding a bit too much like a jail cell closing for my comfort.

We all crouch down on the dirt covered floor behind empty display racks. My stomach grumbles angrily at the sight of them. I would fight a zombie bare-handed right now if someone promised me a taste of some chocolate.

"They must have heard our voices," Payton says. Still holding his arm around my back protectively, our bodies press together. Finn keeps giving me these ridiculous looks that are a mix of jealousy and irritation thrown in with plain old anger. He can say I'm not his girlfriend all he wants, but the feelings he holds for me are so clear he that may as well be holding a sign encrusted in glitter around his neck saying "I heart Emma."

The moans become even louder, and soon a scurry of shuffling noises follows from just outside the store. The front window rattles and thunders as some of the infected start banging their fists against it. I whimper loudly when it seems they will be coming in after us. Payton's hand flies over my mouth and he makes "shushing" noises into my ear. For the record, I'm not the only one being a baby—Marley is blubbering quietly on the other side of Finn and Jake is wincing beside me.

"What if they can smell us?" Cheese whispers from the other side of Payton. "If they're hungry enough they probably won't give up."

"And everyone here really stinks," I add. The odor in the air is a mixture of sweat, dirt, and something I can't quite place—maybe really cheap cologne.

"Who knows how to actually use their guns?" Payton whispers, cocking the handgun Finn had given him. Finn, Zander and Cash are the only ones to hold up their hands, although Zander is holding his so low I think I may be the only one to catch it.

"Wait, are you actually going out there?" Cheese asks.

I peek through a hole in the rack to see more of the infected have gathered to join in on the banging of the windows. Their moans are becoming elevated, more desperate. I train my eyes on the door's bars, waiting for them to move.

"Only if they try coming in," Payton answers. And right on cue, there's a loud explosion as one of the windows breaks open. Everyone yells out in surprise and we cover our heads to keep the shards of glass away. Payton springs into action, holding the gun in front of him and shooting at whatever is behind the broken glass—I'm not about to stand up to check it out.

I can feel reluctance totally radiating from Finn as he stands on weary feet beside Payton and begins shooting his gun as well. I hold my hands over my ears to muffle the loud explosions the guns make and keep my head down to protect it from more exploding glass.

The moans have taken on a new life, now in a seriously agitated tone. The infected corpses on the outside are either really hungry or really mad at themselves for not figuring out how to get in. I scoot over closer to Marley when Cash starts in on the shootout. The guns are so loud I'm sure I'll be deaf for the rest of my life.

Someone starts yelling loudly after a few minutes and I look up to see Payton holding his arms out, telling the other two to stop shooting. "Whoa! Hold up!" he yells once the guns finally quit. "I think we got them all."

The rest of us stand on wobbly legs to find there are no longer infected people banging at the windows. A few are still crawling around on the ground from nonfatal wounds. Paton steps forward and holds his arm out the window, taking care of the last few to move. He hits them each squarely in the skull, just as he did with the woman in the lodge.

Once it's all clear, we follow him outside where there are as many as two dozen dead sprawled about, some even in piles on top of each other. My heart beats wildly at the sight of the corpses and I hold my hands over my mouth. The bodies are completely mangled from an apparent mixture of the virus and numerous gunshot holes. Most of them have the same pale skin with large open sores every-where. Each of them seems to be that of an older adult and there's a fair representation of both men and women, all of which are dressed casually. I can fully appreciate at this point why my mind chose to block something as horrible as this from my memory.

My eyes stop on a woman with blond hair. The skin on her face has deteriorated like all the others and her entire lower jawbone is visible. I stare at the other remaining parts of her. Something about the shape of her small lips, the round curve of her button-nose and the position of her now vacant eyes all look oddly familiar.

The woman looks like my mother.

"Huh," I say aloud.

On second glance, I notice the bullets had torn the woman's torso to shreds. Some of her intestines are spilled across the pavement, looking like slimy red caterpillars. I spin around on my heels to throw up, but nothing comes out.

"You okay?" Finn asks in a gentle tone, resting a hand on my back.

I hold a hand up to stop him from getting any closer. "I really need something to eat so I can properly barf." I spit on the ground once before turning back to the carnage.

When looking at the woman again, I decide I can't be sure it's actually my mother. Her entire eyeballs are a milky white rather than my mother's radiant blue eyes, and her hair is shorter, hanging in unmanaged clumps. My mother would never let that happen to her own longer locks. Then again, these zombies tend to have nappy hair in general.

Jake steps forward to gawk at the same woman. "Is that…?"

Finn follows his gaze and tries not to react when he spots her.

"I'm not sure," I mumble. I walk in a trance over to where the woman's body is, stepping over the slaughtered bodies with great care. My friends loom closely behind me as I stand over the body, assessing what could potentially be the end of my own personal world as I know it. The woman's left hand is missing, so I can't identify her by my mother's large diamond wedding ring. I search her body for signs to prove this most certainly is not my mother lying slaughtered in the street before me, but cry out in surprise when I spot a ring on the index finger of her right hand. I stoop closer to inspect the ring without having to actually touch the hand.

The corpse is wearing the ring I gave my mother as a present for her fortieth birthday.

With my entire body trembling, I bend down and gently pick up her hand. Her skin is leathery and cold—the ring slips from her finger with little effort. I place my mother's hand back on the ground and step away from her corpse, moisture filling my eyes as I look down on the treasure.

Without a doubt, it's the same ring, only with blood and dirt covering it. We were in the Caribbean Islands with a group of their friends to celebrate her birthday when she found the ring. She had all but drooled over the stone's beautiful shade of blue. My dad got their friends to distract her while he gave me the money to buy it. When I gave the present to my mother later that night she cried, saying it would always remind her of the beautiful color of the Caribbean Sea she had visited with her two favorite people in the world. I remember wondering at the time who those two people could be.

The air around me grows thin, the daylight dark. Everything about right now is so surreal and unthinkable —I'm sure I must be dreaming. This can't really be happening. Not to me.

"What the hell was she doing in Iowa?" I hear the words being spoken, but it takes a second to realize they're coming from my own mouth. Searching all around me, I wait for Ashton Kutcher to appear from behind the building and tell me I'm being punked or something more believable. But the same set of familiar faces I've been surrounded by all day stare back at me with the same hopeless, horrified expressions.

My hands fly down to my stomach with the total unease that has settled in. Moving in slow motion, my legs buckle underneath me and I begin falling to the ground. Before I do, however, a set of hands catches me.

Finn looks down at me with the same beautiful, kind eyes I've looked into so many times before. They're attempting to do what they can to comfort me, although he can't seem to think of anything to say.

An abrupt darkness swallows me whole.

Chapter 11

When I wake, I'm alone in some kind of small, but tidy bedroom. An early morning light breaks through the small window over a big oak chest. The house must have belonged to a really old couple—the furniture is ancient and the décor of the room is based around a lime green color. The room even has some kind of funky smell to it that reminds me of old people in general.

The first words I hear from somewhere else in the house are spoken in Cash's moronic voice. "I say we leave her behind. The way she keeps losing it, we'll never get anywhere with her along."

"She just saw her mother's infected corpse lying murdered in the street," Marley's voice says in response. "Have a little compassion, Cash. Next thing you'll want to leave me behind."

"At least that way the two of you could look out for each other."

The fact that Cash isn't smart enough to understand what Marley was saying comes as no surprise, but the sound of a hand slapping skin is. Seconds later, footsteps pound in my direction. Marley soon appears in the doorway looking the angriest I've ever seen her. She quickly changes her expressions when she sees that I'm awake.

She sighs deeply. "Tell me you didn't just hear what that idiot said."

"You mean the part where the world's biggest asshole volunteered us womenfolk to stay behind together, or the part where you slapped him? Just so you know, I'm all for the slapping part."

Her shoulders fall and she sits on the bed beside me. "You're right, he's a total asshole. I don't know why I didn't see it all these years. I guess in all this madness I'm finally able to see straight."

I shrug. "Better now than before something tragic happened, like you spawning his devil child. That thing would probably come out with fangs or something."

She laughs brightly at me, but her face quickly settles into a frown. "Are you feeling okay, Emma? Do you still remember everything that happened yesterday?"

I push myself up on my elbows. "If you are referring to the part where I discovered the woman who gave birth to me had become a mindless ghoul, I don't think there will be anything that will be able to wipe that humdinger from my memory." I look down to see someone has cleaned my mother's ring and placed it on my finger. My insides twist with the sentiment.

Marley is not the touchy-feely type with anyone other than Cash, so I'm not surprised when she doesn't reach out to comfort me. Instead, her entire face falls with sympathy. "I'm so sorry, Em." I'm shocked, however, to see her eyes watering over. Normally they're heavily made up, but from the events of the past twenty-four hours combined with a lack of toiletries, the makeup has begun to fade away and she's starting to resemble a normal human being. When all natural like that she's really quite pretty.

I shrug. "It's not your fault."

She pulls her lips into a sad smile. "I know you don't remember everything, but you've actually been a lot of fun to hang out with through all of this and it's pretty cool to have another girl to hang out with, you know? You and I have always gotten along pretty well, right?"

I smile back at her. "If we had met randomly, in some way other than you dating the moronic older brother of my best friend, I think we probably could have been friends."

"I'm sorry Cash is such an ass to you," she says, rolling her eyes to the ceiling.

I shrug. "I'm sorry I wrote your cell number on the wall of hookers at the rest stop." Technically, Finn had been using the urinal next to me while I did it so he's actually guilty by association, but I decide to take one for the team and don't mention it.

She snorts. "So that was you? I always wondered why all those perverted truckers kept calling!"

Okay, so Marley is pretty decent. She knows how to take a harmless joke for what it is. "Is anyone else here, or is it just us?" I ask. The thought of being alone with only Marley and Cash is suddenly gnawing at my insides. If more infected come around, Cash will be quick to sacrifice me as a decoy so he can escape. But then again, maybe if I'm fast enough I could do the same with him.

"We all crashed in this house last night. The rest of the guys left early this morning with some luggage we found to retrieve our supplies. But I'll tell you what—Finn was all keyed up over leaving you here this morning. I know you guys have been friends forever, but I think he's got some more complex feelings going on."

I give her a small smile. "Apparently all it took for him to realize those feelings was this whole end-of-the-world scenario we seem to be living. Too bad it couldn't have happened sooner."

She raises her pierced eyebrow at me, smirking. "Am I getting the vibe that the feelings may be mutual? Are you into him, too?"

"It's hard to concentrate with our new bodybuilder friend hanging around and getting in the way, but yeah, I think so." Payton is the ideal pinup guy for probably any woman left on this earth, but he can't compete with the charm of my goofy best friend.

Now Marley's expression becomes dead serious—something I don't think I've seen before. I almost clutch her arm and ask if she's okay. "All this crazy stuff that has happened really has me thinking. What if this is it for us? What if today is the very last day we walk on this earth?"

I groan. "You're not going to start up on all that witch-craft stuff now, are you?"

"I'm into the studies of witchcraft. It's not the same as actually practicing the Wiccan religion. That stuff's just really interesting. But that's not the point I was trying to make. I just mean that we really need to start living for the moment. Have no regrets, make no mistakes. You know?"

With the recent death of my mother, I probably don't need to be reminded, but it does make me think. Another day would be totally wasted if I didn't tell Finn how I truly feel about him, even if he does laugh at me when I finally fess up. "I think I do know," I say with a smirk.

A door somewhere else in the house opens and closes, bringing in loud conversation that abruptly ends our chat. Marley clasps her hands around my wrist and her eyes meet mine. "Stay here. I'll get you something to eat and drink." When she leaves the room, the thoughts I've been able to keep at bay start to surface.

My mother is dead and her last meal had quite possibly consisted of another human being.

And what about my dad? Where is he? Had she eaten him? At least I know my mom is at peace now and not walking around trying to attack people. She wouldn't have been very happy about that part—there was never a cruel bone in her body.

These absurd thoughts are thankfully cut short when Finn comes into the room. He looks visibly relieved to see me propped up and conscious. His smile is at its brightest and a warmth passes through me at the sight of him. "Morning. How are you feeling?"

"Hmmm…." I sit all the way up, seeming foreign in my own skin. "You mean at the moment? I would say I'm about five percent hungry and a million percent freaked out. Other than that, I'm awesome."

Finn closes the space between us in just a few strides and wraps me in his arms. This would be an opportune time to let myself cry and mourn my loss, but I still seem to be suffering a high amount of shock. Instead I'm busy focusing on the small muscles in his chest pushed against mine and the musty way he smells underneath the layers of sweat and dirt. His arms are probably a third the size of Payton's, but certainly I'm not shallow enough to let that bother me—or at least I tell myself that.

Finn draws back to search my face, probably wondering why I'm not appropriately upset after everything that has happened. He leans in and presses his soft lips against my forehead, letting them linger a minute or two before moving away to carefully watch me. I think he's afraid I'll lose it again. "Have you been up very long?"

"I just woke," I answer.

"You slept really hard last night. You were having a nightmare and I couldn't wake you up. It was kind of freaky."

I shut my eyes briefly and make a sarcastic hum. "Gee, I can't imagine what kind of nightmares I would be having. That would be a total waste of energy as I seem to be living one."

His reaches out for my hand, watching as our fingers intertwine around each other. "I'm so sorry you had to see your mother like that, Emma. I can't imagine how wigged out you are because of it. If you need to talk, or maybe… you know…like cry or anything, I'm here for you."

I squeeze his hand. "If I decide to blubber, you'll be the first person I do it on, I promise. Are you the one responsible for cleaning up my mom's ring?"

He looks down at the blue stone and pushes it with his thumb. "I figured you would want it. Your mom wore that ring for as long as I can remember."

I look up into his dark eyes. "Most girls my age are worried about juggling a best friend and a guy who they actually want to hang out with. I'm lucky enough to have it all rolled into one. It's so convenient, like one of those bottles of shampoo and conditioner." The minute the words are out of my mouth I want to take them back. None of that sounded like an actual confession of my newfound love for him.

Finn smiles back at me. "You think you're strong enough to walk out of here?"

I nod, quite determined. "That won't be a problem. The farther we can get away from this total nightmare, the better."

His presence alone brings a feeling of familiarity from all the years of memories we've shared. But something new passes between us, doing funny things to my stomach as his eyes hold mine. I've always loved him as the wonderful friend he is, but it's never really been an actual want-to-make-out-with-him type of love before. I wonder if it's possible that I'm seriously falling in love with him; either that or I'm going to barf again.

Finn opens his mouth—surely to pronounce his equally undying love for me—when Payton barges into the room. He studies me for a moment then says, "Time to go." Although he has no way of knowing he just ruined a near monumental point in my relationship with Finn, I feel the urge to kick him.

"Yes, sir," I grumble, sliding off the bed and springing to my feet. For a mere second I lose my balance and Finn has to help steady me. When the room quits swaying I lead him from the room, clutching his hand.

Everyone mumbles some kind of awkward greeting when I join them in the dimly lit kitchen. They each look a bit more refreshed with the night of rest, but stare at me like I'm a science experiment while I chug a bottle of water in one breath and choke down a less than tasty can of cold soup.

When we finally head out of the nightmare of a town and pull the luggage holding our supplies behind, we look more prepared for the airport than anything. We walk through the center of the deserted highway. Two cars—a rusted-out pickup and a newer compact car—veer around us, neither stopping despite our efforts to wave wildly. We probably appear to be infected or just completely nuts the way we're all jumping up and down.

As the afternoon winds down, we discuss the virus and our theories on what is happening, most of which sound like the plot from a major motion picture. Zander thinks something radioactive must have started all of this. Cheese blabs on about some kind of tiny little robots connecting themselves inside our brains. Cash says it probably all started with some bad decision the president made, or something like that—as he speaks I can only think about how we're all probably becoming dumber from having to listen to him. Marley is convinced there's some kind of voodoo involved with all of it, which doesn't go over well with the rest of the group. Jake is even a little freaked out by her after that, going out of his way to avoid walking anywhere near her.

"Why is it we haven't seen any uninfected adults in all of this?" Cheese asks.

Zander nods in agreement. "That's a really good point. We haven't seen any infected kids, either. What's up with that?"

"I'm an adult," Payton interjects.

Cheese frowns over at him. "How old are you?"

"Twenty," Payton answers.

Finn chortles at this. "That's hardly an adult. You can't even go to a bar yet. Besides, who said anything about you being normal?"

I giggle at my friend's returning humor. I've seen so little of it in the past twenty-four hours and was beginning to worry he was broken.

"I'm more of a man than you," Payton returns. "At least I'm old enough to join the military."

Finn nods. "Right. You mean the Army that you up and left?"

"He's got you there," I say to Payton, patting his large arm. Truth is, I'm amused by the banter of the two guys and would love to see it continue on, maybe even to the point they finally rip their shirts off in anger.

"Uh, technically you're an adult at eighteen," Cheese interrupts. "And Payton is obviously not infected." Both are valid points, but I'm irritated that he put an end to the bickering.

"In that case, technically Cash and Marley are adults, too," Finn answers. "So much for your theory on adults not being infected."

"Or your theory on the definition of adult," I add. Cash is most certainly not one, no matter how you look at it.

Cheese shakes his head, unconvinced. "I know I haven't seen anyone over thirty. What if there's some kind of age factor involved?" Although his theory on adults seems is a little far-fetched, then again, so is the whole walking dead thing. Our time would be better spent trying to guess how many times Cash was dropped on his head as an infant.

The conversation quickly shifts to what we would do if this is in fact the end of the world. The younger boys are quite amusing with their answers, varying from running through famous football stadiums naked to taking a bath in the home of Steven Spielberg. When it becomes my turn I'm painfully honest about what I would do. I blame my candor on the trauma from the day before.

"I just don't want to die a virgin," I say. All eight sets of eyes land on me. Payton forces out some kind of a choking cough.

"What?" Cheese asks.

I shrug. "You know, like give away my v-card. Park my pink Porsche down a side alley. Take the—"

Cheese sneers. "I know what that is. I just can't believe you actually said that!"

I sigh. "What did you want me to say? That I want to go to Disneyland? I thought we were being honest here."

Finn twitches around, knowing damn well I haven't slept with anyone, but apparently still uncomfortable with the fact. Apparently no one can come up with a final wish quite as impactful as mine because the conversation is done. As we continue on in silence, I catch Cheese winking at me.

We come upon a small green sign, announcing a town that once had a population of 3,000 citizens. The first buildings to come into sight, however, are merely the skeletal remains of what they had once been. Either the town has recently been set on fire or a bomb has gone off. My pyrotechnical knowledge is limited to an experience with Cash and some other morons lighting fire to a squirrel corpse when we were way younger, so I can't be sure.

"Hopefully we can still find some wheels and a gas station," Finn says to our group.

A few people grunt in agreement, but I moan in agony. My feet and legs are pounding like crazy, feeling as if we've been walking for an entire day. Also, I'm pretty sure my boots were only made to look good and not to actually walk in. Blisters have begun to form on the top of my toes, and something tells me my feet will not carry me any further. Between my poorly chosen footwear and the pink sweatshirt with the school's Panther mascot I'm still wearing from the senior girl's covert operation, it's safe to say I do not look well suited for a zombie attack.

"We've been walking like forever. Can we just stay here for the night?" I look back to the buildings that have been reduced to mere rubble and add, "or somewhere nearby?"

Cash snorts. "We have only been walking for a couple of hours. How pathetic are you?"

Okay, so maybe it hasn't been all day, but I don't exactly have a watch on me. "Pretty pathetic if you ask me," I answer in a quick recovery. "I've been dumb enough to continue traveling with you, haven't I?" I'm delighted to see the return of my sarcasm and to know it hadn't died with the discovery of my mother's body. She would've been proud.

"Someone's coming," Payton says, holding an arm up in some type of Army-like signal that's lost on us plain-folk citizens. We stop moving all the same, collectively sucking in our breaths with the arrival of an uninfected little group of young teenage boys. Cheese's theory on adults and children sure seems to fit as our adventures continue.

A tall, scrawny kid with a freckled face and bright red tufts of hair steps forward. "Any of you been bit or scratched by an infected person?" His voice is deep and his expression is hard, making him sound wise beyond his years. Despite his slender build I'm pretty sure he won't be anyone I'd personally mess with.

"No," Payton—a.k.a. our new leader—answers him. "We're just passing through, hoping to find a way out of here, man."

Carrot Top lets out a cynical laugh that's surprisingly much higher than his voice. He turns back to address his four friends. "You hear that? They just want to find a way out of here."

His minions—more young boys of different shapes and sizes—laugh in response, although there's an overall hesitation to it, like they aren't sure what is so funny but they know they better do as he says anyway. They all look as if they've been homeless for a number of days and there's an overall skittish look about them making me wonder just how much butchery they had seen. A few of them are even covered in soot.

"Is there a problem with that?" Payton asks, interrupting the awkward moment of insanity.

"Only if you thought you were going to drive your way out of here." The redhead lowers his eyes in a threatening gaze directed at Payton. Apparently the kid either has a lot of guts or is completely nuts to be threatening someone of Payton's size.

"Why would that be a problem?" Finn asks.

Carrot Top motions to Payton. "Why don't you ask your friend that? The Army came through and torched the whole town. We haven't been able to find any working vehicles."

"How did you yahoos manage to survive?" Cash asks the redhead.

"There's an old bomb shelter at one of the neighbor's places," Carrot Top answers, unaffected by Cash's insult. "We'd been hiding out there for a few days from the infected when we heard the planes approaching."

Marley's eyes grow wide at the thought of such an inhumane act by our own military. "They didn't bother checking if there were any normal people left before setting fire to the place?"

"Are you starting to understand why I went AWOL?" Payton asks us. I'm among the few who nod in response to that.

"What's the next town south of here?" Finn asks the new pack.

Carrot Top sneers. "If you go south you won't see another town for thirty miles."

"Geez," I groan. "Iowa really is like going to the ends of the earth."

"You should really come and visit North Dakota some time," Payton tells me from the side of his mouth.

"Why do you want to go south?" Carrot Top asks. He watches us suspiciously. Maybe the arsenal of weapons we're toting has something to do with his unease.

"Warmer weather, pristine beaches," I answer. "You know—civilization."

"We don't think they've been infected yet," Payton tells

him. "Going south is probably our best bet of surviving this thing."

"How far south do we have to go?" I ask, beginning to fear Iowa is never ending.

"From what I understand, anywhere south of Missouri and Kansas," Payton tells me.

Carrot Top laughs again. I'm really starting to despise his high cackle. "Good luck if you think you're going to make it that far by foot."

Payton scans our surroundings. "Have any other suggestions?"

"The next town over would be east of here about five miles down the road," Carrot Top answers.

"Why haven't you left yet?" I ask him. I think it's strange they want to stick around by themselves in a virtual ghost town.

"We've been searching for food," he answers. His eyes shift to the suitcases sitting on the ground behind us. "You have any?"

"Some," Finn says. "If you want to come with us, we may be able to spare some."

Carrot Top turns to his friends and they all nod anxiously back at him. "You're on," he answers, slanting his eyes at Finn. I wonder if I'm the only one to see the redhead's eyes twitch.

Chapter 12

W e continue walking down the road for just over an hour when the next town comes into view. This town is much larger than the last and lacks any signs of Army interference. We pass by a few little discount stores filled with knick-knacky crap and a small, ancient movie theatre that ironically announces an upcoming marathon of horror movies.

"I'm not so sure traveling in a larger pack like this is such a great idea," Payton whispers to Finn as we walk through the center of town.

"What did you want me to do?" Finn whispers back. "We're probably safer in larger numbers, anyway. There are more of us to fight."

Payton turns to glare at him. "A larger group also means fewer supplies for everyone. We cannot afford to give them any of our weapons. We just need to find some wheels and get out of town before the Army comes to visit this place, too."

A few zombies wander aimlessly in the distance ahead of us. With a few well-placed shots, Finn and Payton are able to easily take care of them. Otherwise, the town seems to be completely evacuated. Signs that people had left in a hurry are everywhere, from open doors on houses to the mangled, dead bodies lying just feet from their front door.

"That looks like a car dealership up ahead," Zander says when we're maybe a dozen blocks into town. We strain to see what he's talking about and there are joyous cries at the discovery. Carrot Top and his crew have been quiet for most of the journey, but a couple of them whom I guess to be around thirteen race ahead of us to the car lot. The rest of us catch up to them at our established slower pace.

Cars appear to have been taken off the lot recently, leaving occasional gaps in the rows. There are even skid marks from where one of the cars had tried leaving. But those same tire marks lead to a car parked just a few feet away, where a dead woman is leaning out the driver's side with very little meat left on her bones. I turn away, realizing the sight of dead bodies has become a bit too common for my comfort.

"They took all the really big vehicles," Marley says. She's right—only minivans and family-sized sedans remain. I miss the safety of Linda's larger rig, even though it gave Finn the power to drive like a maniac.

"I'll start looking for the keys," Payton says, pulling his gun off his shoulder and holding it out as he walks to the office. Finn and I trail behind, holding hands. Cash and Marley are right behind us, along with most of our original gang.

"I have a bad feeling about those punks we picked up," Cash says, jogging to catch up with his brother. "You shouldn't have said we'd give them our food."

I roll my eyes. "They're a bunch of kids, Cash. It's not like they're going to beat you up and take your lunch money."

Cash struts ahead, ignoring me. Once inside, Payton quickly locates the rack of keys. But someone took the liberty of pulling all the keys off their hooks and throwing them into a pile on the ground.

"Awesome," I say. "It will be just like one of those lame games they play on the Price Is Right."

Suddenly, the sound of a car engine purring to life comes from outside. We scurry over to the window in time to see the tail end of a minivan fleeing the lot.

"Hey! Where's our stuff?" Zander asks. I look back to the group, finding no one had bothered to grab the suit-cases when coming inside. They're nowhere to be seen outside, either. Apparently Carrot Top and his friends helped themselves to our stash and knew how to hot-wire a car.

Words come from Finn's mouth that I don't dare repeat. His angry outburst starts a chain of emotions and accusations flying. Marley and I merely stand by, watching the boys angrily shouting obscenities at each other.

"Everyone just calm the hell down," Payton commands loudly.

Cash and Cheese have actually become involved in a physical altercation, but they drop their hands from each other's shirts at the sound of Payton's booming voice. "I'm sure we will eventually find more supplies."

Marley's mouth is drawn into a straight line and she's almost visibly shaking. "What if this is it? What if we keep going and only find more abandoned towns and dead corpses? Can't we just wait here until our phones work or someone comes to save us?"

She has a point. I open my mouth to let her know I agree, but close it again. What if she's right? What if we're all that's left of this world? I've begun to fear my father was turned just as my mother was and that I won't see him anytime soon, either. Maybe this is it.

There's an awkward pause among us as everyone digests her questions.

Payton looks around the room at each of us, his eyes squinting into a glare. "Don't you guys get it at this point? No one is coming to save us. Our only shot at surviving is to keep going and hope we find some place that isn't infected. If we stay here we may either be torched like that last town, or killed by a pack of hungry zombies." His words are so brutally honest that we stand in silence, looking at each other nervously. He scoops up a handful of keys and passes them out. "Now let's find the vehicles to some of these and get the hell out of here."

Finn and I trail behind the others to the parking lot. Marley's questions are still lurking in the back of my mind. Finn is walking at a much slower pace and his head is bent down. I stop in front of him. "Do you really think we have a shot at surviving this?" I ask my friend. "Because if not we should just do some kind of Romeo-Juliet thing right now and spare ourselves the torture. I'm all cool with the poison part as long as it doesn't taste too funky."

Finn laughs and places his hands on my face. "Em. No matter what happens, I promise not to let you get eaten or turned or anything miserable. I would die before I let anything bad happen to you."

His touch does the usual magic things to my body and I shiver. "I hope you don't mean that in the literal sense, because if you die then I'm really screwed." The muscles in my face try to create a smile, but my heart isn't behind it.

As he looks down on me, I see the same fears and doubts as my own reflected in his eyes, but also the longing for human connection in all of this. More than anything I wish we were back in my room, playing some killer video game about zombies rather than actually living it. At least in the virtual world I had a chance at actually hitting something with a gun.

But then I wonder—would I realize how much this goober of a friend means to me if none of this had happened? Would we forever be stuck in the buddy routine and continue to torture each other with stories of our dates with other people?

Finn's hold on my face becomes lighter and he suddenly leans into me, our lips just a moment away from touching.

This is it.

The big kiss with my childhood friend.

The same guy who purposely kicked me in the shin when playing kick-the-can because he thought it was funny.

The same guy who tried to get me to pee my pants by tickling me in my funny spot while I was sleeping.

The same guy who pushed me and Carolyn down, so he and Chris would win the three-legged race at the homecoming festivities.

The same guy who threw a dart at me when I was flirting at Heidi Hiller's party—no wait—that was me throwing one at him.

I hold my breath in and start to cross my fingers, hoping the kiss won't totally suck, when Cash yells out, "Quit sucking face and get over here to help, boneheads! We're never going to get out of here at this rate!"

Startled, we pull apart, our eyes wide. My breathing comes back to me in a rush and I step back, feeling a fit of hyperventilation coming on.

Was I seriously about to kiss my best friend? What was I thinking?

Finn shifts his stance and looks around the lot. "He's right…maybe we should go help."

"Okay," I say quickly, grabbing a key from him. We busy ourselves among our friends in trying out different cars in the new vehicle section. I try not to let my mind wander back to the kiss that almost happened.

The process of matching a key to a vehicle seems to take forever. After I'm sure I've tried ten different cars, I hear an engine start nearby. Standing on my tiptoes, I find Jake sitting behind the wheel of a red sports car with a giant grin plastered on his face.

"What good is that going to do when all of four people can barely fit in it?" Marley asks. She stands with one leg inside a crossover vehicle the next row over. Jake presses his foot down on the accelerator, letting the engine rev, and his grin increases sevenfold. A second motor suddenly starts before I find Zander sitting inside a silver minivan, pumping a fist in the air.

"Looks like we have our wheels," Payton says from behind me. I jump in surprise—I hadn't heard him approaching. When I turn to look at him I find something hopeful in his eyes, but I'm still too wigged out by the kiss Finn and I almost shared to think of Payton in the romantic sense. A girl can only have so many stressors.

I turn back and join the rest of my friends beside the minivan. "Great. We can face the end of the world like some kind of soccer mom."

Zander shakes his head at me. "Never underestimate the power of a soccer mom. Have you ever seen one mad? They would go completely loco on anyone who did their kids harm."

"Marley and I are taking the Mustang," Cash announces.

"Who said I'm going with you?" Marley asks Cash. I'd

sensed her beginning to withdraw since our private conversation in the old people's home, but it comes as a surprise that she's dissing him in front of everyone.

"Um, guys, I don't care who rides where, but we should probably get the hell out of here," Zander says. He points past the lot to where a small pack of infected are approaching. They're going at the usual slower-than-slow zombie pace, but no one wants to wait around to see just how long it'll take them to reach us.

"Get in!" Payton commands. We all dog pile into the vehicle, knocking Darrin and Cheese to the ground in the process. I help them get up just as Zander slams the van into drive. Those not yet sitting fall over and slam into the side of the van. Finn pulls me down so I'm sitting in his lap. Everyone else holds on to whatever they can when the vehicle starts fishtailing around in the lot, tires screaming in protest.

"It's a minivan, not a Maserati!" I yell at Zander.

We're out of the parking lot and down the road a ways when Cheese screams in his pubescent voice. "Jake! Jake! We forgot Jake!"

No one had remembered our little friend was still behind the wheel of the Mustang. We whip our heads around to see the zombies are just feet away from the lot. My hand reaches for the door so I can jump out after my neighbor boy, but Zander is already making a huge U-turn.

I lean into the front seat between Zander and Payton. "Hurry the hell up!"

"I'm going as fast as I can!" Zander yells back.

The minivan jumps the curb in front of the dealership and we flail around wildly from the impact. Zander drives straight through the sign on rollers advertising "horrifyingly low prices" most likely in anticipation of the Halloween season approaching. Finn's hold on my waist tightens. Contrary to our failed intimate moment, the thrill from his touch is still present. We close in on the car Jake had started but find the driver's door open and the vehicle empty.

"Over there!" Payton yells. We follow the direction he's pointing to a few cars down where zombies gather. With horror, I discover poor Jake lying on his stomach underneath a little four-door car. Luckily the zombies are apparently too dumb at the moment to remember how to bend down. They stand with their bodies pushed up against the car, reaching out to the sky.

"Stop the car!" Payton screams.

Zander hasn't totally stopped the van when Payton jumps from the vehicle, his gun held out and ready to shoot. Finn dumps me off his lap and runs out behind him. I follow, wanting to do whatever I can to help save my little friend.

"Get back in the car!" Finn yells when he sees I'm behind him.

"Not without Jake!" I yell back.

Payton has begun shooting the zombies, but a large gathering still waits near the car. Some of them have figured out how to crouch down to reach for their next meal ticket. When I see Jake behind the mass of bodies he's holding his hands over his face, crying wildly.

"Hold on, Jake!" I yell. "We're coming!"

Payton runs out of ammunition and begins punching the zombies in the face with the butt of his gun, blood and teeth flying everywhere from the hits. Finn picks up the slack and shoots as many as he can without getting too close to hitting Payton. I see an opportunity to run to Jake when the right side of Finn has been cleared.

"Jake, c'mon!" I yell, offering my hand.

Still hiding behind his hands and crying, he can't see

that I'm close. I try to lean closer to him when a set of cold and spongy hands grab on to my back, pulling me away. A horrific smell climbs into my nose and I scream in my little girl voice, reaching in Finn's direction.

Everything moves in slow motion when Payton and Finn both turn to me. Finn reaches out, yelling my name with eyes too wide for his head. Cold lips press down on my shoulder just before a stinging pain pierces my skin.

I only recall one other time in my life when I feared death was a probability, but that had involved facing my dad after taking a carload of girls for a joyride in his Mercedes when I was thirteen. The memory of my dad's anger flashes through my mind when the excruciating pain sinks in through my veins.

The teeth finally leave my shoulder when the zombie's head meets the end of Payton's gun. Finn yanks me toward him before lowering me down into his arms with exaggerated care.

"Hold something against it!" Payton yells at Finn.

I'm only slightly aware of some kind of movement behind me before something warm and soft presses against my shoulder. I jump, fearing another zombie attack, but find Finn holding his shirt against my bite wound.

A round of gunshots rings through the air. Through blurred vision, I watch as the rest of our friends pile out the vehicle, shooting at anything without a heartbeat.

"Romeo and Juliet," I say to Finn, clenching my teeth through the pain.

He guffaws and shakes his head. "You're not going anywhere. Besides, I never agreed to that Romeo crap, anyway." His voice sounds more like a growl but I'm glad to hear a little bit of my old friend shining through, even if he sounds more like he's trying to convince himself of the fact that I'm not going to die rather than consoling me. His free hand brushes my hair away from my face and those annoying teenage hormones kick into place that were missing when we almost kissed.

I groan. "I can't deal with this whole damsel in distress business. Will you please at least let me turn long enough so I can take care of Cash?" If this is the end, I want to make the best of it.

Finn musters a small chuckle but the pain in my shoulder is sharp. I scream out in agony, imagining a million angry cells from the zombie rummaging through my body and turning me like when Bruce Banner turned into the Hulk. The place where its teeth sunk in burns wildly. My fingers dig into Finn's arm when the pain flares again.

"Holy shit! Is there like skin missing from my shoulder or something?" I ask when the pain has gone down some. So much for wearing anything strapless to prom this year.

Jake is crouched down beside us now, his crying escalated. "Is she gonna die?"

Finn is instantly annoyed by the question and gives him a very scornful look. "She's going to be fine, Jake. Just go wait inside the van."

But the whole crew rushes up to gather in a circle around us. They must have taken care of all the zombies seeing as how quiet it has suddenly become. They look down at me with various degrees of shock.

"Oh my god!" Marley cries. "What happened?" She holds a hand over her mouth.

"You have to shoot her, Finn," says Cash. "She's infected." Marley looks at him, apparently struggling with the choice of whether to agree or to punch him for saying such a thing. But she turns back to me with her eyes unbelieving, not knowing what to do.

"If you even touch her you're dead, I swear to god!"

Finn yells at his brother, spittle flying over me. He continues to hold his shirt against my shoulder but his other arm wraps around my torso and he pulls me closer to him protectively.

"What if she's infected?" Cheese asks in a small voice.

"She's not," Finn insists. "So don't even worry about it."

"I for one love my Emma dearly but I'm not going anywhere with her like this," Zander says. "What if she tries to eat us?"

"I'll take her in the Mustang," Payton says.

"I'll take her," Finn tells him. And the macho-match begins.

"I'm coming with!" Jake cries, not to be outdone.

"Boys, boys," I say to them, "there's still enough of me to go around—or at least I think there is." I laugh maniacally at my own humor. The pain is making me groggy, almost putting me into a drunken state of mind. I welcome the thought of any searing alcohol running down my parched throat at the moment.

"At least your mind still seems to be intact," Finn says to me, a sad little smirk playing on his lips.

Everyone's sappy expressions make me want to hurl. I roll my eyes and try scrambling to my feet, but Finn is still holding me down. I glare up at him. "Seriously, I'm fine."

"You two come with me," Payton tells Finn and Jake. He steps forward to help Finn bring me to my feet. "The rest of you follow us in the van."

The others return to the van without protest. Finn continues pushing the shirt against my shoulder and Payton appears at my other side, pulling my arm around his neck. The four of us make our way to the sports car. I'm lifted into the backseat where I eventually settle my head in Finn's lap. He smiles down warmly at me but can't hide the worry that has settled into his eyes. Jake and Payton take the front seats and turn to give me unsure glances.

I clench my teeth in an encouraging smile. "Relax. I promise to let you know if I begin to crave anything other than chocolate."

* * *

I WAKE to find total blackness all around me. For a minute I wonder if I'm dead or even possibly blind from zombie venom. I realize a hand is on my head and reach up in the darkness to find Finn's stubble-covered face.

"I'm here," he whispers. "How are you feeling?"

My eyes take a minute to focus in the darkness until I can at least see the outline of his head and body. In the front seat, Jake is still sitting with his face aimed in my direction, but his head is pressed to the side of the seat as if he fell asleep watching me.

Night seems to have settled in long ago. Payton is still behind the wheel. The lights from the car reveal nothing but the highway ahead of us. A very small ray of light shines on the roof of the Mustang, suggesting the van has fallen far behind. I'm guessing they want to keep their distance in case I go crazy and try to eat everyone.

"I'm thirsty," I say, licking my dry lips. Finn's eyes dart to me so I add, "For water. Or milk. Anything non-bloody." I'm also kind of cold and still a bit hungry, but I don't want anyone to panic with those revelations so I keep them to myself.

Now that all of our supplies we know to be safe are gone, I wonder if we will ever have anything to eat or drink again. Maybe this really is it for us—the beginning of the end. We'll all just wither away to nothing. At least I'll finally shed those annoying extra pounds that kept me from wearing a bikini this summer.

"Hopefully we'll find you some water soon," Finn says, brushing my hair away from my face.

"So do I at least look normal still?" I ask. "Because other than this really intense pain shooting through my arm, I feel relatively normal."

Finn groans. "Everyone seems to think you're going to turn into one of those things based on a bunch of crappy horror movies they've seen. You're going to be okay, Em. I know it."

"I saw it happen," Payton says, interjecting into our conversation without being asked to give his thoughts on the matter. "A guy in my squad was bit and he turned right away. We had to shoot him a few minutes after it happened."

An overwhelming dread takes over me with his words. I have ambitions in life, like going to college and becoming a lifelong student so I can put reality off as long as possible. But certainly college won't be an option if I can no longer speak the English language and only want to eat my classmates. "Sweet," I answer.

Finn tries to meet Payton's eyes in the rearview mirror. "No one was speaking to you, so you can just keep your opinions to yourself."

"It's not an opinion. It's a fact. It's just a matter of time before your girlfriend tries to take a big bite out of you. You might want to make sure your gun is fully loaded."

I push on Finn's face so he has to look at me again. "He's right, Finn. You seriously can't keep me alive if I'm going to try to eat you. It would just be like toting around some kind of really annoying pet."

Finn's whole body moves when he shakes his head in anger. "You said that guy turned a few minutes after it happened. Well guess what? She was bit hours ago. That blows your theory to shreds."

"True," Payton answers. "But maybe because she was only bit in one place the virus takes a little longer to spread. The guy I saw was bit all over."

I snort. "At least you're staying optimistic."

"Ignore him," Finn tells me. "I promised you everything will be okay and I meant it. We're going to find a way out of this mess and we'll be laughing about all of this one day."

"I'm already laughing," I say,

"Just keep telling yourself that, Finn," Payton grumbles over his shoulder. "It's not going to change anything."

Finn helps me when I pull myself up to a sitting position. My shoulder still burns, feeling like the worst sunburn of a lifetime. I pull Finn's Darth Vader shirt off my shoulder to see there is in fact a big gouge of flesh missing and an angry mess left in its place. The wound is just nasty enough for me to become a little light-headed.

"Agh! That bastard took a lot of me with him," I say angrily.

Finn presses the shirt back down, knowing I don't deal well with blood and guts that aren't the product of some gore-filled movie. "We really need to clean it out at some point."

"What's going on up there?" I ask, pointing to a cluster of lights up ahead on the road.

Payton turns the headlights off and slows way down until we're at a standstill. The van lights behind us suddenly turn off, too. In the distance, a line of vehicle lights stretches across the road and even into the ditches, their lights shining on us.

"They've created a barrier to keep us in the infected area," Payton tells us.

"You mean they as in the Army or they as in the southerners who know we've all been infected and don't want to catch anything?" I ask nervously. Neither one sounds like a thrilling option and could possibly end in a lot of guns being shot.

Payton puts the car in park and opens his door. "I think those are Army trucks. I'm going to check it out. You guys wait here."

The slamming of his door wakes Jake from his drooling slumber. My little buddy sits up in his seat with a quick jerk. "I'm up!" He turns back to look at me. "Emma, are you okay?"

"I'm great," I tell him brightly. "I haven't tried to eat anyone yet."

"Knock it off," Finn says sharply.

I giggle at his sour mood. "Finn, face it. This is the end of the line for me. It's either going to happen or it isn't, and I think the odds are really not in my favor right now. Would it make you feel better if I started bawling like a girl?" He still refuses to smile so I lean into him and wrap my arms around his chest. "There. How's that?"

His chest rises as he breathes in deeply for a moment, then exhales. He wraps his arms around me and rests his head against mine. I decide I'm good to go with him holding me like this. Maybe it wouldn't be so bad if he really had to shoot me about now, either.

"What's with all the cars?" Jake asks, spotting the headlights in the distance.

"Payton went to check it out," says Finn. I love the rumbling his chest makes against my ear when he speaks, but the pleasantries are interrupted by the coldness spreading through me like small trickles of ice. It reminds me of the time Finn and I went swimming at my grandparents' lake cabin in early March. The freezing water had stung against our skin like a million needles.

"Are you guys like super cold right now?" I ask. "Or is that just another fun side effect of being bit?" My body shivers involuntarily and Finn holds me tighter.

Jake's door suddenly flings open and flashlights dart through the car. Loud voices bark something to each other about contamination and a set of hands pulls Jake from the car. Jake starts to scream in his very girly pitch and I reach out for him, but Finn holds me back to take his shirt off my shoulder. He yanks on the other side of my totally ruined Foo Fighters T-shirt to make sure my wound is covered and pulls my sweatshirt up higher for good measure.

"Don't let them see your bite," he whispers urgently into my ear.

The front seat where Jake had been sitting is pushed down, and seconds later the next set of hands is coming for me.

Chapter 13

Our whole group is forced at gun point to climb into the back of a really large Army truck, like the kind you always see in those boring black-and-white war movies. Four soldiers continue to bark directions at us as we're herded in like a bunch of cattle. Finn sticks close to my side and holds my hand super tightly, like they won't be able to physically separate us if he holds tight enough. My hand starts to fall asleep but I don't dare tell him to let go.

Marley cries loudly once we're all sitting, and poor Jake appears to be reverting back to his childhood. He sits with his arms clutched around my sides like I'm his mommy. All at once the vehicle lurches forward. Our group is silenced by the fear of what is going to happen to us.

"Where are you taking us?" Payton asks the two young soldiers who jumped in behind our group and now sit on the bench directly across from us.

A dim light shining down from the top of the truck's canopy shows the soldiers to be dressed in full uniform, complete with a hard helmet and some kind of machine guns held up against their legs. The skinnier of the two has the name "Murphy" on his uniform and his big blue eyes are fixated on Marley as she cries, like he's realizing that we're not infected and that we're just a bunch of kids. The taller, beefier soldier is named "Hernandez" and has a short, squat face that reminds me of a bullfrog. He lifts his face to meet Payton's gaze, but looks back without any emotion on his face other than what seems to be a permanent scowl.

Cheese continues to test his theory. "How old are you soldiers? Eighteen? Nineteen?"

The skinnier guy, Murphy, turns to look at Cheese. "Eighteen," he answers, his voice high and unsure. Hernandez nudges him roughly in the rib cage.

"Have you guys seen any infected kids?" Cheese asks him. Murphy subtly shakes his head to confirm the negative. "Exactly! We haven't either. I think all of this might have something to do with adults only."

"Do any of us look infected to you?" Payton asks them. "Cause we're not. What do you think they're going to do with us when we get to your base? I went AWOL a couple of days ago when I discovered the big plan is to wipe everyone out just for living in this area. Are you really going to be able to live with yourselves knowing you helped to murder a truckful of young kids? Look at these guys. Most of them haven't even hit puberty yet."

Cheese raises his hand with trepidation. "Um…actually I have…"

"My point is," Payton says to the soldiers while giving Cheese a scolding glance, "I know this isn't why you wanted to join the Army. The people in this truck are the very ones you signed up to protect. They're one of us, guys. In a few years these guys could be signing up to be a soldier, just like you. They're no different than your little brother or your little cousin that you threw a football around with at the family picnics."

The two armed men turn to look at each other. I know by his apologetic looks that the skinnier one named Murphy has given in long ago, but Hernandez continues to give Payton a hard, skeptical gaze.

"Man, you gotta let us out of here before it's too late," Payton tells him gravely.

Hernandez moves his lip up slightly. I give him my best "I'm a sweet, innocent teenager" look by holding my eyes wide and batting my eyelashes furiously. Hopefully the rest of the gang is doing the same.

Murphy whispers something into Hernandez's ear and the big guy nods once before wrapping his hand around a radio attached to his chest. "Stop the vehicle, over," he says into it.

Another male voice crackles out of the radio. "Say again? Over."

"Stop the vehicle," Hernandez repeats, his eyes still locked with Payton's. "Over."

"Reading you five by five," the voice answers.

"Dear God, he's going to shoot us all right now," I whisper to Finn.

"Follow my lead," Hernandez says gruffly to Payton as the vehicle comes to a stop.

I turn to Finn with excitement and he squeezes my hand in response. Unfortunately, I've turned so my oozing wound can be seen by Murphy. "Hey—what's that?" he asks, standing and pointing at my shoulder.

He reaches down for his gun with delayed speed and doesn't have time to react when his jaw meets Payton's fist. Payton then turns to grab Hernandez's weapon and knock him out with the butt of it in one swift movement. Their bodies lay crumpled on top of each other on the truck's floor.

"Remind me not to piss you off any time soon," I say to Payton.

Finn drops my hand to grab the other gun. We turn to the back and find the other two soldiers standing with their weapons aimed at us.

"Okay everyone, just take it easy," Payton tells them, pointing his own gun back at them. "I just knocked these guys out. No one was seriously hurt. We needed to get out of here before you took us to our slaughter."

"Lower your weapon, soldier," the female soldier tells Payton.

"You lower yours, ma'am," Cheese says from behind her. He holds the gun from Linda's supply to the woman's head. In all the commotion, I hadn't seen him jump from the vehicle. The soldiers probably didn't think of frisking the younger kids for weapons when they first captured us. If anyone from the group would later say they weren't surprised to see Cheese had pulled a gun on the solider, they would totally be lying out of their butt. My money would not have been on the scrawny teen awkwardly approaching his manhood to save us from the situation.

The other solider lowers his gun obediently and puts his hands up before the woman does the same. Cheese has a triumphant, million dollar smile on his face that could light up the world—especially with the blinding flash of metal his braces make.

Payton jumps out the truck and pats Cheese on the back like the good boy he is, then motions for the soldiers to climb in with the rest of us. They sit on the bench across from us with their shoulders slumped and their heads low. I'm guessing they're feeling inadequate for letting a bunch of kids take them over.

"You're not infected," Marley says happily to me. She has finally quit crying, but her eyes are swollen and red.

"Not yet," Cash corrects her.

"Why don't you come over here and see if I'm contagious?" I tell him.

Cash smiles mockingly. "I know you've always wanted to make out with me, Emma. You don't have to fight it anymore."

My snappy comeback is interrupted by the two soldiers stirring at our feet. Finn and Payton continue to point their guns at the four soldiers.

"Drive us out of here, Zander," Payton says. "Keep heading south."

Zander scrunches his face. "Um, why me?"

"I'm guessing it's because of those mad van skills you showed us earlier," I say.

Payton motions at our prisoners with his gun while looking at Zander. "Would you rather stay back here and keep these guys in line?"

Zander nods once. "Good point." He jumps out the back end with his brother trailing behind him. Within a minute the truck jets forward once again. We bounce back and forth when Zander puts his foot down a little too hard on the accelerator. The two soldiers on the floor grumble and rub their heads as they sit up.

The petite female soldier has very feminine features and silky blond hair sticking out from her helmet. She would probably look better fitted in a cheerleader's uniform than in the Army gear that does nothing flattering to her slender figure.

She watches me, her bright blue eyes intent. "How long ago were you bit?"

"I don't know that I would say I was bit. More like

chewed on," I answer, pulling my shirt down to show her the nasty wound.

The soldier leans away with a brutally honest face and the others make a few eeeew noises. Apparently the wound is even more disgusting than I originally thought.

"She was bit more than a couple of hours ago," Finn tells the woman. "She isn't going to turn."

I pat Finn's hand in appreciation, even though it sounds like he's in serious denial over the whole situation. They'll probably have to shoot me eventually—I just hope someone other than Cash is the one who gets the honors.

"She isn't showing any signs," the female soldier marvels, settling her eyes on mine. "Maybe you're right. Maybe she isn't going to turn."

Either Hernandez is scowling at me, or his face is always naturally scrunched up that way. "We heard a theory about this virus with kids."

"I told you!" Cheese says, his voice cracking into another octave with his excitement. "They think kids are immune to this disease, right?"

The female soldier looks to our enthusiastic friend. "They think it has something to do with the brain not being fully developed until later, in your early twenties."

"They really said that?" Cheese asks. She nods and he does a series of air pumps with his fist. From the look in his eyes he's fantasizing about growing up to be some kind of nuclear scientist now that his theory is proving true.

I sit forward with Cheese's excitement rubbing off on me. "If we're talking about fully developed brains here, then Cash will never have to worry about catching this. We could donate him for the scientists to study." Cash is glowering at me when I say this, but I don't care. I'm only looking out for the welfare of our country.

"We may not be able to contract the virus, but they can still try to kill us other ways," Finn says to the woman.

"Yeah, like mistaking us for some kind of happy meal," I say, pointing to my shoulder.

"Do you know a way we can get out of here?" Payton asks the soldiers.

"You'll never get past the barrier they've set," Murphy answers. His eyes dart nervously over at Payton as he speaks, wondering if he's going to try to punch him out again.

Finn sits forward on the bench when an idea forms. "Do you have access to communications with the feds?"

Hernandez grunts. "They have a few feds camped out on our base."

"You need to get me on that base," Finn tells him.

* * *

I'M NOT VERY KEYED up about the plan as Payton and Finn disappear into the darkness with two of the soldiers who are now supposedly on our side. I'm left with a group of boys, Marley, the female soldier and the soldier named Murphy who seemed eager to shoot me upon first discovering my zombie-created wound. I'm growing really tired of people wanting me dead.

Murphy had switched clothing with Finn. My friend had looked majorly hot in the tight uniform, but Murphy looks funny wearing Finn's sweatshirt that hangs off his thin frame and the jeans that are a tad too long. I'm annoyed that those clothes will now probably forever smell off. Thankfully, he stands outside of the truck to keep watch for any signs of danger so I don't have to dwell on it.

Jake and I sit together on one side of the bench inside the truck, but the rest of my "friends" are squished to the opposite end, still insistent on keeping their distance from me. The female soldier is sitting on the bench straight across from us and won't stop staring.

"What?" I finally say to her with my hands thrown out to the sides. "Is there something on my face?"

She shakes her head and grins. "Sorry. I'm just amazed you aren't showing any signs of turning. Do you want me to patch that bite up for you? I would hate to see what happens if something like that gets infected." She laughs but I don't see the humor in it.

I narrow my eyes. "Aren't you scared of getting my zombie germs on you?"

She shrugs. "I'll wear gloves from the kit."

"Well in that case, knock yourself out."

The soldier pulls a first aid kit down from the side of the truck and approaches me cautiously. I move my blond curls to the other side of my head and lean over for her to get a good look. She's making these disgusted faces as she assesses the wound.

"You have an awesome bedside manner, there…" I say, looking at the label on her uniform and adding, "Soldier Schulz."

She shakes her head and flashes an easy-going smile. I picture her outside of the Army as being a lot of fun and able to get along with pretty much anyone. "It's Sarah. And I wasn't exactly trained to be a medic."

"Okay, Sarah, where is it you hail from? You know— before the whole walking dead apocalypse and the Army?"

"Wisconsin. I grew up near La Crosse." She squeezes some kind of ointment onto my wound and I tense up. But rather than stinging my shoulder even more it cools and soothes my shoulder. I let out a satisfied little sigh.

"We're from Minnesota, just a few hours down the interstate from there," Cheese tells her.

I glare over at him with an unspoken threat of injury. If they don't want to sit close to me then they aren't welcome to join in my conversations, either. He lowers his head like a scolded puppy. I turn back to Sarah. "How old are you, anyway?"

"Twenty-three. I joined the Army after getting married and having a baby."

I suck air in through my teeth. "Family life was that great, huh?"

She giggles. "It's not that. I actually love being a mom and a wife. But I also love my country. It was something I felt I needed to do. My whole family was in the service."

"I'm going to be in the Army one day," Jake says from beside me. With one glance I can see Jake is falling for this soldier. Jealousy consumes me—all it took was one little zombie bite and now I'm thrown off to the side like a used Kleenex, no longer his object of affection.

"If there even is such a thing as one day," Sarah grumbles.

I give her a scolding look and cover Jake's ears with my hands. "We're trying to stay positive through all of this, Sarah. You can say big words like apocalypse and infection, but don't crush this little guy's dreams of the future with your crazy talk."

"I'm twelve," Jake says, pulling my hands away from his ears. "I know what all of that stuff means."

I shrug at Sarah. "Still...are you saying that's the overall opinion of the Army right now? Are they thinking this virus is going to go worldwide and we can just forget life as we know it?"

Sarah settles her eyes on mine. "Right now they're just

trying to contain the virus before something like that happens."

"Contain as in murder anyone who has been exposed," Cheese clarifies.

I glance over to the remainder of the group, huddled in their small space. Cash's head is lobbed to one side and he's snoring with his mouth wide open. Marley has her arms wrapped around her body and is using Zander's shoulder as a pillow while his other shoulder is occupied by his sleeping younger brother. Cheese has made his way closer to where Jake and I sit. Our group is definitely an odd bunch, but I still can't help but worry what will happen to everyone—it would really suck if any of them died after all we had been through together.

"What else are they saying about this virus?" I ask. "Other than the whole kids-being-immune-to-it thing? Do they know how it started?"

Sarah leans closer to me and uses a lower voice. "I really can't tell you that."

I frown up at her and use an equally low voice. "Why not? Because you'd have to shoot me? Correct me if I'm wrong, but aren't you already in trouble for agreeing to help us? No offense, Sarah, but if you're looking to protect the Army instead of the civilians at this point, your priorities are majorly messed up."

She sighs deeply and glances out the back where the other soldier is guarding the back of the truck. "Yeah, I guess you're right. I can't say I agree with how they're handling all of this. If my husband and son hadn't already made it safely out of the infected area, I probably would be AWOL right now, just like your friend."

"So how did all of this start?" Cheese asks.

Sarah lets out a huff of air. "Two theories are floating around out there, both involving a fast-spreading virus.

The feds think it's an alien thing and everyone else thinks it's the work of terrorists."

Jake is trembling beside me. I can't decide whether or not I should comfort him. At the moment I think I'm the one who could use some comforting.

"Whoa," Cheese says.

I chew on my lip. "Wait—aren't aliens supposed to be sweet little wrinkly guys that like to eat peanut butter candies and hang out in your closet?"

Sarah shakes her head. "The feds seem to think they're more of the violent variety."

"We're talking real aliens?" Cheese asks her, the excited light behind his eyes blazing up again. "Like they have actual proof of this?"

"I don't know any of the details, but that's the word we got from another unit a couple days back. It's not like the Army actually plans to tell us what exactly is going on." She finishes placing pieces of tape over the gauze. "You should be good for now. Sometime tomorrow you need to put clean dressing on it."

"Hey, I thought you were going to wear gloves," Cheese says suddenly, pointing at her hands.

I turn to him but he gives me an annoyed "go away" look before I can say anything. Sarah looks down at her hands then wipes them off on her pants. I can see a flash of total panic in her eyes.

"I'm sure you'll be fine," I say to her. "You're still in your early twenties, right? If what they're saying is right, you probably have a couple of years before you turn into one of those drooling geeks."

But Sarah's crystal blue eyes meet mine and she silently begs for my help. Her eyes take their time in looking back down to her hands, as if she's moving through a really bad dream. She holds her middle finger out to show me a small gash on its tip.

We look at each other, both too terrified to say what it means.

"Hey, Zander?" I call out casually. "Do you have your gun loaded?"

"Yeah, why?" Zander asks.

"You may just want to have it ready to go," I say, hoping he hears the underlying urgency to my voice. "You know, just in case someone in this truck decides to turn quite unexpectedly."

Zander scurries to stand, his brother and Marley groaning when he interrupts their slumber and they tip into each other.

All eyes fall on Sarah.

The truck is silent.

After a few moments pass, she moves her head up. Her eyes are already becoming unfocused and vacant, reminding me of the woman in the lodge just seconds before Payton had shot her.

Zander aims his gun at Sarah with trembling hands.

Murphy pokes his head in through the back of the truck. "What's going on?" When he realizes Zander's gun is aimed at Sarah, the color literally drains from his face.

I look to him with the goal of answering, but the sadness I feel for my new comrade and her little family is too overwhelming. I don't know how to tell Murphy what is happening. Sarah stands with her mouth hanging open and groans quietly.

Zander lowers his gun and looks to Murphy. "She's been infected."

Chapter 14

Everyone but Sarah is standing outside the truck when the sun begins to rise. The sky becomes filled with the most awe-inspiring shades of pink and blue I've ever witnessed—although I'm pretty much never up this early, so I haven't seen a whole lot of sunrises to compare it to.

Now that we're able to see our surroundings, we find ourselves on a hill overlooking a bunch of cornfields. The barricade we had escaped from isn't far away and there are still soldiers milling about, protecting the border. No towns or rural homes are visible as far as the eye can see, making it totally feel like we're stranded in the middle of nowhere.

Most of the crew looks beyond tired. A few even have dark circles under their eyes. Keeping the overall morale up is going to be difficult when everyone seems to be more interested in taking a long nap than running.

As I'm pondering how any of this could possibly have a happily-ever-after ending, Payton and Finn return in a dark green military jeep with the other two soldiers. Finn gives me an extra bright smile when he hops out of the vehicle, making me flattered that he still worries about my turning into a ravenous monster. I'm something way beyond flattered, however, when he puts his arms around my waist and pulls me to him for a tight embrace. My stomach begins doing somersaults and handstands.

He pulls away from me to assess the group. "Everyone okay?"

He follows my gaze to the truck and discovers that no, everyone is not okay. Sarah is sitting behind the wheel of the truck, banging on the windows. Her face has taken on the telltale pale color and her pupils are glazed over with white. The skin on her cheeks and forehead has begun to disintegrate and her mouth hangs open.

"What the hell happened?" Payton asks, pulling a small black gun from his hip.

"She was just so nice," I say, my voice cracking up with sadness. "Plus she has a husband and baby. None of us had the heart to shoot her."

Cash snorts loudly. "No one bothered asking me. I would've done it."

I have visions of shooting Cash—it wouldn't have to be a fatal shot or anything, just enough to make him shut up. Maybe I could aim at one of his toes or something. "You better hope I don't figure out how to use one of the guns," I tell him.

Finn gently grabs hold of my arm.

Payton gives an impatient roll of his eyes. "How in the hell did she become infected?"

"She cleaned Emma's bite but forgot to wear gloves," Cheese explains to him, glaring at me like all of this is my fault.

Finn sighs and rubs his forehead. "Well we can't just leave her like that."

"What if they come up with some kind of cure?" Marley asks. "We don't have to shoot her yet, do we?"

Apparently I'm not the only one concerned with shooting someone we had just been hanging out with—especially someone who had been so kind to us and seemed so...normal.

Payton sighs deeply before walking toward the truck. "I'll take care of it."

"No!" I yell, leaping out to pull on his arm. But he doesn't stop and only drags me along when I refuse to let go. "You can't just shoot her like she's some kind of animal! She can stay in there for a while longer! She's not hurting anyone!"

Sarah had been my friend for only a very short while, but she only turned because she was nice enough to help me. The thought of her family finding out she's dead makes me cry out. "Please don't!" I beg. "I never should've let her touch me!"

I'm beginning to think that maybe it really is my fault. Maybe I should've refused to let her touch me, just to be on the safe side. We were so busy talking that she had forgotten to put gloves on.

Finn's suddenly behind me, prying my grip from Payton. He spins me around and holds me close when the two gunshots ring through the air. I push my face into Finn's handsomely uniformed chest and he rubs his fingers through my hair. "We will get through this, Em."

Hopefully he knows something I don't, because at the moment we seem destined to live a horribly doomed existence—one in which our best option is to be shot by one of our friends out of mercy.

* * *

FINN BEGINS LAYING out the new plan, which doesn't sound any better than the last. And for the record, their last plan ended very badly with the death of my new friend. As Payton joins in to explain the details of this master idea, there's not a single enthusiastic face among us.

With patience not being a virtue I've ever possessed, I'm the first to speak up. "So what you're saying is that you want us to march up to this Army camp where we will most likely be slaughtered and just turn ourselves in? Does anyone else think this is a horribly crappy idea?"

Cheese raises his hand timidly while looking around to see if anyone else does. Ever so slowly, Jake and Zander raise theirs as well, nodding.

Marley is scowling at Finn and Payton just as much as I am. "What about Emma's bite? They will surely kill her if they see it."

I hold my hand out at Marley. "Yeah, she's got a point. I'm thinking they're more the 'shoot first ask questions later' type of people, based on what we've seen." I cross my arms in front of me and turn to the two masterminds behind this terrible plan. "Either of you think it's a particularly bad idea yet?"

"We're not all going to turn ourselves in. You're going to stay with me," Finn says, wrapping his arm tighter around me. He then turns to his brother. "I think Mom is on the base."

I look up at him. "Why would she be down here?"

I picture her being held captive and imagine he's worried she'll be part of the slaughter. Everyone knows that with her mental status, she wouldn't be capable of defending herself.

Cash frowns. "Did you see her?"

"No, but Payton heard some talk of a female agent nearby," Finn answers. "Apparently they're keeping the federal camp separate from the Army camp. We weren't able to find the headquarters for the feds."

Cash begins pacing. "None of this makes any sense. Why would she be down here? Do you think it's possible she just left us?"

"I don't know," Finn answers, "but we need some kind of big diversion that will catch her attention, and it would be best if we did it as a group."

Marley is still not convinced, along with pretty much everyone else. "And this is the best you could come up with?"

"Do you have any other ideas?" Payton asks with a scowl.

* * *

WAITING until dark would've been a better idea, but no one has the energy or patience to wait that long. We're all anxious to get the heck out of the area, hopefully to some other place in this country where we can relax and enjoy a good laugh about the time ravenous dead people tried to eat us.

From where Finn, Jake, Cheese, and I perch behind a large boulder on a hill overlooking the base, we can see uniformed soldiers crawling about, but not a single civilian is in sight. A few darkly camouflaged tents are scattered about that can serve no purpose other than to provide a meeting place for the Army guys to look all official when they make their plans.

"Maybe they're locking a bunch of people up some-where," Cheese whispers. "You know, like some prisoners of war camp or something."

Finn nudges me in the side gently and points to the camp's entrance. "Here we go," he whispers.

We watch with anticipation as the truck with our friends inside rolls up to the gate. They stop for a brief exchange with the guards standing watch before continuing slowly into the camp. Finn motions for us to follow him around the boulder and through the thick woods at the base of the hill.

I'm still no more athletic than when this all began, and I struggle to keep up with the other three as they dart through brush and around tree trunks. The hard ground is uneven and filled with large rocks that catch my boots. By now I'm grateful that the whole hiking story was a lie Finn told to keep me calm—this is as close to nature as I ever hope to be ever again.

"Seriously," I say, stopping to hold my side when the excruciating pain starts. "I'm really not into this whole running through nature thing. Can we just stop to take a time-out or something?"

Finn stops to peer back at me, torn between being sympathetic and wanting to kick my ass for being so disagreeable. All at once, Jake and Cheese call out to us loudly from far ahead. Finn sprints in their direction, telling them to quiet down. We're safely hidden from the camp but it still isn't very far away.

"There's a really big building back here," Cheese says when we catch up to them.

The brick structure he speaks of looms high in the sky, casting a large shadow at us. Bricks have crumbled down to the ground from lack of maintenance, making it appear quite old. The area around it is massively overgrown with the kind of weeds that would really get under my dad's skin.

Finn frowns at the boys. "This is what you were yelling

about? It doesn't look like anyone has been inside that place in years."

"What if there are people being held in there?" Cheese asks. "You know…people they think are infected but really aren't, like Emma."

"There would be people guarding it if that were true," Finn answers. We look back to survey the still building and find he's right—there aren't any soldiers standing watch that we can see. An unprotected building can't be holding anything too special.

Cheese shrugs. "It can't hurt to just check it out. We have twenty minutes before we have to meet up with those guys again, right?"

Finn glances down at his watch before rolling his head and leading us down the muddy slope in that direction. As we near the building, it reveals itself to us as being an ancient elementary school. The dark bricks that have fallen off over time make large piles on the ground all around the building. Nearly all of the windows are knocked out and have shards of broken glass remaining on them. There are a few tags spray-painted on the crumbling building, but even those are old—declaring the "class of '93" to have once ruled.

A small playground is missing the actual swings on its chains and a teeter-totter has seen its last lean with half of the wooden seat broken off. The metal sign that had once proudly displayed the school's name is rusted out in various places, showing only the letters "mentry scho" as it swings back and forth in the light wind. The building itself is nothing short of super sinister—I fear if I watch it for long I'll see it breathing, maybe even watching us back.

We approach the front entrance to find the doors have been paddle locked with a thick chain running through the handles. Finn leads us to the back where we discover two more sets of doors chained shut.

"What could be so important in here that they've it locked up like that?" I ask.

"They're probably just trying to keep trespassers away," Finn tells me. "I see no other way in. We may as well head back."

Cheese picks up a large rock that was once used for landscaping purposes and lobs it through an already somewhat busted up window. We all cringe at the loud noise the breaking glass makes, but Cheese scurries over to the window and climbs through. Finn does his angry mumbling thing again and we follow Cheese anyway. Finn makes me climb in first and Cheese reaches up to help me down so I land safely away from the glass.

"What was that? Who are you?" I ask Cheese.

He has already taken a soldier by gunpoint and now is becoming this heroic leader. Maybe I shouldn't have been so harsh to judge him right away by his total geekery. But then again, my judgment stands firm when he grins crookedly back at me, flashing metal.

"The way things are going there might not be a tomorrow, right? I figure from now on, I'm not going to take any moment for granted. I no longer go by other people's rules."

I pat his shoulder. "Let me know how that goes for ya."

Finn lands beside me in the glass and we both reach over to help Jake through. "I got it!" he yells, arching his body away from my touch. His Jekyll and Hyde act is making my head spin. I probably should make a better effort not to baby him around the others, even if he's barely old enough to read and write.

The classroom we stand in has what seems to be an entire foot of dirt that has settled over the desks, and even across the cracked chalkboard. Various animal carcasses are scattered about that look to have died years ago from natural causes rather than as a snack of our undead friends. The smell of something very raunchy hangs in the air.

As we file into the hallway my hair gets tangled up in a cobweb, causing me to shriek and wave my arms around wildly. I hate the sticky sensation of those damn things clinging to your skin—it's like a living thing is attacking you. Plus you never know when you'll find some giant, freaky spider wrapped in one of them.

Jake covers his ears and Cheese pokes both fingers in his. They both have this look of annoyance mixed with surprise as they watch me squirm and squeal, trying to get it off of me.

"Geez, Em," Finn grumbles, trying to brush the webs off. "You didn't scream nearly that loudly when that chunk was taken out of your shoulder."

I try to compose myself and wipe the sticky mess onto the door frame. "You know I hate this creepy-crawly crap. It's not my fault."

"Guys, shut up," Cheese says to us. Eyes are turned to the side, he holds his arm out while looking down the equally dirty hallway. "Does anyone else hear that noise?"

I'm still freaking out since the cobwebs won't separate from my hand. Finn elbows me sharply in the side and puts a finger to his lips. I grunt softly, but strain to hear whatever Cheese is all excited about.

Jake's eyes pop open as widely as they can possibly go when he turns back to the rest of us. "There are infected here!"

Then I finally hear it. A low chorus of moans floats through the air, sounding like it's comprised of dozens of difference voices. My skin instantly turns prickly cold and I take a side step so I'm positioned as close to Finn as I can get. His reflex to put his arm around me only does a little bit to take off the terrified edge.

"This has been a load of fun, but what do you say we get out of here?" I plead with them.

Finn lifts his gun and nervously glances down the hallway. "The doors were all locked from the outside. How would they have gotten in?"

I shrug dramatically. My patience is spent. "Maybe they had a key."

Cheese looks from the end of the hallway back to us, his juvenile curiosity peaked. "Let's go check it out."

I shake my head furiously. "I vote we don't. We've managed to go a long time without seeing any more and I, for one, would really not like to relive the whole being bit experience. It definitely is not on my top list of things to repeat."

Finn rubs my arm and a flurry of goose bumps pop up because of it. "Fine, then you can wait here while the rest of us check it out."

I mumble lots of bad words and let him lead me down the hallway with the other two. As we near the entrance to what appears to be a gymnasium, it becomes clear we're about to witness something more than a couple of zombies hanging out. The moaning noises equal the level of a rock concert and the smell of what I guess to be rotting flesh is overwhelming to the point my eyes begin to water.

"Something tells me we're about to make a mistake of epic proportions," I say to the guys as Finn begins pushing on the doors.

I cover my nose and mouth when the strong smell wafts in our direction. Jake turns to look at me and from his big eyes I can guess he's just as freaked out as I feel. Cheese glances back with the same nervous energy. The metal doors squeak slightly in protest as they're pushed to the side just enough to reveal our newest nightmare.

A sea of zombies shuffles about mindlessly on the old gymnasium floor, occasionally bumping into each other and then changing their course of direction. There must be hundreds of them. For the slightest of moments I almost forget how dangerous they can be because they show no violence toward each other. But then I see two collide into each other and one bites the other right on his face, reminding me they're not a bunch of puppy dogs, either.

A few armed men stand close together on bleachers across the way from us, overlooking the zombies with mild boredom as their faces are blank and their posture is stiff. They aren't clad in the usual Army uniforms we've seen all day, but they're definitely in some kind of official military group. Their uniforms are black with matching black berets worn on their heads.

For the massive amount of flesh-eating monsters below, it's unsettling to see very few men keeping watch over them. The zombies could easily overtake them, although they're up high and from what we've seen the infected won't figure out how to climb steps any time in the near future.

"Why would they just lock them up in here?" Jake asks in a whisper.

"Better yet, why haven't they just torched the place by now?" Cheese says in response.

Once I get past the horror of the mutilated human bodies and the totally sickening smell of their rotting flesh, I realize there still aren't any children present. The theory of kids not being able to become infected really seems to be holding true and for the very first time in my life I'm thrilled to be a minor.

A door underneath the armed men opens. Finn pulls the door in front of us shut just a little more and the four of us line up enough so we can each see through the crack. We watch as a new line of armed men enters on the gymnasium floor, each of them holding out large sticks with a flashing blue volt on the end that I guess would electrocute any zombie who gets close to them. The man on the end of the line holds a different kind of stick, one that looks more like something a dog catcher would have with a large loop on the end. The man hooks the loop around the neck of a small female zombie with a big chunk of her brain exposed and only a small handful of blood-soaked hair remaining on her head. She flails her arms around in the air in protest as she's pulled toward him. The armed men move together in perfect synchronicity, disappearing back through the doors while the netted zombie twists around in protest behind them.

"What in the hell was that?" I ask, although I know none of the three guys will have any kind of answer that will hold water. "Some kind of game they have going now to see who can catch the most disgusting zombie?"

Finn turns to me and is about to say something in response, but his eyes suddenly grow wide when looking beyond me. I turn around to find a group of large, similarly uniformed men pointing guns at us.

* * *

FINN TRIES REACHING out for me again, but the metal bars hold us too far apart. My friend is angered by this and kicks the bars repeatedly, cursing loudly. I'm sure all he's accomplishing is bringing severe pain to his foot, but it seems to be another one of those guy things for which there's no logical explanation.

We're in the dimly lit basement of the school. The dank smell of the air comes as a relief after the horrific stench of the gymnasium. The men made us walk down here at gunpoint. Finn held on to me until they forced us apart and threw us in these individual cells. Against my better judgment, I'd shown the men my bite and warned them I would lick them if they touched me again, but my threat didn't seem to faze them—I don't even know that they really even heard me. Not one of my proudest moments, but I'm desperate to not be locked into a cage like some kind of animal.

Cheese and Jake are locked into two cells off to my right. Jake is curled into the far corner of his cell with his hands wrapped around his knees. I'd been able to talk him down until he quit crying and now he's finally sleeping from exhaustion. Cheese gives me this helpless, lost little boy look that I haven't seen him make up until now. I think it's safe to say that collectively, as a group, we're all beginning to lose our shit.

"Who are you people?" Finn yells out, still in the midst of his fit. "What are you planning to do with us?"

I look over at the two soldiers that stand watch, their faces blank. They could possibly be twins—not only do they wear the same black uniforms and matching berets as the men in the gymnasium, but they're equal in height and their faces are equally broad and square. I wonder if they're capable of speaking English as they haven't said a thing since discovering us.

"Maybe they're Swiss or something," I say to Finn. I watch the men closely as I speak. "Dooo…yoooou…speak-a de English?" The men don't even flinch with my question.

"You don't know any foreign languages," Finn reminds me grumpily. His face is hard and he refuses to smile, despite my best efforts.

I grumble at his sour mood. "All those crappy films we used to watch with subtitles should be good for something, right?" He rolls his eyes and moves away from my side of his cell.

"I don't think they're human," Cheese says suddenly. My eyes meet Finn's before we both look over to our young and overly imaginative friend.

"Say again?" I ask him.

Cheese points at them. "Watch them. I haven't seen them blink once and they don't look like they're breathing."

We all stare at the two men for a quiet moment to discover Cheese is right, once again. I look down by my feet in the little cell and find a lone pebble. I pick it up and chuck it at the soldier on the right. When it bounces off his neck he doesn't even flinch.

"What the hell are they then?" Finn asks.

"I don't know. Cyborgs maybe?" Cheese answers. He's showing signs of getting all keyed up again over this never ending, exciting adventure we seem to be stuck on. Licking his lips and wrapping his hands around the metal bars, he leans his head out of the cell to watch the men with wide, alert eyes.

"Or super-soldiers," I say with a shrug.

Now Cheese snaps his head in my direction. "What did you say?"

Finn groans loudly and covers his face with his hands. "And…here we go."

I don't know why Finn has such a problem with my X-Files obsession. He used to come over and watch the DVDs of the show for hours on end with me. But I guess that was all before our sophomore year when I dyed my hair red and started calling him Mulder. I still think it was just one of "those stages" every young girl goes through.

I glare at Finn while answering Cheese. "You know—aliens that look like humans but only want to stop anyone that tries to stop their efforts to take over the world."

"Wow," Finn says, shaking his head in disbelief.

"What if they're aliens?" Cheese asks.

We stare at the two men who still have yet to move during all of this.

"Okay, Em. Let's hear it," Finn says, rolling his hand through the air. "What would Scully do?"

I wrack my brain for some kind of awesome idea the fictional federal agent would come up with, but I've got nothing. I shrug to my friend with my hands up. "I don't know...wait for Mulder to rescue her, I guess."

Cheese speaks up excitedly. "Maybe we should see what it takes to get their attention."

"Good idea," I say. I open my mouth and release every ounce of air in my lungs until my vocal cords ache. Finn shuts one eye in irritation and Cheese covers his ears. Even Jake is on his feet now, holding his fingers in his ears. But the two soldiers still won't look my way and don't even flinch. I stop screaming, deciding they're really beginning to creep me out.

"Holy shit, Emma!" Cheese yells. "Don't ever do that again!"

One of the men's eyes suddenly flickers rapidly—not in a blinking motion but like some kind of light going bad. I make a wailing noise and jump to the back of my cage. "Did you guys freaking see that?" My voice is much higher than normal as I clutch the bars behind me, wishing I could crawl out of the cage.

Whatever these men are, they do not appear to be a part of the human race.

"Don't lose it now, Em," Finn tells me calmly.

I look over at him to see he's getting all worked up, like he's afraid I'll revert back to memory loss, but the problem is that I may have already lost my mind. Why else would I've seen that man's eye flicker that way?

Cheese glances over at us. "Guys—someone's coming."

Heels click on concrete as someone nears our area of the basement.

Seconds later, Finn's mom Elizabeth stares at us.

Chapter 15

E lizabeth looks nothing like an escaped mental patient, dressed in a very high-end, tailored black suit with her dark hair styled neatly into a tight bun on the back of her head. She looks very similar to her older sister Linda, only her eyebrows have the same slight curve as Finn's and she's a bit shorter. I marvel at how pulled together she appears despite everything that she has been through and everything that's happening now. She bears no resemblance to the insane woman I've grown up knowing all these years.

"Mom!" Finn gasps, grasping the metal bars. "I can't believe you're okay! What are you doing here?"

Elizabeth doesn't answer. She doesn't make any kind of recognition that he has even spoken. She turns on her high heels to face the soldiers. "That's my son—what is he doing in there? Release them!"

I have never heard her sound so bossy like that. I obviously haven't seen her since she was committed—Finn even refused to go visit her, but she seems different now. I have yet to see her smile or show any of the bubbling Elizabeth who likes to paint and do other artsy crap. This Elizabeth is cold and hard, not showing any kind of emotion.

The soldiers step forward in unison to unlock Finn and my cells before moving on to where our younger friends are locked up. I wonder what kind of command Elizabeth had secretly used to make the two robot-men move so rapidly in response.

Finn and I run to each other and embrace tightly. Hands down, it's the best hug I've ever had. He buries his face in my dirty blond locks and then kisses my neck, causing a parade of shivers to travel down my spine. When we pull away and look into each other's eyes for an exaggerated moment, the desire to make out with him slams into me. By the way Finn is looking back at me he's quite obviously thinking the same thing.

Jake coughs loudly, ruining yet another moment between us. We break apart, but Finn holds on to my hand, awkwardly watching his mom. They may as well be complete strangers the way they stand and regard each other. My heart breaks a little for my friend.

"What are you kids doing here?" Elizabeth asks. She speaks with casual curiosity, like she has been living at home this whole time and is running into us at the supermarket.

Cheese now stands freely with us and Jake pushes up against my side. I have a hard time knowing if I should baby him right now or continue to treat him like the little stud he so desperately wants to be. I give in and wrap my arm around his back, but he isn't bothered by my contact this time. He even seems to relax a little.

"We were going to head north like you told Aunt Linda," Finn tells his mother, "only we were separated from her when we were near the Cities. I think she was taken to some kind of Army camp—she told us to run from the area. We met up later with an AWOL soldier who told us the Army is planning to wipe Canada out and our best bet was go south. Plus he heard there was a female agent down this way, so we were hoping..."

Elizabeth sighs. "I don't know what he's talking about. This virus is strictly contained to the Midwest area. You would've been better off going north."

Finn narrows his eyes back at her. "What are you doing here, Mom? We haven't heard from you in months. Where did you go?"

"I was called down here to help contain this," Elizabeth says to her son. But she doesn't answer his other questions and she has been missing for months, so there's obviously more to her story.

"What's with the robots?" Cheese blurts, motioning to the two soldiers now standing taut behind us. Panic fills me when I realize they aren't standing very far behind me. I shuffle closer to Finn and find his hand with mine. Something just isn't normal about the two men—they're so stiff and artificial. They almost remind me of the creepy Chucky doll Cash passed down to Finn when we were in elementary school. I keep waiting for the soldiers to turn their heads and ask us if we want to play.

"There's no need to panic," Elizabeth tells us. "This will all be under control soon."

"Elizabeth," Finn addresses his mother with sarcasm, "there's something really off about these goons over here. Are you going to tell us what's going on?"

Elizabeth motions to the two soldiers in some sort of odd hand signal and they promptly leave the room. I give them my own special hand signal as they pass us by. Once the men are gone, Elizabeth rests her fingers on Finn's arms. "I think right now we need to focus on getting you kids out of here until we know it's safe."

"Our friends are on the base somewhere," I tell her. "Someone who shall remain nameless had this brilliant idea that some of our group should create a diversion by turning themselves in. But how is it that you're all dressed up and ordering these super-soldier guys around?"

"It's part of her job," Finn answers.

"Her job?" I ask, snorting as I say it.

"I don't understand," Elizabeth says.

Finn shakes his head. "I sort of broke her when I told her the Army was planning to bomb the area. She had a bit of a memory relapse yesterday."

Everyone looks at me and a light bulb seems to turn on in my head. "So wait. You actually work for the Army?" I ask. "Are you kidding?"

"FBI," Finn corrects me. "Try to keep up."

I seem to be growing more confused as this day progresses. Apparently I'd acquired a lot of important information in the short time my brain was on hiatus. "So what about that whole bit where you thought you were having Michael Jackson's baby?"

"That was real but she had to give it up for adoption," Finn answers, his words hurried.

I blink rapidly when the overall confusion becomes too much to process.

"Cash is with them, too," Finn tells her. "We befriended a few soldiers who were trying to help us."

Elizabeth removes her hands from Finn's arms. "Now is not the time to trust the Army. We have to find them all, before it's too late."

"Too late for what?" I ask. Obviously I have no qualms about Cash being tortured or whatever she thinks the Army may do, but my friends are with him.

Elizabeth does not answer me. She's too busy pushing us out of the room into a different hallway from the one we were brought through. Cheese and Jake scurry to keep up. The hallway is seriously direful and seemingly never ending. And of course, it had to be covered in cobwebs. My eyes must be as big as saucers as I try to maneuver through without touching any of them.

"What is with this place?" Finn asks his mom.

"Back in the fifties it was a bomb shelter," Elizabeth answers.

I clutch tightly to both Finn and Jake's hands at this point, still fearing what may lie ahead for us. Elizabeth's refusal to actually fill us in on what is happening has me pretty freaked out. She's obviously not who I thought her to be, but there seems to be more going on she's not willing to share. I only hope she at least has her son's safety in mind, above all else. Finn keeps squeezing my hand obsessively as we walk together. I'm guessing he's involved in a major struggle with his own thoughts on the issue.

We take another turn that brings us past the opening to a well-lit room. I catch a glimpse of more soldiers and more cells through the door's crack, only these are filled with people who are either infected or look like they may have been at one time. I pull on Finn's hand when I step back and peer inside in the room.

My jaw involuntarily drops at what I see.

In one of the cells closest to the door, an elderly man wearing nothing more than a pair of blue pants that have been ripped to shreds reaches out when he sees me. His wrinkled skin is a blotchy white color and looks to be paper thin as I can still see the bones and tissue underneath. His white hair sticks up like an old man's Mohawk and his dark, sunken eyes give him a very sullen look. As he continues to hold out his bony arm, he opens his mouth. I can see his teeth are barely staying where they're supposed to be.

"Help me," he whispers, his voice seriously strained. My hold on Finn becomes so fierce that he winces until he sees what I'm shrinking away from. His eyes grow as wide as mine feel and he pulls me into him.

Shockingly, many of the people locked up also look uninfected, but appear as weak and sad as the old man. A few of them turn to look at us, but otherwise remain motionless. Very faint moans drift out from the room, but they sound more like actual crying than the death moan that we've come to dread. Something tells me these people are being used to discover a reversal to the infection.

A group of somewhat normal-looking people dressed in white lab coats are standing on the far side of the room and freeze in place when they spot us. Elizabeth has discovered we quit following her and comes back now to collect us.

"Go about your business," she says sharply to the coated crew. They pause for a minute to consider us, but then continue on as they were told. I continue to clutch Finn tightly until we're out of their little lab area and walking up a set of cellar steps.

"That place was wicked cool," Cheese whispers to us.

I turn to him with my face still pale from everything we had seen. "Those were people back there, dude. Not one of your little comic book shows or whatever, but real, live people. Do you need your head examined, or what?"

He seems to still be caught up in planning his life as some kind of world-dominating scientist. He mumbles to himself and seems to get all revved up about something. I turn away from him, disgusted.

I push my lips up to Finn's ear and speak as quietly as I can so Elizabeth will not overhear me. "What do you think they were doing to all those people back there?"

Finn leans into me, his eyes still on his mother's back. "I don't know, but I'm not sure we want to find out."

We emerge outside in an entirely different area from where we originally entered the school. In fact, the old building is nowhere to be seen. I guess with all the walking we've done it's obvious to everyone else that we were in some kind of tunnel but I yell out "whoa" in surprise.

A small parking lot ahead of us is filled with a fleet of black, four-door sedans. The entire area is gated off many feet over our heads with barbed wire spanning across the top of it. An eerie tingling sweeps through me. This looks like some kind of Nazi camp rather than…well, whatever that nightmarish place was.

Elizabeth leads us to one of the black grandpa-style cars and hands the keys to Finn. "You need to drive out of here as fast as you can. Head east for now. I'll get your friends and meet up with you as soon as we can."

"Can't we help you?" Cheese asks her. Apparently he has both world-dominating scientist and action hero in mind for his future careers.

"It's too dangerous for you kids," she says. I don't like how she can't seem to look directly at anyone when she answers them. This woman has been lying to me for the past how many years—I certainly wouldn't put it past her to be lying to us now.

Finn makes a point of meeting his mom's eyes with his own. "Are you sure?"

Elizabeth opens the door to the vehicle and looks off into the distance. "Yes. But if you see any military you need to turn around before they see you. Remember, head straight east."

I part Finn's side long enough to walk around the car and climb into the passenger's side. Jake and Cheese take the backseat as Finn slides in. Elizabeth shuts the door behind her son and we see her dip her head once on the other side of the glass in some kind of goodbye gesture. She turns on her heels in one abrupt movement and walks back toward the underground entrance.

"Okay, that was totally whacked," I say. "Is it just me, or did she purposely avoid all of our biggest questions? And what was with those creepy soldiers? Do you think there's some big super-secret she's purposely keeping from us?"

My friend looks at me with a dead serious expression that I rarely saw on him before today. He steers the car out of the parking lot, squealing the tires on the road with his reckless driving. "I don't know, but that wasn't my mom."

Snapping out of the shocked state I've fallen into takes me a good minute. When my eyes come back into full focus again I thrash my head back and forth like I've just woken from a really bad dream. "What do you mean that wasn't your Mom? Since when did you start doing drugs?"

Finn glances in the rearview mirror a few times, like he's afraid we're being followed. "What? You're saying walking dead people are feasible but you can't open your mind enough to believe that wasn't my mom back there?"

I pause to consider this. "Okay. You may have a point there. But I don't know why you wouldn't think that was Elizabeth."

Finn laughs, making me believe that if we actually do survive this and don't get eaten alive, it's possible we will eventually die from madness. "You don't think I know my own mother well enough to spot the difference? She may be a federal agent, but the Elizabeth we all know would've been hugging me and crying, considering she hasn't seen me in nearly half a year. She also would've been really freaked out to learn her sister is missing. She didn't even flinch when I told her. Trust me, it wasn't her. Either that or she has been completely brainwashed."

I roll my eyes to the top of my head. "How could it not be her? Do you think she's got like some kind of evil twin that you didn't know about?"

"She's a robot, just like those soldiers!" Cheese declares, leaning over the seat so his head is right between us. Using my index finger I firmly push his forehead away, forcing him back into his seat. The kid clearly needs to be on some kind of calming medication.

Finn shrugs. "I don't know what that was, but I sure as hell don't plan on leaving until we've rounded up the others."

"Wait, we're going back there?" Jake asks. His voice is high and shaking with frazzled nerves.

I turn to him and try to gently explain what is going on —through my head, anyway. "Jake, we can't just leave everyone back there. Maybe if it were just Cash down there we wouldn't have to worry about it, but we owe it to the others."

Jake still seems anxious and he leans forward in his seat. "So that lady back there who Finn says isn't his mom —what if she gets to them first?" His question is pretty dangerous for me to try to answer, so I don't—it continues to hang out there like the stained underwear at a slumber party that goes unclaimed. I glance over at Finn and can tell the question is weighing heavily on his mind, too.

Miles down the road, serious déjá vu sets in—it's the same road that led us to the Army camp just a few hours earlier. The sun's low on the horizon, creating pink and yellow hues across the sky as it slowly sinks behind the ground. The car lights automatically flip themselves on but Finn turns them off with a flick of his hand and parks the car behind a large rock on top of the hill.

"You so better not tell us to wait here," I warn him as soon as he turns to me. "I won't do it. I'm done being told what to do by you."

"I'm not that stupid," he answers. "But guys, we have to stay together and keep quiet. I really don't know what we're going to find down there."

"Hopefully anything other than more infected or freaky super-soldiers," I say.

Finn checks the large gun he's still toting around before we pile out of the car to make another line of Finn holding my hand, and me holding Jake's. Poor Cheese is left all alone with two free hands, although I decide maybe it wouldn't be such a bad thing when I trip a couple of times and almost pull the others down with me.

The camp below is beginning to light up with the start of nightfall. Large strings of what look to be party lights run from tent to tent and larger, more powerful lights shine over the tops. The temperature has dropped along with the light, although I think much of the chill comes from my own fear.

We stop behind a group of bushes to peer down at the Army soldiers. They've all gravitated to the center of camp where a large cluster has formed. A buzz from their excited conversations fills the air.

"What are they doing?" Cheese whispers.

"Why are you asking us?" I whisper back. My tolerance for being annoyed with him today has run out. "We obviously don't know any more than you or we wouldn't be standing here, spying on them like a bunch of idiots."

The sharp squeal of a microphone is amplified through the air before a man's voice comes over a speaker system. His words are faint and mumbled from where we stand. The scene combined with the dull words carrying through the night make me think of the old tapes we had to watch in history class of Hitler giving one of his infamous pep talks.

"We need to get closer so we can hear," Finn says. He turns to Jake, whose eyes are as big as saucers by now. "Are you going to be okay with this, little man?"

Jake's eyes dart unsteadily between me and Finn, reminding me of those annoying squirrels that run all over the yard like they've had too much caffeine. The poor little guy is not holding it together through all of this.

"I think he's next in line to lose his mind," I whisper to Finn.

"Whatever you do, don't let go of Emma's hand," Finn tells him.

"You, either," I tell Finn.

Our human chain once again descends down a hill toward the camp. The base is not fenced off like the place where Elizabeth had been, but there are guards watching at various points. We find a spot between tents where either a guard has left to listen to the announcement or just isn't manning his post. At this viewpoint we can finally hear what is being said clearly over the speaker.

I catch my breath when the man giving the speech comes into view as well. The voice belongs to Payton.

Chapter 16

Payton's expression is hard as he looks over the soldiers. "I want to stress how important it is to stop this group of children before they're able to penetrate the quarantined area."

I suck in my breath.

"Holy crap," I whisper to Finn. "Tell me this isn't happening. Is he talking about us?" But apparently I'm not whispering as quietly as I thought. Finn clamps his hand over my mouth before I can say anything more. I look over to him to see if he's actually hearing what Payton is saying, but he shakes his head, willing me to shut up.

What is going on? This wasn't part of our original plan to find Finn's mom. Payton continues speaking to the soldiers for a few more minutes, but I'm too wrapped up in my own thoughts to hear what he's saying. Why would Payton suddenly be leading a mission to capture us? Apparently the Elizabeth-bot informed the Army of our little visit. But if their mission was to detain us for some reason, why would she have let us go in the first place?

Why didn't she just bring us to their camp when she had us?

I pull my friend's hand from my mouth and stare at him. "Are you following what is happening right now? None of this is making any sense. Why would he be in charge, anyway? It just takes one look to realize the guy is AWOL."

When I look back, I see that Payton is gone from his little pedestal and the soldiers are beginning to disburse. We continue to crouch in our hiding spot, my legs prickling with needles from the awkward position. The purring of many different engines start up, and headlights flash across the camp as the vehicles leave.

"Did you guys see that?" Finn asks. He points to a tent not far from where our traitor of a friend had been standing. "I think I saw Marley's hair."

I didn't see anything, but once all the headlights are gone Finn leads us over to where he thought he saw our friend. I personally think I'm doing a good job at being covert as we sneak through the camp, but Cheese hisses at me more than once to be quiet.

Most of the soldiers are gone, having left on the convoy in search of us. Two remain outside of the tent, seeming to be keeping guard. One of the soldiers is not much taller than Cheese and barely looks old enough to shave. He has a baby face that makes him look more like fifteen, and dark hair that tries to kink despite being the regulation military length. The other guy can only be described as ginormous. He's like a skyscraper against the tent, with hulking muscles and the broad set face of a real manly-man. His close shaven hair is a funny white-blond shade that has to have been dyed to be such an off color.

"Cheese, get your gun," Finn whispers. "You take the

little guy and I'll take the big one. We're not going to shoot them, just bring them inside the tent with us."

"You can't be serious," I say. "You guys are going to take them on by yourselves?"

The big guy has arms the size of a ten-year-old's body. He could easily throw Finn over his shoulder without blinking. My friend may be adept with guns, but he does not possess much more athletic ability than I do and is sometimes lucky if he can just walk straight without tripping.

"You two stay here until I motion for you," Finn tells Jake and me. "Got it, Em?"

"You won't hear any protests from me," I answer.

I can hardly stand to watch the two as they sneak off in opposite directions, looking like a couple of boys getting ready to play tag. My hands fly over my face. I part my fingers just enough in time to see the two of them springing into action. The big guy towers over Finn, telling him to put the gun down in a voice bigger than he is. A lot of shouting goes down between the four of them while they try to decide who has the upper hand. I anxiously look around, hoping there isn't anyone else around to hear their exchange. The vision of the big guy squishing Finn like a dinosaur would squish an annoying bug keeps crossing my mind and I struggle to push it away.

Finn and Cheese somehow convince the two soldiers they mean business. The bigger guy finally places his gun on the ground. Finn motions with his free hand for me and Jake to join them. With some initial hesitation from both of us, we drag our feet over and follow Finn inside the tent. The two soldiers are quiet and obedient with the guns still directed at them.

"Hey, guys!" Zander greets us casually once we step inside. Our friends are sitting in a circle around a table with playing cards in their hands. They each take their time looking up when we enter, like they've been waiting for us to show up for a night on the town or something. Not a one of them appears to be stressed or upset in any fashion. Here I thought we would show up and they would cry out in excitement when they saw us, jumping and screaming for joy. Maybe Cheese's hero complex is starting to rub off on me.

I gasp. "Seriously? You guys are playing cards right now?"

Cash sneers in response. "What did you think you were going to find? Us bound and gagged? These guys are part of the U.S. military, Emma."

"A girl can still dream," I say, narrowing my eyes at him.

The big soldier grunts in his deep voice. I turn to him with my hands on my hips. "What is going on around here, anyway? Why did our friend randomly take over and tell everyone to go chasing after us?"

The large soldier looks back at me with his hands still up but doesn't say anything. Apparently, when you're all big and strong like that, you don't have to answer to anyone unless you really want to.

"Payton said that?" Cash asks.

"We saw him just a few minutes ago," Finn answers. "He was speaking to everyone like he was in charge."

Marley shrugs. "If you can figure out what's going on, then you're one up on us. He disappeared right after we got here."

Cash is looking harshly at his brother. "Where did you nimrods go? We were starting to think you ditched us."

"You're lucky you weren't here alone," I say to him. "Or we totally would have."

Cheese steps forward and the words spurt from him in one breath. "We found this super-secret lab where they were running tests on zombies and there were these robotic soldiers that answered to Finn's mom."

"Wait, you found Mom?" Cash asks, setting his hand of cards down on the table and standing to face us. Finn and I exchange a weary look. We both know his brother's tiny brain is not capable of comprehending anything too mind-blowing.

"Not totally sure on that one," Finn finally says.

Cash scowls at us and crosses his arms in front of his chest. "How can you not be sure? Either you found her or you didn't."

"Okay, we didn't," I say, looking over to Cheese with my eyebrows raised. He knows not to contest me by the look I'm giving him so he presses his lips together tightly.

"But how is it that Payton is suddenly in charge?" Finn asks. When none of our friends seem to have an answer, Finn steps closer to the shorter of the two soldiers. "This crew is hungry and tired of running. We would really appreciate some answers from someone."

The scrawnier, baby-faced soldier looks up at his much larger friend. The big guy shakes his head in warning.

Baby-face sighs, his shoulders slumping as he looks down. "Our camp has totally been overrun by the FBI people who came in. They're calling all of the shots and no one is contesting it."

"Miller!" the larger soldier barks at him. "You're talking to a bunch of civilian children." The two exchange an intense stare before Miller looks away.

"Exactly, Jags. They're kids," he answers. "What are they going to do about it?"

"What is the FBI telling you to do?" Finn asks Miller.

"That's classified," Jags answers.

Miller faces Finn, but I can tell he's watching from the corner of his eye to gauge his buddy's reaction. "They want us to detain all the children since they cannot be infected by this outbreak."

"Why? What are you supposed to do with us?" Cheese asks.

"Miller!" Jags yells at his fellow soldier in warning.

But Miller is obviously too far into this to stop now. "They want to study all of you to figure out why you seem to be immune to it."

"Like 'study' as in probe us and shit?" I ask. "Isn't that kind of un-American of them?"

"But that doesn't make any sense," Cheese says before anyone decides to answer me. "They just had us in little jail cells and let us go. Why would they do that?"

"Maybe that really was your mom," I tell Finn. My eyes look back at him with hope that he'll forgive me for questioning him again.

"So you fools did see her!" Cash says angrily.

"What else is the FBI saying about all of this?" Finn asks Miller without addressing either Cash or me. I can't decide if he's angry at me now or if he doesn't want to admit he may have sounded a bit crazy with his earlier theory.

"If you think they're telling the Army anything of importance, then you really don't know how it all works," Jags says to Finn. "We're given orders from our commanding officer, and he doesn't fill us in on all the details. Quite frankly, I have no intention of following through on any orders that involve harming innocent children from this country. When I joined the Army, I did it to protect my fellow countrymen."

"So glad to hear it," I tell him as I reach out to punch him playfully in the shoulder but think better of it when he gives me a cold look. I bring my fist back down to my side, throwing him a toothy, nervous smile instead.

"Do you know a way to get us out of here safely?" Finn asks the two soldiers.

Jags frowns. "What's in it for us?"

"I thought you just said you wanted to protect your fellow countrymen," I say, trying to mock his tone of voice.

"Whatever the FBI is planning, it can't be good," Finn adds. "How exactly do you think they're going to run these tests on us? I really think there's more going on that they aren't filling you guys in on."

Jags looks over at Miller then back at our friends still gathered around the table. He puts his hand on his neck and rolls it around, grunting in frustration. His eyes finally settle back on Finn. "It's not going to be easy," he warns.

* * *

BUT JAGS WAS WRONG. Sneaking out of the camp by foot proves just as easy as coming into it had been, even with our group having more than doubled. Payton's lynch mob was heading east, so we go in the other direction. Jags warns us that the perimeters set by the Army will be much more difficult to pass, but for now we're just glad to be away from the strange place filled with robot soldiers and Elizabeth's creepy doppelganger.

So many factors have already made this adventure of ours terrifying, but the sun has completely set and we run through the dark with very little moonlight showing the way. The whole scene is completely eerie on so many levels —especially when I look over at anyone and their eyes seem to glow white in the darkness. I'm reminded of our younger days when Finn and I would make up horror stories with flashlights shining on our faces. If only we knew we would one day be living the worst horror story of them all.

We don't see any vehicles on the gravel roads— although it's nighttime, and I also wonder if we're really, truly at the ends of the earth. I cling to Finn's hand so tightly he flexes it a few times so I'll lighten my grip.

"Is our master plan really to run through the dark all night?" I ask anyone who will answer. "We're going on days of very little sleep here. I feel I'm speaking for the group when I say we have to take some kind of time-out."

Jags stops from up ahead and looks back at me in the scant moonlight. "We passed through a small town just a few miles out where we maybe can rest for a little bit, but I don't think we want to stop for very long."

I grumble at his answer. "A few miles? You can't be serious. These boots may be fashionable, but I'm going to be forever crippled if I have to go much farther in them. I already have a million blisters."

"Would you rather someone carry you?" Cash snaps.

I open my mouth to answer, but Jags suddenly marches over to where I stand and swoops me off my feet and into his gun-sized arms. I'm stunned into total silence. This guy is certainly massive, but he's holding all 125.8 pounds of me like I'm a sack of flour.

"Put her down," Finn demands. Apparently my BFF is not willing to share me, but I'm okay with that. Once all this zombie stuff is over I plan to make him more than a friend.

"Are you going to carry her?" Jags asks.

"Yeah, are you?" I ask Finn with a smirk. We both know that the last time he attempted to carry me it ended with my head connecting with a lamppost and me losing consciousness. Finn rolls his eyes at me and our journey continues on.

As we trudge along, the swaying movements from being nestled in the arms of the soldier nearly lull me to sleep. Our group remains totally silent—we're all completely exhausted by now. How much longer can we continue walking along the countryside like this? If our only hope of survival is to walk our way down to Florida, someone may as well shoot me and end this misery as soon as possible. Being that I'm borderline unconscious, time passes in a blur as we continue on. Before long the cluster of lights is closer and we enter a painfully small town that appears to be void of any activity—either human or inhuman.

The buildings and houses show the usual signs of being abandoned at a moment's notice, but at least this town hasn't been torched like the time we met Carrot Top and his gang. We pass a few blocks of the average-sized, run-down homes before finding ourselves in a little downtown area that spans two entire blocks and is filled with seemingly unsuccessful shops. Just like most of the other towns we've passed through, we don't see any other humans and the usual odd feeling is in the air, like there had been some kind of mass abduction. We don't even see any maimed bodies.

As much as I hate cats because of the way they always are sneaking around and can't ever be trusted, it's still unsettling that we haven't seen a single one. Usually, every town has at least a few strays wandering about. Are the animals as keen as we are as to what it going on, or are the zombies just that desperate for any kind of meat?

"There's a small bowling alley at the end of the block," Jags tells us. "We can rest there for a little while." He sets me back down onto my feet. Finn is beside me in a second flat, his face showing serious irritation that Jags had been carrying me in the first place.

"Somebody is jealous," I whisper playfully.

He wraps his hand around mine and places a soft kiss on my temple that brings a spark to my skin. "I was afraid of losing you to those giant muscles."

"Maybe you should start working out," I say teasingly. We both know I'm not a big fan of the overly muscular type, but it's fun to mess with Finn all the same.

Our group follows Jags all the way down the block like a bunch of mindless sheep until we reach the bowling alley. Not surprisingly, the door is unlocked and we're able to waltz right into the place.

The building has a stale, musty odor to it of old cigarettes mixed with funky bowling shoes. But the warmth of it is quite pleasurable, considering how cold the fall nights are becoming. We stand for a moment in the darkness until someone finds a light on the wall. The place slowly flickers to life under the spotty fluorescents. Cheese stands by the light switches with a giant grin on his face.

"Holy retro," Marley says with a little smile.

The building is certainly older than any of us and has a definite 70's vibe to it. The carpet has obviously not been replaced in more than a few decades and screams out in bright orange, blue and gold colors that mirror the stripes on the walls. The six small lanes are a blond wood and outlined with more blue stripes. Bright blue plastic chairs surround each scoring system. Although seriously tacky and extremely outdated, the place makes me yearn for simpler, less gloom-and-doom type days.

Back in the days of non-walking-around dead people, Finn and I would sometimes drive to Mankato and bowl on the weekends. Neither of us were league material or anything—I was sometimes lucky just to keep my ball in my own lane. Regardless, we had a blast together and it was something to do. If we weren't worried about preserving our lives at the moment, this place could be a lot of fun.

Cheese scampers between the lanes and disappears behind the pins. Others are busy finding a place to sit at the bright orange tables on the carpeted area. Aside from the fact that everyone looks frazzled from lack of sleep and we all have some kind of gun strapped to our bodies, it almost feels like we're preparing for a fun Saturday night on the town. I realize with a start that I have no idea what day of the week we're on anymore, but decide it probably isn't necessary anyway. It's not like we have any pressing appointments.

"Do you think it's safe now for us to eat food, considering we can't get infected and everything?" Zander asks from beside me.

My eyes drift over to the concession area. Behind the counter there are half a dozen rows filled with different candies and an array of chocolate bars. The brightly colored packages are as wonderful to behold as an 'R' rated movie to a nine-year-old.

Chapter 17

The limited food we've had access to—in the last twenty-four hours anyway—have been anything but satisfying. My love for chocolate has been well established and I have a necessary daily intake in order to stay mentally balanced. Come to think of it, maybe that would explain my little bout of amnesia Finn is telling me I recently suffered. My mouth waters at the thought of all that chocolaty righteousness just sitting there, waiting for us to sink our teeth into it.

"How about we let Cash try one first?" I say.

"I say ladies first on this one," Cash answers, holding his arm out for me to lead the way.

I shrug and drop Finn's hand to walk toward the heavenly selection. "I guess we know I'm not going to catch anything by it, and I'm not a pansy."

Finn grabs my arm before I get very far. "Hold on, Em. We don't know that for sure."

I point at my shoulder once again. "Um, zombie bite here, remember?"

"I'll try one," Marley offers.

I look over to see her eyes are fixated on the candy as much as mine. But it's no surprise. How could anyone resist such a beautiful display of high calorie snacks?

Cash snorts. "You two are seriously considering becoming infected just to feed your faces with a little chocolate? I've always said women are inferior to men, but this is ridiculous."

Before I have a chance to respond with something witty, all at once loud disco music begins to play and the machines power up on the lanes. Colored lights flash over the lanes like it's prom night. More than a few of us jump in surprise to the sudden intrusion of the alley's previous silence.

Cheese emerges from behind the pins with another goofy smile plastered on his face. "My grandpa owns a bowling alley up north. I know a thing or two about how these places operate."

I take advantage of everyone's stunned reaction by dashing over to the concession stand, and Marley is soon behind me. So many candy bars sit there just waiting to be chosen and I'm starving for a sweet treat. I scoop a few different bars into my hands and inhale their delicious, chocolaty scent that I've been missing. In the midst of all this madness, it's like I've rediscovered an old friend.

"Em," Finn warns sternly. "Think about this for a minute. We don't really know how this virus is spread. Maybe you can't get it by saliva. What if it's spread through infected food? Is it really worth risking your life for a little bit of chocolate?"

I don't answer him. My eyes and hands are busy rifling through the amazing selection.

Miller, who has been quiet up until now, watches us all like we've lost our minds. "He's right. I don't think eating that would be such a good idea."

I find my favorite candy bar and drop the rest of them. Marley is one step behind me with a different selection.

"A bunch of chocolate, and you two are totally losing your minds," Finn grumbles. "Em, please don't do this."

When I almost have the succulent chocolate bar filled with nougat, caramel, and nuts to my lips, Finn springs forward and grabs it away from me, sinking his own teeth into it. I gasp and hit him on the shoulder. "So it's okay for you to eat it but not me?"

He gives me a frustrated glare. "If you won't listen to me, then I at least want to test it first."

I try to pull the candy bar from his grip, but he snatches it to his side. "Just wait. If nothing happens to me, then you can have your own."

Fireworks may as well be bursting around Finn. He's obviously willing to risk his life for me and it beats any old John Hughes movie any day—well at least some of them—*Sixteen Candles* will forever remain epic in my book. I lean in and kiss his cheek, pleased when my teenage hormones burst in approval. When I lean away from him, there's a very satisfied smile on his nougat-covered lips.

At this moment I know I'm head over heels in love with my old buddy. "You have…a little something…" I tell him, wanting to use my finger to wipe it off, but he sucks his lip in before I get a chance.

Marley is only halfway done with her candy bar when Finn is taking his last bite. Miller looks like he'll explode from anxiety just watching all of us. Jags is busy standing watch at the front door, seemingly oblivious to anything else that's going on.

Cash and Darrin are coming at us now with their eyes big like begging puppy dogs. "Not yet," Finn tells the two boys. "Maybe later."

"I get to shoot you all if you go crazy," Cash says, watching us from the orange table.

He places his gun on the tabletop in front of him, like some kind of warning. I'm amused to see how worried he seems to be about his own girlfriend, unless maybe she has already dumped him in private. At least his brother is man enough to step up and take care of me. How the two of them were birthed from the same set of parents or even the same species, I'll never understand.

"How was it?" I ask Finn, still standing close and watching him as he seems to savor every bite.

"For my last meal, it was pretty damn good," Finn says with a sly smirk.

I wrap my fingers with his and lean into him, forgetting about all the people watching us. "If it ends up being your last meal, I'll have one, too. Romeo and Juliet all the way, baby." Finn appears to swallow with great care as our lips linger just inches from each other. Our eyes silently pass all the things we can't seem to say at the moment.

"Who's up for a few rounds?" Cheese calls out.

Finn and I both flinch at the interruption. I look over to see Cheese grab a black bowling ball from the ball-return.

Finn presses his lips to my forehead. I sigh when I realize the big kiss isn't going to happen. Not now, anyway. "I'm all over it," I yell back to Cheese, running around the counter. If a cold shower really works for guys, I'm hoping a round of bowling will work for me.

I pull on Jake and Darrin's arms. "Come play with me, guys. We'll have candy bars when we're done to celebrate."

"I thought we were here to rest because your fancy boots can't take anymore walking," Jags barks at me. Apparently he has been paying attention, after all.

I walk behind the other counter across from the concession stand. "That's why I'm switching to bowling shoes, soldier."

One of my secret fantasies has always been to work at a bowling alley and I probably get a little too into the whole process of handing out the shoes. But hey, this may be the last thing I ever get to do, so I want to make it count.

Those of us willing to have a little fun join in for one of the most exhilarating bowling matches of my life. My frequent rendezvous to the alley in Mankato with Finn have paid off—I actually do halfway decent and make the others look like amateurs.

During the game I look over to see apparently someone has filled Jags in on the situation. He watches Marley and Finn on high alert, maybe waiting for the opportunity to shoot them. I'm reminded of the time Payton had been so willing to shoot me just seconds after saving my life at the lodge. Why would he go to all the trouble of helping us and then suddenly want to help the very army he absconded from to capture us? Something just doesn't add up, although I do really suck at math.

Finn hasn't taken me in a long time, so my bowling skills are somewhat rusty. But it's amazingly awesome to throw ourselves into a fun, mindless task where we aren't running for our lives. Finn pulls me down to sit in his lap as we wait our turns, making it seem like a real date. We may have been on a thousand adventures together, but I guess it took something a bit more serious for us to realize we have deeper feelings for each other. Every time my friend gives me his lopsided grin, I'm tempted to ask if he wants to check out the backroom with me for a little while.

Everything would seem to be downright perfect right now, if only there wasn't the constant worry that something could easily turn horribly wrong at any moment. Our spirits soar to the point that a few of us are able to shake around between frames to the outdated music and laugh happily together. After all, we're just a bunch of kids trying to survive this whole thing. No one—other than Cash, who watches with a seemingly permanent scowl—could judge us for just wanting to take a moment to finally have a little fun.

Marley takes advantage of the fun-filled moments by eating a bag of nuts in front of the rest of us once she has decided she isn't going to turn. I'm fairly certain she mostly does it to get a rise out of Cash, who is already completely irritated by her anyway.

We're nearing the last frame when I miss throwing a spare. Everyone yells in support of my narrow fail until Jags whistles loudly from the entrance of the building. He's pressed up against the door, looking out the peephole with his gun raised on alert. It's unnerving to see someone dressed for war becoming ready for combat.

"Someone hit the lights! Hurry!" he yells.

Cheese dashes back behind the pins and Zander jumps over to the light switches on the wall. Within seconds, someone kills the corny music and disco lights. Shortly after that, the main lights go black and we're standing in complete darkness.

"Oh shit!" I yell nervously when I've lost all my bearings. I hadn't looked around to see where everyone was positioned before the lights were killed. I'm still at the mouth of the lane while Finn and the others were crowded around the scoring system.

"What's going on?" Finn's voice yells out from what feels like impossibly far away. I know he's probably addressing Jags at this point, but I'm so freaked out that I can't stop my mouth from moving.

"Just experiencing a little technical difficulty here," I

say nervously. Panic sets in while I feel the air around me with my arms. If there's one thing I hate more than getting tangled in spider webs, it could possibly be standing all alone in the darkness with the threat of mindless zombies attacking.

"A whole horde of infected are coming this way," Jags's voice answers Finn. "They were probably attracted to the lights and music you yahoos were using."

"Don't you have an army-issued flashlight or signal flares of some kind you can use?" I ask Jags, taking a step closer in the direction that Finn's voice had come from.

I don't like the stillness the whole place has suddenly taken on with the new darkness—it's creepy not being able to see even a hint of my friends. The only light is coming from the small window above the door where Jags is standing, and I can barely make out the top of his head.

"Everyone stay calm. Follow the direction of my voice and slowly come back this way," Jags tells us.

"Where is everyone?" Marley whines from the distance. Her voice comes from somewhere on my right, but it seems as if a whole football field separates us. I take another step and run into someone who "oomph's" in response. My hands bat the air in search of a face but I have to lower them until I find the top of a fluffy head of hair.

"Finn?" I ask hopefully, even though I know it's not likely him—the head is quite a bit smaller than that of my would-be-boyfriend.

"No, Emma. It's me," Jake answers. My hands discover his face, and I run my fingers around it nervously. My fingertip lands on something squishy, apparently poking him in the eye. "Ow! Knock it off!" he yells.

I'm just relieved to have found another person standing so close to me. My hand travels down his arm until I find his hand. I grip it tightly inside my own. "Stay with me," I tell him, taking another step toward Jags's voice.

"Somebody, turn the light back on so I can see where I'm going," Cheese begs from behind me. He would've been standing behind the pins when the lights had gone off. I freeze in place, debating whether to try and coax him our way or to continue in my search for Finn. My heart beats so fiercely in my chest that I can hardly think.

"Just stay there," Jags's voice orders from somewhere in the darkness.

"Cheese, is there another door in the back?" Finn asks.

"No," our young friend answers, his voice wavering.

"You still have your gun?" Finn asks grimly. I'm getting dizzy from all the voices swirling around me and wish they were closer. Apparently my depth perception in the dark royally sucks.

"Yeah," Cheese squeaks. His newfound hero complex is MIA, although I would be just as freaked out if I were standing alone. Holding the hand of a twelve-year-old boy doesn't do a whole lot more to comfort me.

When I take another tentative step forward, my shin connects with something metal. The pain is instantly hot where I imagine a goose egg will eventually form. "Ouch!" I yell out.

"Em, you okay?" Finn asks. His voice is getting closer.

The pain shoots up my leg and I begin to dance around. Unfortunately, I drop Jake's hand in the process. "Son of a—" I collapse down to the floor when tripping over my own feet.

"Emma?" Jake cries out from somewhere above me.

"What's going on over there?" Finn demands. "Emma, are you okay?"

Loud banging noises erupt at the entrance of the building and a few of us cry out in surprise. The infected dead are coming. If there are too many of them, our chances of survival are probably slim to none. Turning the lights off seems to have been a really crappy idea at this point.

"They're here!" Jags tells us, as if we already didn't know. "This old door won't hold them for long! Someone find the light switch and turn it on when I say. If they get in I need to be able to see what I'm shooting at!"

"Jake!" I cry out, swiping at the air for my little buddy, but not finding anything to hold onto.

Odd little noises come from all around me in the darkness, but I can't identify the source of them. I try to scramble back onto my feet even though I can't will my stubborn feet to move. The pounding at the door becomes louder and louder. Someone cries behind me.

Suddenly, a low moan starts up from somewhere nearby. Fear ripples through me, seizing my chest. There's an infected person inside. Did they find another way in? Has someone in our group turned?

This is it. I'm going to die from a heart attack after everything else we've been through.

My happiest memories flash through my mind with the heightened level of fear. Most of them have to do with either my parents or Finn. I realize with sadness that I'll never again experience my mom's burned lasagna or my dad's really strong margaritas that my parents never realized I enjoyed right along with them. I still hold on to the hope that my dad's alive out there somewhere, and not infected with this obnoxious virus.

The whole Romeo and Juliet pact I couldn't get Finn to adhere to seems like the easiest way out at the moment. If only I could find him, maybe I could talk him into it now. I don't know how thrilled he would be about having to actually shoot me before the infected get to us, but I could probably provoke Cash enough to do it for him.

The moaning behind me becomes deafening.

"Finn?" I cry out softly, praying he's okay and not the one who turned.

"I found the lights!" a voice sounding like Darrin's calls out—I can't be sure it's him as the kid hardly ever says anything.

"Hit them!" Jags yells from the entrance. "I can't hold them off any longer!"

The fluorescent lights flicker and hum over us. With tears that refuse to fall blurring my vision, it takes a minute longer for my eyes to adjust. Aside from the continued banging at the door, an abnormal stillness fills the room. I tell myself it's because everyone else is also trying to adjust their eyes, but I shudder. With the harsh cast from the artificial lights and the disturbing life the air has taken on, my breath becomes tight.

Something's terribly wrong.

When my eyes are totally focused, I first discover Jake curled into a little ball and sobbing on the floor just feet from me. All that's missing from him looking like a two-year-old is a thumb to his mouth. The poor kid is going to need some serious therapy if we're somehow able to survive this. But then again, we probably all will.

"Jake," I call quietly to him. "It's okay, buddy. Come here." Reaching out for my friend, I beckon him to come to me. He won't move and continues to cry much like he had when stuck under that car in the lot, just before I was bit.

The moaning starts up again, but it's even louder and sounds much, much too close for my comfort. With all my attention focused on helping Jake, I wasn't able to get a good look around the room to find the source of the too-familiar noise. My heart rate slows to a dangerously slow level.

Someone in the bowling alley has definitely changed.

If it's Finn, I may as well give in and run to the pack banging on the door. I hope that they would pull out one of my major body organs first to end the misery as quickly as possible.

I suddenly feel movement just behind me. Ever so slowly, I turn my head to see what's behind me before screaming for my life.

Chapter 18

At this point I know the following things to be true:

1. My mother is dead. Her horrifying death is something I have yet to come to terms with. My brain has gone through some seriously damaging events in the past few days, and it will take time for everything to process before I'm able to properly mourn. I was never much of a crier before all of this, but now I know something inside me has completely broken.

2. I'm one hundred and fifty percent in love with my best friend and it's not just because he seems like one of my only options at this point. While we have yet to share a kiss to discover if there's any chance of us being anything more than buddies, I'm hoping we will have the opportunity to actually be alone again sometime to test this theory out.

3. A time will probably never come in which I'm rid of the most annoying person I've ever known in my lifetime. My best friend's brother has always been around to harass me, and more than once, I hoped he would catch this virus thing that seems to be going around. But I've put up with

him for this long, so maybe it won't literally kill me to have him around as long as we both continue to survive.

4. My family unit has changed to include a whole gaggle of pubescent boys, my gay ex-boyfriend and a few AWOL Army soldiers. They may be an odd crew to hang out with, but they're my crew and I may actually be growing fond of a few of them—even though they've started to smell like something you would find in the bottom of a gym locker.

5. Being bit by another human really sucked at first and hurt something awful at the time, but it may have proven in the end to be a really good science experiment. At least now I know that I won't die from zombie slobber if there are any future attacks.

These are all solid, tangible facts that my mind can process and that I've come to terms with in the past few days. But now that our harmless fun at some random bowling alley in the middle of what feels like the ends of the earth has been interrupted by more of the rotten, totally annoying, never-ending hungry infected human corpses that I've come to despise even more than my best friend's brother, it would seem there are some things I still can't deal with.

My only female companion on this nightmare of a journey turning into something we're going to have to shoot being the first of them.

Marley stands with her mouth agape and her arms reaching out for me. Her vacant eyes are searching to the ceiling above and her face has broken into the telltale signs of infection; red boils erupting from her face, oozing with blood. She doesn't resemble the same witchcraft-believing, goth-loving, sometimes fun-spirited person we've all come to know so well in the past few days.

I scamper to my feet, feeling like there's someone else

in control of my body when it won't move as quickly as my mind wants it to. My screams of shock and fear mixed together have brought a number of people into immediate action that feels slow and drawn out, like some kind of ending scene in a really crappy movie in which everyone dies.

Jags—our giant defender of all that's evil—is busy trying to hold the door shut with his massive body, but my would-be paramour and his moron of a brother spring forward for what I hope to be my rescue. Cheese is also running to me from behind Marley with his gun drawn. For a sliver of a second I'm afraid he'll take aim at her when I'm standing mere feet away. From the corner of my eye, I can also see Zander barreling in my direction. I fear from his body language that I'm about to be the subject of one of his biggest tackles on record.

Watching Payton shoot my newly acquired soldier friend just the other day had been hard enough, but the thought of someone killing my old cohort in front of me makes my stomach and my mind both whirl around.

From some deep, dark place, visions of our family maid being beheaded in front of my eyes begin to play through my memory in disturbingly full color. Other less-than-pleasant memories try to break through behind it from all the things I'd temporarily forgotten. My scream becomes trapped in my throat, and I'm virtually unable to move despite the immediate threat from Marley.

All at once, I'm propelled backwards with a hit so hard I finally understand the meaning behind the saying having the wind knocked out of you. My back slams against the floor, bringing fresh pain to my body. Zander lands on top of me, resulting in both of us letting out a very loud "oomph."

A gun goes off, roaring like shots of thunder in the small alley.

Zander's wide eyes are staring down at me from just inches away. I peer around his large mass to discover fragments of skull on the floor beyond where we lay. I turn back to bury my face in Zander's chest, not wanting to see any more of Marley's innards that cover the floor. Moisture blurs my vision, but I know the tears are from the weight of my friend on top of me. I haven't been able to shed proper tears for my mother—I certainly won't find it in me to mourn the loss of anyone else.

I'm dead inside.

"Em! Are you okay?" Finn asks from somewhere in the immediate vicinity.

Someone is crying in the room—most likely Jake. Zander hoists himself off me and then offers his hand, helping me to stand on my feet.

"Thanks," I tell my friend. But I'm just about knocked right back off my feet when Finn collides into me. His hands fly up to the sides of my face.

"You're okay? You didn't get bit again?" He leans back to examine my body for any sign of injuries.

"I'm okay," I say. "I'm okay." I think the second confirmation was for my own benefit.

Finn yanks me into his chest and wraps me in his arms, kissing the top of my head. We nuzzle our heads together as we embrace. Both of us are laughing nervously out of relief. "I thought you were the one who turned," I whisper with my lips against his ear. "When I heard the moaning…" I shake my head.

"I was sure it was you," he says to the side of my face, his breath hot against my ear. We pull our faces back in to face each other so our noses and foreheads are touching.

I close my eyes. "It's my fault she turned," I whisper. "I never should've suggested we eat those candy bars."

"Look at me," Finn commands. I do as I'm told. "You didn't make her do anything. She wanted to eat one just as badly as you did. I think everything we've been through has made us each a little bit mad." He looks down at me with serious intensity. This is a tender side of my friend that I get a rare view of, and the impact of it causes my breath to catch in my throat.

"Everyone else okay?" Cheese asks loudly.

Finn and I pull apart to look at our young friend. He stands next to Marley's remains, but purposely looks past them with obvious care not to see any of it. Eyes wild, he makes jittery movements, reminding me of a dog having just heard fireworks. Zander stands nearby with his arm around his little brother, who also seems pretty shook up. Miller holds a hand on Jake's shoulder, but Jake's tears have dried—he isn't the one crying.

My eyes finally settle on Cash, who is crouched next to his dead girlfriend's body. I actually experience a glimmer of guilt for all the crap I've given him over the years with the sight of him sobbing. I didn't want to see her body, but it's too late now. She was most definitely shot straight through the brain—a gaping hole in her forehead gives a clear view of her remaining brain matter. Her lifeless eyes point up at the ceiling and her mouth hangs open in a last silent moan that won't ever escape.

"Cash," I say, stepping toward him. I figure if I'm the only female in the room it's my duty by default to comfort him, even if we are life-long enemies of sorts.

"Stop right there!" Cash yells, holding his hand out. "Don't you dare come any closer!" His eyes are burning into me with disdain. I push up against Finn, who begins rubbing his hands up and down my arms.

"She didn't do anything, Cash," Finn tells his brother in a sharp voice.

"The hell she didn't!" Cash snaps. "It was her bright idea to eat that shit in the first place!"

"I hate to break things up, but I think we have bigger problems on our hands right now!" Jags yells in a strained voice from behind us.

We turn to see him pushing his back up against the door with such force that his face burns bright red and the veins in his neck unnaturally bulge. Some of the infected wave their hands through a crack in the door, moaning with excitement.

Zander, Finn, and Miller rush into his direction. Cash is still giving me a death stare, so I shuffle sideways until I'm standing close to Jake. I set my arm on my little buddy's shoulders and he hugs my waist tightly.

I look back to the doorway. My quarterback friend is trying to look past the flailing arms to the street outside while the guys beside him stand with their guns aimed at the arms, ready to shoot if they break through the door.

"How many are there?" Finn asks.

"Can't say for sure, but there are a hell of a lot of them," Zander answers.

In a flurry of events, the door suddenly bursts open, pushing all four guys down to the ground with it. The infected pile in the same way rats would scurry through underground passageways, although fortunately at a much, much slower speed. Their blank eyes stare into the room and their mouths hang wide open while their arms grasp at the air in the typical Thriller pose. I decide I'm getting really sick of these things.

I yelp at the invasion and pull Jake closer to me, wondering what we're supposed to do. I don't have a gun on me at the moment, which is probably a blessing—with my inexperience I would have better luck at shooting one of the guys. Without a back entrance, there isn't anywhere else to go. We're trapped.

I look over to Cash and find him scrambling to his feet with his gun pulled. But glancing back to the doorway now flooded with the infected, I know there are too many for him to shoot on his own.

Jake and I hug each other tightly. "Just keep your eyes shut, bud," I whisper.

When the first large male walking corpse jerks down to the ground only feet away from us, I flinch in confusion. Then a second, small female without any arms jerks until she's lying on top of him. One by one, the infected fall, landing either near or directly on top of my four friends.

"Finn!" I yell out. He's busy fighting off a smaller woman who seems to have stumbled on top of him. Her mouth is mere inches from his neck when she jerks around and falls flat on his chest.

I'm even more confused when bright lights and loud noises from the street outside all swirl together. Suddenly, there are more Army soldiers entering the bowling alley with guns drawn, yelling and shooting in a flurry of movements. They're quick to take down the remaining dead with their handguns, some of them even using knives. Jake and I both hold our heads down as the shots ring loudly through the building.

When the room becomes nearly silent, I finally look up. A bulky, tan-skinned soldier stands tall in the middle of the new group and asks in a gruff voice, "Everyone here okay?"

My guys help each other back onto their feet. Finn runs back to me, letting me pull him close for another embrace. He surveys the room while making small circles with his hands on my back. The others from our group look upon the pile of carnage with matching bewilderment.

Miller and Jags are engaged in a conversation with some of the soldiers—I catch them giving their names, ranks and division numbers. I don't miss the murderous glare Cash still gives me each time I look his way. Marley's body is still positioned near his feet, so I have a hard time looking in his direction anyway.

"I think everyone is okay," Finn tells the soldier. "You guys showed up just in time."

The soldier lowers his gun and gives us a kind smile. "You're lucky we came when we did. You would never have been able to fight all of them off by yourselves. What are you kids doing here, anyway? Why haven't you moved on to one of the safety zones yet?"

"Most of us came down from Minnesota," Finn tells him. "These two soldiers agreed to help us. It's kind of a long and complicated story."

The soldier motions for us to follow with a wave of his hand, and most of the other soldiers begin vacating the building. "You can fill us in on the way to our camp."

No one in our group moves, however. We stand in place and shoot each other nervous glances. Even Finn is less than thrilled by this proposal. Our experience with the Army hasn't necessarily all been pleasant.

"What's the matter?" the soldier asks. "If you stay with us, we'll keep you from getting attacked again."

"We were just at an Army camp a few miles down the road, and that didn't end so well," Finn tells him.

The soldier frowns at this. "Whatever happened there is beyond our involvement. Our base is twenty miles south of here in the nearest safety zone. We heard about a division of the military and came to help get things under control."

I eye him suspiciously. "What is your eventual goal in all of this, soldier?"

"It's Lieutenant Colonel to you, Miss, and we're the good guys. Our eventual goal is to put an end to this outbreak and ensure people like you are kept out of harm's way." His voice is smooth and clear and his words are confident and strong. Times like these I'm proud to be an American and I'm glad to know these guys have our backs, regardless of what Payton and his mob are planning.

"That's good enough for me," I decide, pulling on Finn's arm.

"Wait a minute," Finn says, refusing to budge. He looks back at Mr. LC. "Have you been in contact with a soldier by the name of Payton?"

Mr. LC scowls and shakes his head. "That's not a name I'm familiar with."

"Do you know anything about the FBI's involvement in what is happening?" Finn asks.

"We're aware of a breach of command somewhere in the system. The FBI may or may not be involved in said breach. We're trying to sort the facts and make sure no more civilians are harmed in the process."

Finn is still hoping for some kind of assurance that his mom is in fact alive, but wasn't the woman who tried luring us into a trap. He sighs deeply and looks around at our group. Cash won't acknowledge his brother but the rest of the group nods, one by one. With that, the decision is made—we will go along with this new batch of Army soldiers to their camp. I only hope it's nothing like the last nightmare from which we had narrowly escaped.

* * *

THE "SAFETY ZONE" turns out to be nothing like the Army camp. We pull into a small town surrounded by secure fences with barbed wire and hundreds of soldiers, but there aren't any tents. The atmosphere is very somber here. We're all given a very thorough security screening involving body scans and having to answer really strange questions about our family history and actions in the past twenty-four hours before being cleared to enter.

The town has been taken over by the Army. A newer development of homes on the edge of town has been converted into safety houses for the non-infected. The neighborhood looks to be only a few months old with blankets of new grass that have darkened with the chill of winter. Unscathed swing sets stand in a few of the yards as well as basketball hoops and discarded play toys. The neighborhood in general looks un-disturbed. It's a welcoming sight to come upon something where there aren't any signs of panic or mayhem.

"Your group will be assigned a home for the time being," a young, pimple-faced soldier with a pale white complexion and strawberry blond hair explains to us as the truck parks along the street. He's incredibly lanky and looks to be the same age as me, but his voice is abnormally deep and he seems wise beyond his years. "Keep in mind everything is just on a temporary basis until we regain control of our country."

"Who has control now?" Finn asks.

The soldier stands and motions for us to exit, saying, "That's classified."

Our group piles out of the back end of the truck, one at a time, until only the pimply soldier, Finn, Cash and I remain.

"I'm not a part of this group," Cash says bluntly, unmoving.

"Like I said," the soldier says, turning to him, "the arrangements are temporary. Just be glad you've got a bed to sleep in. Thousands of citizens are unaccounted for, possibly shacking up in random abandoned homes, worrying whether or not they'll get attacked in their sleep."

"Or maybe they've all turned into flesh-hungry monsters," I'm quick to remind him.

"Hey, Emma," Cash calls out. Chills run up my spine —I don't think I've ever heard my name spoken with such hatred.

Finn has been holding my hand since leaving the bowling alley, and he squeezes it now in a gesture of encouragement. The rest of the crew, already standing in the street, has stopped to peer into the truck, all eyes on Finn. Slowly, I turn to face him as well.

"Do you even feel remorseful for what you did? Do you even care that Marley is dead? She was your friend too. But instead of mourning, you seem to be cracking jokes at her expense—and your mother's."

I stare back, not sure how to answer. Of course I'm horrified by what happened to Marley, and actually do feel responsible for her death—regardless of what Finn thinks. But in this new, insane world we've come to know in the past few days, I've been forcing my mind not to think of the things that will make me crawl into a ball and become unresponsive. Things like my mother's death are too much for me to process.

Finn looks kindly upon his brother. "Cash, you know she feels bad about Marley. We all do. But it's not fair to throw Emma's mom into this."

Cash glowers back. "If you're going to continue to defend her then it's time for you to make a choice—her or me. I'm not going to stay here with her. If you choose her, I'll leave and you won't have to see me again."

I drop Finn's hand and take one step closer to Cash. "No. I'll leave. I'll ask to be reassigned to a different zone."

"No!" Jake yells from the street.

"That won't be necessary," Finn says, putting his arm around my waist. "If you're going to make me choose, then I choose Emma. I'm not going to let her be ostracized from the group for something she didn't do. I love her, Cash."

If someone had told me a few months ago that he would be confessing his love for me to his moronic brother, I would have laughed them out of the room. But we've been forced to become older and wiser in our quest to live and make it through all of this—at least Finn has.

My breathing slows, and I turn to my friend. "Don't do this. You can't choose me over your family, Finn. If something has happened to your mom, then Cash is all you have left."

"I knew you'd pick your pathetic girlfriend over me," Cash sneers.

Finn's eyes radiate warmth and tenderness. "Emma, you're my family just as much as he is. I don't want to have to choose between you, but I'm not going to leave your side through all of this. If you go, then I go."

"So who's staying and who's going?" the lanky soldier asks, making a disgruntled noise.

"We'll go," Finn tells him.

Zander takes a step closer to the truck. "Then the rest of us are going, too."

I shake my head at him and sigh. "No, Zander. This is ridiculous. No one should have to choose sides."

"I agree," Finn says, glancing back at his brother. "We'll stay in a different house on this base until you have cooled off. We can't separate the group now—not after all we've been through together."

"You've made your choice," Cash says in a low voice. He walks forward, roughly pushing his shoulder into me as he passes by.

* * *

THE SOLDIER LEAVES us at the doorstep of a random house. Finn and I walk inside all alone, our hands clasped together. I'll never forgive myself for making Finn choose between me and his brother, even though he had insisted it was his choice. But we're only a few blocks away from the rest of the gang, and I hold on to hope that Cash will come to his senses and forgive me—however, I'm not holding my breath for something that improbable. Cash will always be Cash.

Upon entering the house, we find it incredibly bright and airy. A grand stairway in dark mahogany wood fills the foyer, an impressive chandelier dangling over it. The smell of something wonderfully rich—possibly tomato sauce—makes my stomach growl anxiously. We know very little about this safe zone, but I hope this means there's uninfected food available.

After taking a little tour of the great room and kitchen on the main floor, we return to the bottom of the steps. The house is quiet and obviously vacant at the moment, although there are signs of recent life—dirty dishes in the sink, an open paperback book laying on the coffee table, and a pair of military boots at the bottom of the stairway.

"Would have been nice to know who else is going to be here with us," I say nervously, eyeing the boots. "Just because we're all survivors in this doesn't exclude the possibility of being roommates with Jack the Ripper."

Finn turns to me, his eyes wide in mockery. "You're right. John Wayne was from Iowa."

"The actor?" I ask, puzzled.

He grins slowly. "No. John Wayne Gacy, the serial killer."

"Well that's a relief." I sigh and let my shoulders drop. "Finn, I'm so sorry you had to leave everyone to be with me. I really wish you wouldn't have done that. You know I could probably survive a day or two on my own——"

My friend clamps his hand over my mouth. "Stop. I don't want to hear any more apologies. You know I never would have let you leave by yourself, so just get over it. Okay?"

My eyes are wide, but I nod obediently.

His grin grows larger. "I'm going to remove my hand and kiss you now, okay?"

Again I nod, a smile forming under his fingers.

When he pulls his hand away, our lips crash together—I nearly chip a tooth in the process. It's a pleasant surprise when the kiss doesn't totally suck. His mouth and tongue are warm and soft as they devour mine. His hot breath causes every bit of me to tingle delightfully. As our hands grope each other's bodies, I realize that this kiss has surpassed all others—even the epic make-out session with Eric in the back of his dad's Mustang.

"Finn," I mutter, gasping to find my breath, "do you know what would be totally awesome right now?"

From the spark in his eyes, I know he enjoyed himself just as much as I did. He makes a "hmmm" noise, then leans down to kiss me again.

Trying not to get lost in the moment—although it's quite fabulous—I push him away. "If we were to take a nice long, hot shower. Seriously. We both smell really, really funky." Finn laughs between a series of little kisses. "I mean it!" I insist, laughing, but still pushing him away.

He sighs and rests his head against mine. "Fine, but I call dibs on the shower." All at once he spins around and dashes up the stairway, taking two steps at a time. I chase him, although my shorter legs won't allow me to travel quite as fast. Once at the top of the stairway I squeal and leap onto his back.

Finn laughs and struggles to free himself of me, but opens the first door to reveal a small bedroom with an unmade double bed. I jump off his back and race him to the next door, screaming wildly as he tries to push me aside and opens it before I can.

We both stop short when the door hits the wall beside it.

Clad in nothing more than a white towel barely covering his lower half, Payton stands in front of the sink with a toothbrush in hand.

Chapter 19

Payton's eyes are just as wide as ours must be, but my surprise is mostly due to the shock of seeing him shirtless. The guy's muscles are even more impressive than I'd fantasized them to be. I think if I were to bounce a quarter off his pectoral muscles, it would bounce back at us with enough force to take out an eye.

Payton draws in a breath of air and drops the tooth-brush to grip the towel securely at his waistline. "Emma! Finn! You're okay! How did you get here? Where are the others?"

Once I remember I should be afraid of this traitor who once claimed to be our friend, I take a step backwards until I'm pushed up against Finn. My boyfriend (it's probably safe to assume that by now) pulls on me so I'm standing behind him.

"What in the hell are you doing here?" Finn snaps. I nod—it's a good question. What exactly would Payton be doing in this safe zone, and why is he acting like nothing strange happened back at the other Army camp?

Payton draws his mouth into a thin line and motions to

the door. "Give me a minute to get dressed. I have a lot to tell you."

"We are so not going to listen to anything you have to say right now," I mumble from behind Finn's shoulder, but Payton has already shut the door to the bathroom.

Finn draws the gun from his jeans. "Em, run downstairs and hide. Don't come out until I come down for you."

"What do you think you're going to do?" I ask. "We both need to get the hell out of here, Finn! That psycho is obviously on the bad side of all of this, and you don't stand a chance of taking him over with your wimpy little gun!"

"Just go," Finn says more forcefully. He's busy trying to push me toward the stairway and I'm trying to hold my ground when the bathroom door again opens. Payton stands in the doorway still shirtless but wearing his uniform pants. He's holding a large gun directed at us.

"Are you kidding me? Again?" I groan. I hit Finn's shoulder. "I told you we should've gotten out of here!" Payton is quite obviously more than AWOL at this point—more like completely WACKO.

"Put your weapon down!" Payton barks at Finn.

Finn slowly draws his hand out and lets the weapon fall to the ground. "Who are you guys, really?" Payton asks with narrowed eyes.

I roll my eyes to the ceiling. "Holy crap, Payton. We're the same people you met back in Minnesota. I'm the same one you wanted to shoot once before. You know, right before you were about to get your brains blown out by that old coot, and we saved you? But you are not who we thought you to be, are you? We should be asking who or… what…you...really?" Once again, he has me flustered to the point I'm stumbling over my own words. I blame those ridiculous pecs of his.

"Why?" Payton asks. "What did you see?"

"You led the lynch mob out after us back at that Army camp." Finn says, much more gracefully than I would have put it. "Are you going to explain to us what that was all about?"

"That wasn't me," Payton insists. His eyes narrow and he moves the gun so it's pointed directly at me. "When all of us were walking together a couple of days ago, sharing what we want to do if this really is the end of the world, what did you say?"

I groan and throw my arms up to my sides. "Come on! Are you being serious?" At this point I'm sure he must be doing all of this for his own amusement. Why else would he choose to ask me such a mortifying question?

He shakes his head firmly, his hands still wrapped tightly around the gun. "I need to be sure it's really you. Just answer the question."

Glancing to Finn first—who is actually giving me a hint of a smile—I answer, "I said I didn't want to die a virgin. Happy now? I really hope you're enjoying yourself."

But Payton is not happy. He continues looking at me with a funny distrust. He motions at my shoulder with the gun. "Let me see your bite."

I snort. "Now you're just trying to get me to take my clothes off." I can't imagine what all of this is about, and he's really starting to irritate me. We're the ones who should be questioning him to see if he's still our friend, or if he has turned to the dark side as we suspect. Next thing you know, he'll be wearing a black mask and breathing funny.

"Just show me!" Payton barks, his level of tension elevated.

"Take it easy," Finn warns him. I can feel my boyfriend leaning forward, poised to jump if Payton really decides to shoot me. I'm really hoping it doesn't come to that, however. I'm guessing a gunshot may trump a human bite as far as the pain factor goes.

"Okay!" I bark back, pulling my shirt down. "Are you happy now?" To my surprise, I find the gauze covering the wound to be soaked in blood. Something bright green oozes from underneath the sides. I intake a sharp breath of air—the color is rather funky and almost appears to be glowing.

"Let me see it," Finn says, leaning in.

"Not without gloves!" I snap, pulling away. But his fingers gently lift a corner of the tape off my skin, and he makes a horrible face with his discovery. The dense air against the wound makes me squeal out in pain.

"Sorry," Finn says. "Em, it looks bad. I think it may be infected or something."

Payton lowers the gun and lets out a sigh, his shoulders dropping. "Sorry, I couldn't take any chances. A lot of shit has been going down. Is the bite really that bad?"

A second later, Finn's fist is thrown into Payton's jaw, making a dull popping noise. Payton blinks and takes a staggering step back while Finn shakes his hand violently, flexing his jaw and mumbling many swear words.

"Don't ever point a gun at her again," Finn glowers. "You got it?" Payton bobs his head in affirmation and rubs his jaw.

I cradle Finn's wounded hand and beam up at him. "Finn! That was freaking awesome!" Truth is, I'm getting highly annoyed with Payton wanting to shoot me and glad Finn actually did something about it.

"Sorry," Payton says. "But if you knew what I've been through, you would understand."

"What have you seen?" I ask. "Pretty sure at this point we could trump your story."

Payton laughs. "I don't think you have a chance. We better clean out your wound. Someone on this base can look at it later. Then we'll get you guys something to eat. I'm guessing you're starved by now. Then I'll tell you everything I know." He turns back to the bathroom.

I take the moment to balance on my tiptoes and give Finn a hero-worthy kiss. "That was awesome, Finn. Seriously."

He looks down at his hand and shakes it lightly. "It didn't feel very awesome. He's right though, we need to do something about your shoulder." He doesn't have to say any more. I know by the face he made and the awful color of my wound, there's something horribly wrong.

* * *

THANKFULLY, the Army has supplied the house with food they know to be safe to ingest. Payton shows us the stash in the kitchen that he calls "MRE" packets. I look at the small wrapped items and decide MRE stands for "may require e-magination." I'm still cautious, taking into consideration the different interactions we've had with soldiers in the past couple of days, not to mention Marley's ill-fated snacks.

Finn and I devour some kind of meat out of the packets. It actually turns out to taste pretty decent. My stomach rolls angrily with the introduction of new food, and I try to remember the last time we ate anything. The bottles of water we're each given disappear in nearly one breath, so Payton gives us more. I drink until my stomach feels so full it's in danger of bursting.

Payton sits on the couch across from us with his hands held together and his elbows resting on his knees, watching.

For the first time, I notice the area underneath his eyes has become dark and sunken in. He doesn't look malnourished or anything—I got a good enough eyeful of his body to verify that earlier—but there's something behind his eyes now that's older, possibly even wiser.

"Is your shoulder feeling any better?" Payton asks.

I shrug. "The pain's just enough to remind me that we're not stuck in some crappy nightmare."

"We need to get a doc to look at that once the sun is up," he says. "If it's infected, you could get violently ill."

"Are you going to tell us your story now or what?" I ask.

He huffs a large breath of air out of his cheeks. "I brought everyone into the camp just as we planned. We were taken to a smaller tent where a couple of soldiers were ordered to keep watch over the others. Then I was taken to another location—an old school."

My eyes light up. "Ohmigod! That's where Finn and I were, too! We saw them playing this wacked zombie rodeo thing where there were these really weird guys dressed in black, then we were kidnapped and taken down into the dark basement where—"

Finn nudges me sharply in the side. "Let him finish first, Em."

Payton raises his head and nods to me. "I was taken into the same basement to meet with a few of those strange soldiers. At first I thought they were from a foreign Army or something, but their movements were just so…precise. They seemed to communicate without having to even speak to each other."

"What do you think they were?" Finn asks.

Payton swallows hard. "Not human."

"Ha!" I cry out, hitting Finn in the arm. "I told you!"

Payton bites his lip. "Whatever they were, they were

able to do some pretty crazy shit. One of them held on to me and…" His eyes dart back and forth between Finn and me when he seems unable to finish.

"Oh," I say quietly. "They probed you, huh?"

Payton squints and jerks his head toward me. "What? No! You're seriously twisted, Emma! It was nothing like that."

I hold my shoulders up in a large shrug. "How was I supposed to know? So what did they do to you then? Have out with it!"

Payton looks past us, fixating his gaze on something else in the house. "At first I thought maybe I was going crazy or having some kind of out-of-body experience. I mean it was just too insane to believe."

"All right already!" I exclaim. "What happened? Spit it out!"

His eyes fall back on mine, and I can see the hint of a scared little boy. "I saw myself, standing right in front of me. One of the guys in black just morphed in a flickering movement until he looked like a carbon copy of me. I even reached out to push on his chest to make sure I wasn't hallucinating." Finn and I sit in stony silence, staring at our AWOL friend. Payton falls back on the couch, defeated. "You guys don't believe me, do you?"

"Actually, it would explain why we ran into someone pretending to be my mother," Finn tells him. Here we go again. Every time I begin to feel like Finn is smart enough to get us through this whole debacle, he's quick to prove me wrong.

Payton sits straight again. "Your mom is the one who busted me out of there."

I hold my hands up. "Wait a minute, guys. We agree there's something unusual going on as a whole, but who are these freaky clones? What are they doing, and what do they have to do with this other big problem we're having—you know, the whole dead rising again thing? And what do you mean Finn's mom busted you out? How did you know it was her? Was she wearing a name tag that said 'Finn's mom,' or what?"

Payton shrugs. "I don't know all the answers to your questions, Emma. Whatever was going on, they didn't seem to intend to hurt me in any way. I was locked away in some dark hole until Finn's mom came to set me free. I think it was her, anyway."

"And this woman looked like…" I ask, motioning for him to elaborate.

"Almost as tall as me, but real skinny with brown eyes and brown hair," he says. "It has to be his mom—she looks a lot like him."

"It's your mom!" I tell Finn, slapping his arm again.

"Or her clone," Finn corrects me.

I roll my eyes.

"She said she was trying to find her son and his friends—that's when I put it all together. She told me she knew what was going on and knew a way out of the school. When we heard footsteps, she told me to run to the end of the hallway and wait for her in the furnace room. I waited for over an hour, but she never joined me, so I felt my way through the darkness until I came into the light. I found my way back to the camp, but you guys were all gone by then."

"So you just ran off and left her there?" I ask. "You sure are stretching this AWOL thing out as far as you can, aren't you?"

He rolls his eyes to the ceiling. "She told me to go on without her if anything happened. She seemed like the type who could fend for herself. She nearly shot me trying to decide if I was one of those clones."

"Well what did she say was going on?" asks Finn.

Payton shakes his head. "We didn't exactly have time to discuss things."

"We have to go back," Finn says. "They must have cloned my mom and have her held captive somewhere."

"You can't go back," Payton tells him. "The clones—or whatever they are—are the ones doing the bombing, and they're still planning to wipe out all of the Midwest. Every human soldier I've come in contact with disagrees with all of this. Whatever is happening is not a result from the U.S. Army. These clones are leading the attack. I'm not the only one to go AWOL in the past couple of days because of it."

"Even better reason to go back," Finn says. "Someone needs to stop them."

I snort. "What—you're going to stop them? I think we've already established these clones aren't human. You don't know what they're capable of. Maybe they would decide to probe you, Finn. I don't think that sounds like a very pleasant experience overall, and let's face it—you're not exactly the fighting type unless a television screen and game controllers are involved." I motion to his wounded fist as proof.

"She's right," Payton says to Finn. "The soldiers running this camp are well aware that the Army has been divided with these clones, and they're planning to evacuate in the next couple of days. Going back now would be more like a suicide mission."

"Finn, your mom is an agent for the federal government," I say. "Something tells me a bunch of high school kids aren't going to be able to do anything she can't already." Or so I say. I can't stand the thought of my boyfriend going back to that creepy place—especially with the potential of probing.

Finn shakes his head and stands up. "I can't just turn

away from her, Em. She may not be able to save herself this time. She's been missing for the past six months. Maybe these clone people are holding her hostage."

"Well you can't do it alone," Payton says, standing beside him.

I groan in anger and stand in front of them. "You two can't be serious. Payton, did you see the little Frankenstein lab they had set up in that school? Something majorly whacked was going on there. You guys can't go back! Your plans always suck!"

"Em, it will be okay," Finn counters, lacing his fingers with mine.

"No! It won't! I lost my mom and I can't stand the thought of losing you, too!" Real, actual tears are filling my eyes. I know I'm being selfish in asking him to choose me over a family member once again—even though I actually like Elizabeth. But for the first time in days it feels like we're safe. I don't want to go back there. I can't. Pretty sure my legs wouldn't carry me back there if I tried. Fear has won over every other emotion in my body. Well, except for maybe the ever present hormones.

Finn wraps his arms around me and buries his face in my hair. "I promise to come back to you, Em."

The crazy flurry of emotions raging through me become so consuming my eyes won't stop watering. Before I understand what is happening, I'm crying. Full out, tears raging down my face, snot dripping out of my nose. Once I realize I can feel something again, the tears won't stop coming. Too many emotions are involved. My arms clutch Finn's warm body and I push my snot-filled face into his chest, finally letting loose.

* * *

WHEN I WAKE, my body is sprawled across the king-sized bed in the master bedroom that has been impeccably decorated in sophisticated gold and brown tones. The only sound to be heard is the hum of a large fan that spins lazily at the peak of the vaulted ceiling, bringing a welcoming movement of air across my tired, dried tear-streaked face. Light spills in through the large bay windows, bringing the first morning light. I wrestle away the sheets that have wrapped around me like some kind of sea urchin in my slumber, and leap to the doorway—tripping twice in the process—with a spreading panic that I've missed Finn and he's gone.

Once in the hallway I hear voices drifting up to me from the main floor, low and serious. I fly down the stairway so quickly I nearly wipe out. When I enter the great room I'm surprised to find everyone gathered— Zander, Darrin, Jake, Cheese, Miller, Jags, Payton, Finn, and even Cash. I run a hand over my wild hair and stand straight with my hand on my hip, attempting not to look exhausted from coming down so quickly.

"Emma!" Jake says brightly. A flurry of other greetings is directed at me, but my eyes settle on Cash. He stands behind the couch and stares out the window on the other side of the room, looking like he'd rather be anywhere else.

"Hey, Cash," I say to everyone's surprise. But he won't turn and acknowledge me. I timidly cross the room to where Finn sits. He reaches out to pull me into his lap and kisses my neck before wrapping me in his arms.

"Pretty much everyone has agreed to go back with Finn," Payton tells me, his voice gentle, begging for forgiveness. "We also agreed it would be best if you stayed here, considering your bite and everything you've been through."

"My bite is fine," I say through clenched teeth. "And I'll go if I decide I want to. You're not the boss of me."

I look around the room. Most of the guys hold their heads down sheepishly with the guilt of deciding my fate against my wishes. The group, in general, looks to be freshly showered and wearing newer clothing they must have found in the abandoned homes. The shirts for everyone but Zander are one or two sizes too big, only Zander's is this ridiculous golf print that in any other set of circumstances, I know he wouldn't be caught dead wearing.

"I don't want to go with, either," Jake tells me in a small voice. I study him for a moment, wondering if he's being sincere or if the other guys bullied him into saying that so I would have a reason to stay behind. Then I remember the sight of him huddled in the little jail cell crying, and curled into a ball under the car while zombies surrounded him. The young boy who looks back at me has seen far too much at his age—there's a permanent fear lurking behind his eyes. He may not be "team Emma" anymore, but that annoying motherly gene in me is yelling loudly like one of those annoying older, balding guys at the basketball games Finn is always dragging me to.

"Shit," I mutter under my breath.

"We'll come back as quickly as we can," Finn whispers into my ear. "You and Jake will be safe here."

I look over to Cheese…Darrin…Zander. They have the same look as Jake, only they're quite obviously trying to hold a brave front with the rest of the guys. "Are you sure everyone needs to go?" I ask. "Wouldn't it be better if you stormed the fort with fewer people?"

Payton shakes his head. "We need as many as possible for our plan to work."

I stand when the panic escalates. "Whatever your little plan is this time, I don't want to know, Payton. Your plans never seem to go the way you hope they will. How can you plan against something you know nothing about, anyway? How are you guys even going to be able to tell a clone from a normal soldier? Have you thought about that?"

But I already know the difference is easy to spot. The way the soldiers and robot Elizabeth had acted was glaringly obvious—especially when one soldier's eyes had twitched like a computer screen on the blitz. I just want them to think they're doomed for failure.

Finn reaches up to take my hand. "Em, we'll be okay."

My eyes tear up again when I look around the room. These once stinky, but thankfully now clean, misfit group of guys have become my family. I still hope my father is somewhere out there, unscathed, but it doesn't seem possible I'll find him any time soon. Losing Marley had been extremely hard—I'm sure losing any more of them would be nothing short of heartbreaking. I can't even pretend to wonder how I would deal with losing Finn.

"When are you leaving?" I ask softly. Finn squeezes my hand.

"In an hour," Payton answers. "We're going to bring one of the big trucks around and gather supplies, restock on ammunition."

My stupid lip won't stop quivering. "So this is it?"

"We'll come to let you know when it's time for us to leave," Payton says.

"We should start getting ready," Jags tells him. He stands near the doorway with Miller—they both seem to be high on alert by the way their bodies are held erect. I just hope they're not crazy enough to lead my non-military friends into a bloodbath, or even a really quick death, without a lot of blood.

Payton nods in agreement and stands. One by one, everyone files out of the room in silence, most of them catching my gaze as they leave and giving me a halfhearted smile of some sort. Cash is the last to leave me and Finn alone.

"Cash," I say gently. He stops moving but doesn't turn to face me. "I'm really sorry. Marley was more than just a friend of mine—she was like family. I wish I never would have brought up the idea of eating those stupid candy bars." The tears are rolling down my face again. Crying two times in a row has to be some kind of record for me. I guess with the end of times near I'm finally able to let myself feel something for these people I've come to love. After all, life is short—then zombies eat you.

Cash turns to me now, visibly stunned. He nods once. "I'll make sure your boyfriend gets back in one piece."

"That would be good," I answer, my voice cracking. "Thanks."

Cash forces a small smile in return before he's gone from the room.

Once the front door closes behind him, Finn stands in front of me and wipes my tears away with his sleeve. His dark brown eyes look down on me with a mixture of love, sympathy, regret, and fear. "Is this for real? Emma Ferdig is actually crying? Again?"

"Shut up," I say, trying my best not to smile. My fingers pick at the button of the navy polo shirt he changed into. The ill-fitting material hangs off his frame, seeming excessive enough to fit Payton. My friend looks better suited for a preppy keg party than a mission to rescue his mom from a bunch of inhuman creatures.

"We're going to be okay," he tells me. "All this drama is going to be for nothing."

My eyes travel back upward to meet his. "I sure hope you're right."

"I know I am." He leans in to kiss my forehead.

"You know, being in love with your best friend doesn't totally suck," I say with a short giggle, wiping the snot away from my face.

Finn smirks and pulls me tight against his chest. "So I've heard."

My own smile falls away. "Are you really going to leave me here?"

He lowers his face closer to my own. "No, I'm going to come back for you."

"Well, just to put a little more pressure on you, I'm totally going to do the Romeo and Juliet thing if anything happens to you. Only…I'll…you're…be Romeo."

He laughs. "What was that?"

I grin even though my pesky eyes are welling up again. "Just shut up and kiss me."

When our lips meet, I'm able to forget about the fact that I may never see him again. I'm able to forget that I've lost so many people close to me, including my mother and maybe even my father. But I'm not able to forget that I have yet to shower and smell terrible.

My focus becomes geared on the delicious way his lips and tongue taste against mine, the way he kneads my hair with his fingers, and the way my body melts into a buzzing warmness the longer our kiss continues. Whatever may or may not happen to him on this quest of his, at least we will always have this moment to hold on to.

Then I become angry with myself—angry that I didn't realize what a wonderful boyfriend Finn would have made all of these years, angry that I'd taken advantage of his friendship in so many ways until now, angry that this may be the last chance I ever have to show him just how much I really love him. The kiss becomes red-hot with my anger but I withdraw all at once, panting hard with a sensation that someone is beating on my chest.

"They said you guys won't be leaving for an hour yet, right?" I ask.

The look passing through his eyes becomes something desperate—something primal. I imagine it's the same look I'm giving him at the moment. "Let's go," he says in a low voice. Holding hands, we race up the stairway to fulfill my end-of-the-world quest.

Chapter 20

After hugging every last guy in our party goodbye, Jake and I stand side-by-side on the curb in front of the house—arms looped around each other—until we can no longer see the truck. Even though I've just experienced the most mind-blowing ten minutes with my boyfriend (seven and a half of those actually being foreplay), the buzz of our jaunt has been replaced with a total and complete emptiness.

I imagine it's akin to losing a pet of some kind, although my parents never allowed me to have one after the time I won a fish at the fair—they said I was too lazy just when I refused to clean its bowl and threw it in the toilet tank. I didn't understand what the big deal was—my dad once told me that thing was clean enough to drink out of incase of an emergency.

Looking down at my little buddy, I force myself to smile. "Did you see there were movies in this house?" I ask him with a raised eyebrow.

"Like porn?" he asks.

I gasp and slap him on the chest lightly. "No! Not porn! Aren't you too young to even know about that shit?"

He shrugs. "I was pretty young when I found my dad's stash."

I lead him back to the house. "I'm going to finally go take a shower and try to find something that doesn't smell like ten day old feet. How about you watch Barney or something while you wait for me?"

Jake pushes me away. "Give me a little more credit. I've seen all five of the Saw movies."

I snort. "Well, that would certainly explain the fall of today's younger generation. Between that and all the war games, you kids should be completely numb by the time you're adults."

"Assuming we live that long," Jake says, his voice filled with gloom.

I have nothing to say in return—he's right.

* * *

THE SHOWER IS hot enough to leave my skin red and raw, as if it could burn away all the horrible memories. I even take the time to shave my legs, hoping Finn had been too caught up in the moment to notice they were beginning to resemble those of a dog's. Ten minutes in, the water temperature drops, and I squeal from the sudden icy cold pellets.

I step out and towel myself off, taking special care not to disturb the wet dressing Payton had just taped to my shoulder. I didn't remove it, thinking I couldn't stand to look at the nasty wound again. We got the address for the doctor from Payton and plan to go there just as soon as I'm ready.

Although the house is new and decorated appropriately for the current trends, the woman of the house was either really old or had a serious fashion handicap. The best I can find to wear in the spacious walk-in closet is a pair of mom jeans—covering my entire waist and needing to be rolled on the bottom numerous times—paired with a plain white sweater. I try not to look in the mirror, reminding myself that we're in apocalyptic times where fashion no longer applies, but I catch a glimpse of my reflection and frown back at it. I look like my grandmother just before she had died at age 87.

My hair has been pulled back into a ponytail for most of this adventure, but still became pretty tangled with all the running and traveling. It becomes painstakingly time consuming when I try to brush all the snarls from it. I consider looking for a pair of scissors.

"Emma?" Jake calls from the other side of the door. "Are you okay in there?"

Frustrated, I decide to ditch the horrible de-tangling nightmare and leave my curls straight. I reenter the master bedroom to find my little buddy lying on his stomach in the king-sized bed, watching the flat screen television on the opposite wall. He gives me a funny half-smile when he sees the ridiculous getup I'm wearing.

"Nice pants," he snickers.

My eyes shift away from him to the television, finding he has actually picked one of my parents' favorite classics from the 80's—Cocoon. "Have you ever seen this before?" I ask, pointing my brush at the television.

Jake rolls his eyes. "No. And it's really dumb. I figured it would be about a bunch of aliens doing experiments on humans or invading their bodies like in the real alien movies. But it's really lame. I think this guy has a thing for one of the aliens—she looks just like a normal person but she's not very hot. She has boy-hair."

"Show some respect. She was hot in the 80s," I tell him, my voice trailing off. Or so my parents told me. But his words run through my head again and I freeze in place.

Aliens doing experiments on humans or invading their bodies.

Could that possibly be what is really going on? Sarah, the female soldier who turned after dressing my wound, told us the feds were considering a possibility that aliens were involved. That would maybe explain how they were able to clone Elizabeth and Payton and how that soldier's eyes had flickered. Maybe it would even explain the humans we had seen in those cages who appeared to be subject to some kind of weird science experiment.

"What's wrong? Jake asks.

Realizing my jaw is hanging down, I quickly snap it shut and turn to face him. "Jake, what if it's not terrorists who brought this virus to our country?"

Jake shrugs. "I don't think anyone ever said that it was, Emma."

I dip my head at the television. "What if it's aliens, just like Sarah said?"

My little friend flips around so he's sitting on his butt. "I think we already discussed that option." Then something in his eyes shifts. "Wait. You're not going to lose it again, are you? Finn said I need to take you to see someone immediately if you start acting funny."

I grumble and sit on the mattress next to him. "Just hear me out. We know these things—whatever they are—have some crazy ability to do things science nerds have only ever fantasized of doing. They were able to clone people, Jake. What if they brought some virus that caused this whole zombie outbreak? We heard them say they wanted to stop us before the rest of the country found out what was going on. What if they released this virus accidentally, or what if it did something they hadn't been expecting? Maybe they were testing it on people in that lab to see how they could fix it."

So maybe some of my theory had already been considered, but I think for the first time it's really hitting home that aliens may be the cause of all this. Not computer generated or Steven Spielberg created but honest to goodness, real live aliens.

Jake nods his head and pulls on my arm. "Yep, it's definitely time for us to go see that doctor guy."

I laugh. "I know you're just a kid, but you have to admit some of it would explain everything that has been happening. What I still can't figure out is why that Elizabeth-bot just let us go. And why are young people immune to this whatchamacallit? If these clone people are actually aliens, Finn and the rest of those guys won't stand any chance against them. I think we should stop them, Jake. I don't think they thought this through enough."

He grabs my other arm now. "No way, Em. We're not going anywhere. I promised I would make sure you didn't do anything stupid."

I snort and pull away from him to tap him on the head. "Well that was a dumb promise. Have you met me?"

"Let's just think about this for a while," Jake says, sounding wise beyond his years. "First we have to get your shoulder treated. You promised Finn and Payton that you would. If you still want to go after that, we would have to find someone to help us figure out how to get there. We came here in the dark, in the back of a covered truck. I have no idea what direction we even came from."

"That way," I say, pointing to the front side of the

house. But I know he's right. I probably wouldn't even be able to find my way out of this small camp at this point. What I wouldn't give for a cell phone right now or even one of those CB things Finn had used in the combine.

I cave in and agree to see the doctor. Now that I'm actually clean and feeling amazingly woman–like, I walk with more of a springing step when we get outside. The sun is actually doing its job today of warming the air. This gloomy new world of ours appears somewhat brighter under the rays, although there are still clusters of gray clouds looming off in the distance, threatening impending darkness.

A group of young boys and girls are gathered in the front yard of a nearby safe house wearing ill-fitting clothing that obviously does not belong to them. A girl no older than fourteen seems to be in charge. Seeing all of them with lost looks plastered on their faces in this new world of ours is startling. They gape at me with their mouths wide as we pass by and I wonder if I suddenly look ancient to them, considering most of the adults in the area have turned by now. Then again, it could be the ridiculous clothes I'm wearing.

What if this is truly it? Will children only live to early adulthood and then die if they don't find a way to stop this virus? Once again I'm fearful that I may someday be in the position to parent some of these children, should the other adults of the world not survive this. In that case we're all doomed.

After directions from a couple soldiers we run into, we discover the doctor in a house a couple of blocks down. The house is very similar to the one we've been assigned to, only this one is very sparse in decorations. Either the last owners had moved out or the Army decided to strip the home of any personality to make it look more official.

A doctor, who doesn't appear to be much older than I am, introduces himself as Doctor Martin. He's short and round all over, with small hazel eyes peering out behind plain, rectangular glasses that keep sliding off of his nose. Although he's wearing the standard-issued Army uniform, he seems uncomfortable in it, like he would rather be wearing a lab coat. I quickly learn his bedside manner has a lot to be desired. After I introduce myself and Jake, he stands silently beside me and folds his hands, waiting for me to speak.

"So you've gone to med school and all that?" I ask suspiciously.

"Mhmm," he hums in a lower voice, staring a hole into me.

"So you're like a real doctor then?" I ask.

His glasses nearly hang off the tip of his nose so he pushes them back up with his finger. "I'm like a real doctor. Yes, I graduated high school a few years early. This is part of my internship, although I doubt any of this will mean anything to anyone one day. If I'm lucky enough to survive there may not even be a university that can verify my credits."

I flinch at this. "Wow. You're certainly not going to win any awards for Mr. Optimist of the Year, are you?"

"What is it you needed to see me about?" he asks sharply.

"I have this nasty bite," I say, pulling my shirt down. "My friend Payton told me I had to come see you about it."

The doctor throws me a baffled expression and takes a step back. His eyes dance between my face and the wound too many times to count—it's like he doesn't believe what he's seeing and that maybe I'm just messing around with him. Either that or he's got some crazy song stuck in his head and is trying to dance it out. "What kind of bite would this be, exactly?" he asks, his voice high and tight.

"One of those infected jackholes bit me," I say. "Just make sure you put gloves on if you're planning to touch it. The last time someone touched it with their bare hands it didn't go so well." I flinch at the memory of Sarah turning.

"Obviously," the doctor counters dryly, pulling on a pair of latex gloves and moving his head close to my shoulder. He carefully removes the dressing and pushes on the sides of the wound while inspecting it, causing me to yell out "y-ouch." He steps away from me in a flash.

"How long ago did this happen?" he asks with the most interest I've heard come from him in the past three minutes.

I groan. "I don't know. I've lost track of time. It's been a couple days, maybe?"

He removes his gloves and takes a step away. "This is not a common infection."

"Then what is it?" I ask.

His lips pull into a tight line. "I can't say that for sure."

I peer around him to where a female soldier sits across from Jake, shifting through piles of paperwork at a kitchen table temporarily serving as a desk. She's twice the size of the doctor with jet-black hair pulled into a tight bun, and an unpleasant scowl planted on her lips that makes her appear to be a very angry person. Jake watches her with trepidation, as if he's waiting for her to start screaming at him.

"Is there anyone else who can look at it—maybe like an older doctor or some other grownup who has maybe been around a little longer than you? Maybe they would know."

He throws the gloves into a silver canister and pushes his glasses up again. "Considering this was a bite by a deceased human being who technically shouldn't have physically been able to do anything in the first place, it's a relatively new type of infection that very few other doctors would even know about. As far as this stuff goes, you can consider me a specialist."

I bite my lip and consider him for a moment. Although he certainly doesn't seem to have a whole lot of personality, he's a man of science and my doctor who would be bound by some kind of confidentiality, so maybe he'll have an open mind. I fidget in my seat and look around the room before my eyes settle back on him. "Do you think...you know...maybe it could possibly be...like some kind of...alien virus?"

Now his dark, neatly trimmed brows knit together and cause a sharp crease above his eyes. "I can't discuss that. It would be considered classified information."

Bingo.

There is it. Looking back at his beady little eyes, I know he knows way more than he's willing to tell me, only he doesn't want me to know that.

Having a mind of its own, my left hand darts out to grab him roughly by his collar while my right produces the gun I'd stuffed into the back of my mom-jeans. The gun feels surprisingly sturdy in my grip, although the metal is cool against my sweaty skin. I do believe this is the very first time I've pointed a deadly weapon at a person— surprisingly, it isn't even at anyone who is infected.

The doctor holds his breath and beads of sweat spring into existence along his short hairline. He watches me, fearful.

"Emma!" Jake yells from the corner, jumping from his chair.

The husky female soldier behind the table jumps up, watching us in shock. But I do my best to ignore my little buddy and the woman who could probably crush me with one hit.

I puff out my chest and lower my voice, hoping to sound like a real threat. "Listen, doc, the love of my life and a handful of these goofballs who have become my only family just went on a miserably planned mission to rescue a woman from these freaky people who seem to be capable of cloning other human beings. If there's any information you are in the know about, you need to tell me right now. Anything at all you may know that you'd like to share."

He blinks rapidly at me from behind his thick lenses. Suddenly, up comes the finger, pushing the glasses back. "I guess it's not like I would be giving away any doctor-patient information…"

I nod with heightened enthusiasm. "You would have the potential of saving a bunch of lives. Just think of all the awards you could get for something like that."

After a moment of thought he licks his lips and lets his shoulders fall. "It doesn't even matter at this point if they decide not to give me my medical license. This is probably the end of life as we know it anyway."

I punch him in the shoulder. "That's the spirit!"

* * *

AGREEING to see Doctor Martin keeps proving to be the best thing I've ever done. He cooks up this great story for the guards at the entrance of the base, saying I have a crit-ical medical condition that needs to be seen by one of the doctors in the next safe zone two hours away. I no longer have the gun pointed at him, but he knows I've it tucked it under my leg just in case he would decide to signal for help.

"But we're getting ready to move everyone out," the young and equally inexperienced male guard at the gate tells the doctor. He literally looks like he was in the middle of boot camp when this began. Tall and skinny with hardly any muscle mass, he has this massive Adam's apple that bobs up and down when he keeps swallowing nervously. He glances back at the crudely built tower enough times that the other guard climbs down to get involved.

"I have this nasty skin condition," I say, pulling the fugly white sweater down enough to show them. The young soldier and the not much older, but slightly more muscular soldier from the tower both lean into the doctor's rough-terrain jeep, trying to get a better look. From the look on their faces, I know right away that our plan will work.

"It's very contagious," the doctor adds. The soldiers back away in sync and exchange a worried glance.

"What about the kid in the back?" the guard from the tower asks. His voice is gruff and his deep set eyes give me the willies—thankfully he's on the good side in all of this. He looks like the kind of guy that could deliver a "can of whoop ass" if you only asked.

We all turn back to Jake, sitting behind us. He waves at the soldiers, stone-faced. "He has the same thing," Doctor Martin says quickly.

"Only you don't want me to show you where it is," Jake says. I stifle a sudden burst of laughter with a bout of fake coughing, leaning over to hide my smiling face.

Doctor Martin pats me on the back. "I'm afraid if we don't hurry she may not have much longer."

"Just let them through," the watch tower guard says to his fellow soldier. Then to us, "Be careful out there. You'll want to hurry back before the feds decide to wipe everyone out."

I suck in my breath and look up at him with tears from the laughter welling up in my eyes. Using the crackly "sick voice" that always seemed to work on my parents when I wanted to skip school, I say, "Thank you."

After we pull away from the camp and are a safe distance from the guards' sight, I turn to give Jake a high five. "Good job, little man! That was a really good one."

He shrugs. "After hanging around with you the past few days, I guess I've learned a thing or two about being a smart-ass."

Laughing, I turn to the doctor and cup my hand on his shoulder. "And look at you! I'll bet you didn't know you had such awesome acting abilities!"

"Don't touch me," he says bluntly.

"Sorry," I say, quickly withdrawing my hand.

I turn back to Jake. "Are you sure you're going to be okay going back there again?" But at this point in the game, he's already scarred for life and has probably seen enough to have earned his first tattoo.

He shrugs and looks out the window. "I wouldn't want to stay back there alone. Besides, I know this is something you have to do."

I reach across the back to squeeze his knee. "Jake, it's all going to be okay—you'll see." Whether or not we survive this, I have to keep telling myself we will or I may finally lose my mind entirely. The edges of his mouth tilt up but he's unable to smile.

In addition to being a good actor, it turns out Doc can add "racecar driver" to his resume. We make haste to where he knows the camp is located like nobody's business —another bonus of having met him. Jake and I certainly wouldn't have been able to find the way on our own.

The still vacant fields and abandoned towns pass us by in a constant blur. The only other signs of life are in the form of a few deer grazing on a field of grass that has begun to turn brown from the winter that looms just around the corner. I wonder if the animals can get the virus—it could be amusing watching a crazy deer.

The usual scattering of corpses is seen here and there, but I don't dwell on it, and don't stare at them or wonder their stories. My only focus right now is getting to Finn in time to fill him in on everything the doctor knows.

The feeling that we're all alone in this—mixed with the fact that we don't see a single other vehicle in motion as we travel—brings an unsettling fear in the pit of my stomach. How long do we have until the "Army" or whoever finally bombs this area? At least a bomb would be more of a pleasant demise than death by zombies.

As fast as we're going, our friends must have been traveling at a speed equal or greater. My heart thumps wildly in my chest when I begin to fear we won't reach them in time. But we finally find the familiar truck parked next to the boulder overlooking the now vacant camp where Finn and I had hid with the boys on our latest excursion.

I urge the doctor to hurry along, my gun pointed at his back as we hop out. The guys are just beginning to pile out from the back end of the truck. Jake scurries along, never leaving my side. Payton is among the first to appear, scowling when he sees us, then quickly drawing his gun and taking direct aim at me. His eyes are filled with conflict.

"Seriously?" I yell at him. "I thought we were past that by now!" I'm livid. How many times is he planning on trying to shoot me? Is there something about me physically that makes him want to shoot for the sport of it? Do I repel him?

"Emma?" he asks, keeping his gun pointed on me. "Is it really you?"

"Your boyfriend seems like a great guy," Doctor Martin mumbles from the side of his mouth.

"He's not my boyfriend," I snap. I grunt angrily and pull the corner of my sweater down with my free hand for Payton to see. "Creepy green oozing wound—you happy?"

At this point I would just forget the sweater and run around topless so he'll quit questioning my authenticity, but the gray clouds have blocked the sun and our breaths puff out white against the brisk air, so that may prove to be stupid in the end.

Finn comes bolting around the corner, but stops short when he sees me. A delayed moment passes as he tries to register everything. He hasn't missed the fact that Payton is once again pointing a gun at me despite his warning earlier, but I think he's still in shock at seeing me holding a gun to a stranger and doesn't know what to do.

"Em?" he finally asks. "What—"

"Who's this guy?" Payton breaks in, motioning to the doctor.

"This is the doctor you wanted me to see," I tell Payton impatiently. "Would you put the damn gun down now? I'm really not in the mood to play human decoy with you again."

The rest of the guys have heard us and now gather behind Finn in a tense circle, watching with the same level of confusion. Miller's hand slowly reaches for the gun at his waist. Jags almost looks like a sumo wrestler with his thick arms crossed over his chest and his mouth drawn down at the sides as he looks down on me.

Payton lowers his gun when he's finally convinced I'm not a clone. I would punch him if I thought I could put any kind of dent in him from doing it. "Why are you holding a gun to him? You don't even know how to remove the safety."

The doctor turns to take a step at me but a metallic click causes him to stop short. We turn to see Finn suddenly pointing his own gun at the doctor.

"But I sure as hell do," he says. "Back away from my girl." I drop the weapon and run to my boyfriend, slamming my body into his and nearly knocking the gun from his grip. I hug him tightly and his free arm wraps around me to squeeze for a moment. He quickly kisses the side of my head, leaving a warm spot in my hair. "I thought we agreed you were going to stay put, Em. What's going on?"

I pull on his arm. "Could you just hug me again, for a little longer this time? It's freaking cold out here!" The chill running through me makes me wish I had grabbed my old funky clothes for extra layers.

"Emma," says Finn impatiently.

I sigh and push up against him anyway. "Okay! Geez! I brought our new doctor buddy down here to fill you guys in on this top secret stuff he has been privilege to while working for the Army."

Finn frowns at him. "You're a doctor? Like a real doctor?"

I slap my boyfriend on the chest. "He graduated from high school early," I say sharply. "Have some respect."

Doctor Martin shrugs. "I decided to finish my internship with the Army. I had no idea what I was getting myself into at the time, obviously."

Payton makes a sound that's something between a snort and a laugh. "We all chose a really crappy time to serve our country."

"You don't have to keep pointing that gun at me," Doctor Martin tells Finn. "I probably would've come along willingly, even without your girlfriend pulling a gun on me. She just had to ask nicely."

"Sorry," Finn and I say simultaneously. Finn lowers his gun.

"Well, what is it? What's this information you know?" Cheese asks the doctor, stepping forward. Eyes bright and wide, he waits for the news that will most likely blow his socks off. It reminds me of a puppy with his tongue hanging out, waiting for a treat.

Doctor Martin shifts his weight, uncomfortable with all the staring eyes focused on him. "Emma's theory is right. This all started with an alien virus."

Chapter 21

"Ha!" I cry out, hitting Finn's chest again. I turn back to the doctor. "Can you write that down somewhere for me—you know, for posterity's sake?"

"And you know this because…?" Finn asks him, motioning with his hand for the doctor to continue on.

Doctor Martin's skittish eyes turn back to my boyfriend. "I joined the Army six months ago when word of this virus was first circulating throughout the FBI. As you can imagine, it was kept extremely classified, and on a need to know basis."

"Why would you need to know?" Payton asks.

"I was just getting to that part," the doctor answers impatiently. Beads of sweat swell at his hairline as he licks his lips. "Can I maybe have some water? We didn't have time to grab anything before Emma forced me to drive here."

"I'll get some!" Darrin volunteers, running back to the truck. We continue staring at the doctor until he has a bottle of water in his hands. He takes a long swig, nearly emptying the liquid before our eyes.

"Thanks," he tells Darrin, pushing those annoying glasses up once more. "I graduated from Harvard at the top of my class, so I guess the Army had been vying for me for quite some time. Once they had me, I was immediately given a young soldier as a patient who had been infected with some unknown virus."

"This is good stuff, right?" I ask the group.

"Shut up, Emma!" Cash snaps, not turning away from the doctor. I'm actually delighted to hear Cash acknowledge me in such a familiar way. Things are really beginning to look up.

The doctor casts a questioning gaze between me and Cash before continuing. "Anyway, this nineteen-year-old who had been working closely with a couple of FBI agents came in with this unusual green-colored bite on his leg. They told me he was bit by some homeless man in the street, but I graduated from Harvard. I'm not stupid."

Cheese snickers. "No shit."

"They only referred to him as 'Patient X' and wouldn't tell me his real name. I didn't have any prior history or—"

I roll my hand through the air. "Just cut to the good stuff, Doc."

Doctor Martin rolls his eyes. "So I was working in the lab late one night and heard these voices coming from Patient X's room. They were real urgent and sharp, like they were arguing about something really important. I didn't think they knew I was still there, so I snuck back into my office and watched them from the monitor in Patient X's room. The General of the Army was sitting at the bedside of this guy with a couple other high ranking officers and this woman from the FBI."

"This was about the same time your mom went missing," I whisper to Finn.

"The agent was telling them an outbreak was likely and

it had to be contained before it got out of control. The General sat there shaking his head in denial, I guess, while the other officers argued with the woman over how they would even begin to contain something alien that they knew very little about."

"Maybe they just meant alien as in foreign," Cheese counters.

"No, no," the doctor replies. "They went into great detail describing how they didn't know the first thing about a virus that came from another planet, and if word got out it would cause a worldwide panic. The General was more concerned about how this would play out and how it would have the potential to make the Army look bad."

Payton glowers at the doctor. "You never told anyone before this?"

Doc Martin shakes his head. "I guess part of me was in denial that it was real and that something like that could be happening. After that night I did some of my own research to see what we do know about alien life in general. The first records I found involved the Roswell incident, of course, but with my heightened security level I was able to access the Army's most confidential records. Turns out other places around the world have experienced more recent encounters. This female agent was responsible for uncovering a string of viruses that showed up in other countries. They all had the same characteristics—young men and women bit by an infected human that resulted in a green, almost glowing color."

I nudge Finn. "Sounding familiar?" But he's too engaged in Doc's story to acknowledge me in any way.

"I found pages and pages of reports from this FBI agent, giving the Army her best guess at what was really going on. From her research, she was able to conclude that anyone whose brain wasn't fully developed would be unaffected by this alien virus at first, but for everyone else, they would immediately become an animated corpse, only hungry for other human flesh. She said the virus could be contracted through blood, saliva, or infected food. One thing she wasn't able to conclude was why the aliens were releasing this virus on humans, or what its true purpose was."

"Whoa," Cheese says, being the only one to verbalize a response.

"But there's something more…something about the bites that I didn't tell Emma," Doc Martin says, turning to me.

The way he says my name makes the little fuzzy hairs on the back of my neck stand at attention. A trickle of fear runs through me. My heart takes on a different pace, slow and unsteady, my body shuddering with every beat. As if moving through a fluid dream, I turn to face the doctor head-on.

Finn squeezes me with his arm. "What is it?" he asks the doctor on my behalf.

Doctor Martin bows his head at me, an apology. "I figured it would be safer to tell you when you were reunited with your friends."

Something tells me this will not end well for Team Emma. My lips are wet with perspiration while my tongue and lips are completely dry. I force down the ball of fear forming in my throat. "Whatever it is, Doc, you better come on out and say it real quick-like. I'm about to have a heart attack here."

"The agent said there was a way to reverse the effects of the bite, whether for an adult or a child, but there seems to be a time limit in which it can be done," he says.

I scowl. "What effects? I'm fine, other than some fluorescent green puss."

Again, the finger pushes up the glasses.

"Dude, don't you have some kind of rubber band you can put around your head to keep those damn things up?" I snap.

Doctor Martin's eyes grow wide, completely stunned by my outburst.

Finn waves his hand. "Ignore her. It's how she deals with stressful situations."

The doctor turns to Finn, apparently better able to deal with his calm reactions. "The night I saw the agent meeting with the General in Patient X's room, she was trying to warn them that there wasn't much time. She was scolding the General for not letting her know as soon as they became aware of the situation and said she may have been able to help him if she had only known sooner."

I can hear Finn swallow behind me. "Did she say exactly how much time he had?"

Doctor Martin looks at me. "She said in her experience, most victims only lasted a maximum of four days."

Dread drifts through the air, as if everyone is collectively holding their breaths because actually breathing will, in itself, doom me from having a chance of surviving this. Even I'm holding my own breath, but mostly because I'm worried I may not have many more to take.

"So what's the cure?" Finn asks with an edge of anger to his question.

"She didn't say. It wasn't in her reports, either," says Doctor Martin, shaking his head. "I'm sorry. I wish I had more answers."

"Well that blows," I say back. All this running and walking and trying to escape creepy dead people for nothing. I may as well have just let our housekeeper have at me. At least it would have been one final kind gesture toward her for all she had to put up with over the years.

"What about Patient X?" Cheese asks. "What happened to him?"

Doc Martin watches me as he speaks. His small eyes are doing their best to ask for my forgiveness from behind those eternally annoying glasses. "The morning after their secret meeting, I found him lying in his bed. He was dead, Emma. You may not turn into a zombie from this virus, but there are only so many days your body can carry it before it gives in. You probably don't have much longer."

For a moment, we're all so quiet with this revelation that you could literally hear a pin drop—well maybe not on the dirt ground we're standing on but maybe on one of the vehicles nearby or something.

Finn's grip on me becomes so tight I can't breathe. Then I realize my chest has seized all on its own, keeping the air from passing through. All this time I thought I was immune from turning into something horrendous that would want to eat my friends and family. Turns out there was something I still wasn't immune to, something that only Finn's missing mother may know how to reverse.

Then Jake cries out, "No! No! Emma can't die!"

I suddenly notice a gathering of snowflakes swirling above us in the sky, signaling the start of a winter storm. I watch them whirl around until they fall on my boots and disappear.

Just like the snowflakes, I'm about to disappear.

This is the moment I've dreaded, the very reason why we kept running, even when it seemed hopeless. We all seemed to believe if we kept running, we would never die. But what exactly had we been hoping to find in the end? A magical place where the infection hadn't spread? A castle surrounded by gumdrops and cotton candy? Our hope of escaping these aliens is ridiculous. We never should've hoped for anything more.

There still may be hope for my friends, only because none of them have been touched by infection. Stone-faced, I lift my head to study each of them, one by one. I'm too choked up to give any formal kind of goodbye—okay, maybe I just really hate public speaking. At any rate, I wouldn't know what to even say to them.

Jake seems to be nearing hyperventilation. I want to reach for my little buddy, but it feels as if my arms and legs are encased in stone. He has certainly become the little brother I never wanted, and I'm actually pretty fond of him by now. I worry what will happen when I'm gone— who will teach him the facts of life? What if he's raised by this pack of wild boys and never learns any civilized views on everything?

Zander stands soberly at his side, his arm draped over Jake's shoulders. Giant tears roll down his face. He tries to smile when I look at him, but his lips only quiver and jump around. Even though the whole romance thing hadn't worked out so well between us, I'd discovered him to be a loyal friend through all of this. His other arm is around his little brother, who I know is going to be okay despite the blank look he gives me when my eyes roll onto him.

Miller and Jags are wearing matching expressions of pity. I don't know what will happen to any of our Army friends if any of this is ever resolved, but I can see Miller one day growing up to be a loyal husband and father, while I picture Jags entering the world of professional wrestling.

Cheese stands with his hands twisted together awkwardly, not sure what he should be doing as I watch him, but his eyes are filled with tears. I know he's a smart kid, but I still hope one of these guys will teach him the lessons on how to embrace his geekery. Once his voice levels off, girls may even find him endearing.

Payton holds his jaw tight. He's angry at the whole

situation. Not counting all the times he tried to shoot me —I've lost track of just how many times exactly, but more than enough—he has been a real comrade through everything and I know he'll keep my new family safe. Hopefully there's some equally attractive girl who has survived this somewhere out there for him so they can go on to have a family of freakishly good-looking children together and teach them as toddlers how to fight off the infected.

I catch my breath when I discover Cash to be among those crying. I know he's having the same awkward emotions toward me that I have come to accept for him. He's seriously annoying and knows every single one of my buttons to push, but he would've made a great brother-in-law one day—family gatherings surely would've been lively. Now I wish that I'd gotten the chance to see Cash on Christmas morning in his pajamas, assuming he would wear something more than just his underwear. If not, scratch that thought. I'm actually quite saddened to think we'll never pick on each other ever again. I only hope he's able to find a surviving female who can put up with him the way poor Marley used to when she was naïve and not forced to think of him as the last guy she would be with on this earth.

Finally, I tip my head back to look up at Finn. Tears fill the corner of his dark brown eyes that usually bring me so much joy and comfort with a mere flash. A million memories rage through me as our eyes hold each other.

Marley had said we need to live for every moment and not have any regrets. Looking back at my lifelong friend, I realize I have a whole butt load of them—probably somewhere in the thousands. And a lot of them actually have to do with Finn—all the things I wish I would've said and done a whole hell of a lot earlier. But none of those regrets are recent. I'd done my best to show him just how much I loved him.

Most of all, I'm certainly grateful that I'd brought the doctor down here at gunpoint or I may not have had a chance to say goodbye. As much as these people once to irritated me something awful, I've learned to deeply care for each and every one of them.

The most I can hope for all of my friends now is that they'll somehow find a cure and be able to go back to their old lives—live in our horrendously boring little town with no worries bigger than the next lame quiz or what crappy movie to rent. What I wouldn't do at this moment to go back to the days of being bored, the nights of having no other plans than to watch movie marathons with my best friend and talk trash about his idiot brother.

Something suddenly shifts in Finn's eyes. Behind the sadness and pity, I still find something warm and glowing radiating onto me. But it's something other than the usual teenage boy hormones, beyond the pure love and adoration he had shown when we were doing the horizontal bop less than 24 hours ago.

My eyes leave his and drift down to the succulent mouth I've come to know the curvature of so well. Only I find it curled upward at the edges, his lips pulled into a tight line.

Finn is smiling at me.

"Guess you'll get your Romeo and Juliet ending after all," he whispers.

###

About the Author

When not writing from one of the 10,000 lakes in Minnesota, Jen Naumann is either rocking out at concerts, riding Harley, helping her husband farm, or chasing down one of their four active children.

Visit Jen website for all the latest news and updates on her books, and sign up for her newsletter.

Keep reading for a preview of *The Time Zombies Became the Least of My Worries*...the exciting conclusion to Emma's story!

The Time Zombies Became the Least of My Worries

PROLOGUE

Do you seriously believe that saying "Everything happens for a reason"? Do you really think you flunked that super hard test in physics your junior year because you were *meant* to spend your summer vacation being tutored by one of the hottest senior guys, like you were some kind of idiot? Do you honestly believe you spent a hundred dollars on a third-row ticket to see your favorite band in concert, and came down with the stomach flu just so you would be forced to watch your life-long crush take his girlfriend at the time in your place? How about the time you bought that cute little black dress for your sixteenth birthday that turned out to be see-through in the deejay's ridiculously bright-lights, and the entire school had a good laugh at your polka dotted thong? What could *possibly* be the reason for that? So maybe you've never had anything quite like this upsetting happen to you, but you get the idea.

I personally think the saying is stupid, and must've been made up by some eternal loser who wanted to feel better about their miserable life. What reason could there *possibly* be for me to lose my mother and one of my best friends to a zombie infestation? Or for myself to get bit by one of those creepy walking corpses, only to find out I'm going to die much sooner than planned?

Maybe all of this happened because I decided to have pre-marital sex with my best friend, Finn. It's not like it was a one-time fling, although it may literally end up being one in the end since I was told I don't have long to live.

Then again, maybe I'm just going to die young because life really *sucks*. Crap. I guess that qualifies as something happening for a reason.

———

ONE
(Emma)

The "old" me would've been extremely uncomfortable with the number of people staring at me. She would've made some smart comment like, "Keep your eyes to your-selves," or "What's the matter—haven't you ever seen so much awesomeness in one person?" Sometimes I miss the wittier, more naive version of myself. That girl used to know how to craftily change the subject.

Believe it or not, being the center of attention makes me squeamish. Often times this level of self-awareness makes me do something incredibly clumsy, like the time I was asked to say something to the entire high school when voted as one of the candidates for homecoming queen, and bumped over the deejay's can of soda into the micro-phone. The dumb thing shorted out, squealing like

Freddy Krueger's razored fingers on a really clean chalkboard.

Yet I've been through so much with these guys that each of them has become more like family. I know they're only staring because they're devastated, and don't really know what to say. What *do* you say to someone in my situation? "That sucks?" In a way, I guess you could say that I've maybe matured a little during our adventures together.

"So…what do you guys say we focus on someone else for a minute? Like maybe Doc Martin over here? We just barely touched the list of reasons why he looks completely ridiculous in his Army uniform. He looks like he's ready to attend 'take your kid to work day' or something, am I right?"

Okay, so maybe I haven't matured.

The Army doctor who gave us so many answers we've been searching for pushes his eternally slipping glasses back up the bridge of his nose before crossing his arms, and frowning down on me. I vow to crush his stupid spectacles with my foot, even if it's the very last thing I do before I die. And I mean that literally.

Finn huffs before leaning in closer to me. "You feeling okay, Em? Are you in pain?" My best friend of *forever* has only made "boyfriend" status very recently, and already he's playing the part a little too perfectly with his doting brown eyes paired with his extremely sappy, wet kisses to my cheek and forehead. I guess these are things a good boyfriend does, but it still feels kind of strange coming from the guy I took to the comic book store, waited overnight in lines for concert tickets and the newest electronic gadgets, and used to make fun of before I started properly dressing him.

I sit up on the hard ground, rolling my eyes to the frozen sky. "I don't feel like I'm going to die *right this minute,*

Finn. I told you I feel fine, other than the fact that I'm freezing my *ass* off."

The snow has begun to accumulate into small, wistful piles, and I swear I can see the start of icicles forming on my eyelashes. Puffs of white burst from the lips of everyone gathered around, making us look like a bunch of compulsive smokers. I've never inhaled any kind of tobacco or hashish in my life, but can say with confidence it's not one of the things I will regret never having tried. But the thought of it gets me thinking of all the things I *do* wish I would've done, like shaving my head, learning to speak Chinese, or getting some kind of tramp-stamp tattoo.

The news that I may not have much longer to live because of the stupid zombie bite on my shoulder is a lot to swallow. But quite honestly, I'd rather go out this way than actually be eaten alive by one of those things, or even turning into one of them like the older adults do. Even my poor friend Marley with her whole death-by-chocolate scenario had it better than my neighbors back home who were gutted in the street while probably still alive. I don't care who you are, or what shameful things you may have done in your life, that kind of death falls under the category of cruel and highly unusual punishment.

"Everyone, back *up*," Finn snaps, draping his arm around my shoulders. "Give her some room." Our friends shuffle back only a little, giving each other the same look: *poor, helpless Emma and Finn—their love story will forever go down as being a tragic one, with the likes of Titanic and The Hannah Montana Movie.*

I groan at my boyfriend's overly doting attitude. "*Finn!* Stop treating me like I'm on my death bed! There's still a chance we can find your mom and get a cure for this thing, right? I mean, c'mon. It's not like this is the end of the world."

The others still have these sad, pathetic frowns as their eyes water, showing very little hope for any happy ending. I study my young neighbor Jake, who oddly reminds me of that chubby kid in the *Goonies* movie who cries like a goober when his hand is about to be cut up in the blender. Okay maybe I *am* exaggerating a *little*—but his eyes are pretty wet. I guess everything suddenly seems magnified to a more intense level when I know my last few breaths on this earth are numbered.

When I look back up at my beautiful boyfriend, knowing I can count on him to stay dry-eyed, he actually looks like a thirteen-year-old who was just told there's no Santa. I cross my arms and sigh. "Ugh, not you, too."

Grab it now on Kindle Unlimited!

Acknowledgments

To my husband Brian, my four children (Owen, Sam, Jamie and Lindsey), my parents, my brother Rob, my sister Jodi, all of my in-laws, my friends, extended family and the members of my small community for your unwavering support—I'm really blessed to have all of you in my life;

To my fabulous and amazing friends Jody "Ferdig" Skogsberg, Carolyn Zierke and Billie Gervais for always being there to put up with all of my crazy ups and downs—love you guys more than you will ever know and I cherish you all;

To Janet Krinke for your eternal support and friendship through my adventures—you are one of the few who really gets my inner-geekery and I appreciate all that you do (especially sticking it out through my painfully rough drafts);

To my sweet friend Mindy Jagerson for always staying positive and always being there when I need to get out of the house and do something fun—you keep me sane;

To my fellow author Maria Monteiro for your friendship, encouragement, support and ideas—you have helped me in so many ways and I'm grateful on a daily basis that we found each other (although we have yet to actually meet!);

To my amazing mother for all your help even though zombies aren't your cup of tea;

To my dear friend Liz DeVelder for your fresh and helpful insights;

To Danielle Krause and Pam "Eagle Eye" Berndt for helping to clean this up—you guys rock;

To Nicole Krinke for being the most horrifically beautiful zombie girl and letting me throw you out into the woods wearing your gorgeous, brand-new prom dress;

To my editor Megan Schoeneberger for all your hard work;

And finally to the awesome, unique and fun group of people I've met online who are into zombies the way I am —this one's for you!